LUCID ORIGIN

BOOK THREE OF THE DESIGNED SERIES

LUCID ORIGIN

BOOK THREE OF THE **DESIGNED** SERIES

KATE TAILOR

FIFE
PRESS

an imprint of
YOUNG DRAGONS PRESS

OGHMA

CREATIVE MEDIA

Bentonville, Arkansas • Los Angeles, California
www.oghmacreative.com

Library of Congress Cataloging-in-Publication Data

Names: Tailor, Kate, author
Title: Lucid Origin/Kate Tailor | Designed #3
Description: First Edition | Bentonville: Fife, 2021
Identifiers: LCCN: 2021934698 | ISBN: 978-1-63373-640-5 (hardcover) |
ISBN: 978-1-63373-641-2 (trade paperback) | ISBN: 978-1-63373-642-9 (eBook)
BISAC: YOUNG ADULT FICTION/Science Fiction |
YOUNG ADULT FICTION/Loners & Outcasts |
YOUNG ADULT FICTION/Action & Adventure
LC record available at: https://lccn.loc.gov/2021934698

Fife Press hardcover edition June, 2021

Jacket & Interior Design by Casey W. Cowan
Editing by Gordon Bonnet & Amy Cowan

This book is a work of fiction. Any references to historical events, real people, or real places are used fictitiously. Other names, characters, places, and events are products of the author's imagination, and any resemblance to actual events or places or person, living or dead, is entirely coincidental.

Published by Fife Press, an imprint of Young Dragons Press, a subsidiary of The Oghma Book Group.

To my Heart and my Tiny

ACKNOWLEDGEMENTS

THIS BOOK IS POSSIBLE because of a group of speculators, an accountant, a podiatrist, a Belgian, a set of crazy aunts and their husbands, two lovable children, a father, a missed mother, an extra mother, and a great group of Oghmaniacs.

C H A P T E R
01

EVERY NIGHT RALEIGH dreamed of being buried alive. In the darkness, with no light, it was impossible to tell how large the room was or if she was still in the bunker. That's why she had a night light and why she appreciated the sound of her own scream as she awoke. Yells that echoed back to her, proving that this room had carpet, a hall outside, and that it wasn't a concrete tomb underground. It had been two weeks since her harrowing experience of being trapped underground, and she didn't know when she'd lose the sensation of being trapped, if ever.

Now she stood in her room, her forehead pressed to the cold window. The winter days were mercilessly short, but the sun slid across her face now, promising her better days. When she looked outside the first thing she sought was the sky, cataloguing how it looked in her mental journal.

Today was overcast, as were so many winter days in Chicago. From her second story room she could see the patio in the back yard and the one tree on their side of the fence. It wound its naked branches up, as if, like her, it sought relief in the sun.

She pulled her sweater closer around her rather than step back from the pane of glass. The starvation had caused her to lose fat and muscle, and the bit that she retained wasn't enough to insulate her during these cold months. Her face didn't look the same as it had. Not only was it thinner, but her eyes looked different, but she couldn't quite say how.

A soft knock drew her attention from the yard. "Raleigh?" Rho spoke in a soft voice, the one he'd been using more since she'd returned. The one that hinted that he considered her somehow fragile now.

Her eyes darted to the clock. It was eight in the morning. "Come in."

"It's the phone. It's for you." Rho offered her the cell phone.

For her? Who would call? Tau, Kappa, and Collin were holed up with her in the townhouse. A few blocks over Gamma, Upsilon, and Dale still were in hiding. Just last night she'd had dinner with them. Everyone she knew was here, safe. "Who?"

"Gabe."

She wasn't ready for that call yet. Soon she'd have to help Grant and Able go after Sigma, but she was too weak. Rho's knitted brow hid under his wavy hair. Something was up, maybe he didn't want her bargaining any deals with Grant and Able after all. She took the phone.

"Raleigh?" Gabe's voice came through loud and clear. Audible enough that Rho could hear it from his short distance away.

Raleigh studied Rho before she spoke. "Gabe. I thought I was going to have some time before we helped you find the kidnapped Modified."

"Yes, to recover, but this isn't about them. It's about your family."

Raleigh staggered back a step, her side prickly against the cold sill. "My family?"

"We've had our eyes on them. We don't think Sigma will go after them, but we were already watching them after you went off the grid and figured that keeping an eye out a little longer wouldn't hurt. For their benefit."

Grant and Able had their eyes on everyone, and she didn't pretend to be surprise or offended now. "What happened?"

"Thalia was in a car accident late last night."

Her sister's snarky smile darted across her mind. "Is she all right?"

Silence. *"She's in critical condition. We can send a plane to you, so you can go home. So you can help."*

"No, a commercial flight would be faster."

"Do you need us to buy you a ticket?"

"Yes. I'm in Chicago."

"Hold on."

Gabe's end of the line went silent, and Rho moved closer to her, his voice low. "If your sister is hurt, then we should go, too. We can help." He reached out his hand, pressing it softly to her shoulder.

"Grant and Able have eyes on my home."

"And they're our temporary allies. If Gabe wanted to, he could trace this phone, he could have stopped us before now without this. It's your sister."

Gabe came back on and said, *"There is a one o'clock flight to Denver. You're on it."*

Rho held out his hand for the phone. Raleigh handed it over. "Gabe?" Rho asked. "Can you get Tau, Kappa, and I on that flight, too? I'll text you the names on our licenses."

"Yes," Gabe's voice said clearly. Rho disconnected and then texted him.

Thalia was hurt and four states away. Would she get there in time? Would she and the Designed be enough? She needed their help, but it wasn't her place to force them out of hiding.

"Will the others want to go?"

"Kappa will come. And Tau…."

Rho stared at her when he said Tau. Raleigh gripped the edge of the sill wondering if Rho'd guessed that something deep and hungry lay between her and his brother. "What about him?"

"The bunker shook him up, he won't talk about it. He's worried about you, asks how you're doing all the time. I'm sure he'll want to come. I've told him that he's free to work with Mu again, but he's insisted on staying near you. I think there are things he needs to talk about, but not yet."

Raleigh and Tau had already discussed their relationship. One that had managed to thrive while they themselves withered away in that bunker, but somehow couldn't survive now that they were free.

Rho held up his hand. "Don't look guilty. I'm not jealous that my brother can talk to you about things he won't say to me. I'm happy that the two of you put aside your differences. He really hated you for a while. We need the two of you to get along. If he confides in you, that's great. The smoother we can make things between you and my brothers the better."

Raleigh jumped at the sound of Collin's fist hitting the doorframe as he entered. "Rho, what's up?"

"Kappa, Tau, Raleigh, and I are going to Denver."

"What? We're not ready to negotiate with Grant and Able."

"It's Raleigh's sister, she needs us, they're getting us there."

Collin's face didn't show any compassion at the news. "Not me?"

"No, just the four of us."

"I could have your back."

Raleigh didn't want Collin there. He'd been antsier, his anger rash and ready to bubble over at the smallest infraction.

Rho shook his head. "Not this time, and you should ease up on your Lucid usage."

Collin's eyes glared at Raleigh. "She told you to take me off it."

Raleigh squinted at Collin. "No, I didn't." But she wouldn't argue that it was a good idea. "And I don't have time to think about that now. We need to get packed, we need to get to Colorado."

She moved around Collin and headed towards the closet. Grabbing her bag she began to shove in the few belongings she had. Not that any of her clothes fit her well these days.

Rho said, "Collin, it's my decision to pull your Lucid back. After everything we've seen with Adam, I think that Chi might be right. It might be too much of a sacrifice to have you take it."

"I can control it." Collin held back the urge to fidget, but Raleigh could sense his restlessness. The largest problem that existed for Lucid is that anyone who used eventually succumbed to the addiction.

Rho didn't repeat what she thought and what they all knew. "Our trip will give you a few days alone to taper off in your own way. I'll leave enough so you don't stop cold turkey."

"I should have your back," Collin said. Facing the closet, Raleigh could imagine the expression that Collin wore now, his already hard face became a mask when angry.

"I'll have my brothers and Raleigh for that. Now, Raleigh's right, we have to pack, this isn't the time."

Collin tensed, ready to argue further, and then retreated. His feet slapped heavy against the floor, he wasn't going to drop this anytime soon. Rho sighed and rubbed the back of his neck before following him out.

The Receps and their addiction was a problem, but right now Raleigh could only think about Thalia and hope she could get there in time.

THE FLIGHT ARRIVED five minutes early, but Raleigh's legs couldn't carry her fast enough. She followed closely behind the guys as they traversed the parking garage, sidestepping around cars while searching for their rental.

"This is it." Kappa stopped at a car near the end of the line and pressed a button on the key remote. It chirped in response.

Rho slid his finger along the spotless cherry red exterior. "It's red, that's going to stand out."

Tau loaded the bags into the trunk. "Hate to break it to you, but we're not going to be covert. Grant and Able booked our tickets, they'll be watching us the whole time. The synthetic is gone. Sigma isn't going to jump us in a parking lot. You're going to have to get used to not looking over your shoulder."

Rho didn't protest further, glancing into the front seat. "Raleigh, take shotgun so you can navigate."

Raleigh slid onto the black leather seat, and Kappa took the driver's seat. He reached up to adjust the mirror. For a moment the mirror reflected the image of Tau and Rho, before Kappa turned it away. Two men who had made her heart run the gamut over the past year. Thoughts of them both in the backseat right behind her normally would have been more than enough to occupy her time, but they couldn't distract her from her sister and the hollow sensation of helplessness that filled her chest.

Rho passed the phone up to her. "Call your parents, let them know we'll be at the hospital."

Raleigh took the phone and began to call home, but stopped. Her mother would fuss and talk. She had every right to be emotional about Raleigh finally coming home. That would take time and energy she didn't have. "We're driving to the hospital, I'll text

Patrick, my uncle." She typed a simple message and then watched it send. The phone vibrated a moment later. With a room number for Thalia and a promise that he'd meet her in the lobby. No other questions or admonishments about her absence over the last few months. No guilt.

The small car hugged the looping exit ramps away from the airport. Mountains dominated the western horizon. She knew the outline of them by heart, the dips and the peaks the same way she could trace the features of Tau's face. The thin high-altitude air filled her lungs and was more satisfying than sea level, because it meant she was home.

Time struggled past. They moved fast, but the minutes drew on—taunting her for being so far away. Her mind tried to predict what Thalia would need as a gnawing fear broke her confidence. What if there was nothing to be done?

They reached the hospital, and Raleigh undid her seatbelt. The car had barely come to a stop, and she was out of the door. Each of her strides were long, straining the muscles of her legs as she avoided the patches of ice. The guys stayed in step behind her. Her heartbeat echoed in her ears, alternating between a sharp pain of worry and the hurried elation of nearly running.

When she reached the doors, they were slow to move, taunting her, whispering that she hadn't made it in time as they slid open. The scent of cleaner hit her upon entering, threatening to bring up a dozen memories. It was in this building that she'd learned of Lucid less than a year ago.

She paused, searching for Patrick. On her tiptoes she glanced at each of the faces in turn, not seeing his in the mix. "We should go up without him."

Rho's fingers found hers and gave a faint squeeze. "Give him a moment, he said he'd meet us."

"There you are!" Patrick darted out of a stairwell and around the other visitors. He shrugged off the formality of being a physician and donned the giddy kindness of an uncle. He wrapped her up in his arms as a way of greeting. "Thank god you're all right."

"What about Thalia?"

"I'll take you to her." He traced his gaze over Raleigh's shoulder to Rho and the others.

"Uncle Patrick, these are my friends. Rho, Tau, and Kappa." They had aliases on their false licenses. When she'd lived undercover with Gamma and Upsilon she would never have used their given names. But now she didn't care, even though the monikers caused her uncle's eyebrow to hitch up even further. She added, "They're here to help."

He nodded. "Nice to meet you. Come, Thalia's in the critical care unit."

The hospital was Raleigh's domain, not Thalia's. Her feet knew the checkered patterning of the hallway by heart. It had been years since the building had been able to evoke fear in her, but her heart twisted now as she rode the elevator to the critical care unit.

An unlucky horseshoe of patient rooms surrounded the nurses' station. The rooms had one large glass wall that faced the center and only a curtain to keep a patient's privacy. Inside the first room Raleigh sensed a man with a heart attack, only his toes were visible through the door. She fought the urge to stop and tell her uncle about it. One over lay a woman with a stroke. Over her shoulder she caught Tau's glance. He too found it hard to be in a place like this. A place where people pled for help, but they weren't in a position to save everyone.

Patrick walked ahead. Raleigh heard him clearing the four of them to visit Thalia. Crowds were discouraged in these rooms, where at any given moment a patient could quickly ail, and the room would flood with doctors and nurses. The nurse looked over, waving at Raleigh. These were her people, and they had long memories of the good she'd done in the past. No one stopped her or her three friends now.

They stepped into the last room, and Raleigh understood Thalia's familiar presence before she saw her. Her sister, so close to her in age, was one of the first people she'd grown used to the sense of—the chewed painted nails, the way stress made her queasy, and a laugh that echoed in her chest when she was happy.

The crash had caused broken ribs and bruising. Most troubling though, and the reason Thalia was in this room, was the inflammation in her spine caused by the trauma. "She can't move her legs," Raleigh said to Patrick as they stepped in.

"No, not yet. We're working on it."

"And she's had a concussion," Tau added.

Patrick's eyes darted to Raleigh's guests, as if seeing them for the first time. Rho shut the door and drew the curtains across the large window.

"Raleigh?" Thalia said, her voice small. Oxygen ran in and out of her nose through narrow tubes, and IV bags bulged overhead with nutrients and medicine. Some of which must be pain killers, because Thalia had a fuzzy euphoria quelling her pain.

Raleigh walked over. "Oh, Thalia."

"I was in an accident." Pain nipped the edge of her words. Her pink hair matted to her head before splaying against the white pillow. Her skin was only a few shades darker than the linens of the bed. Too pale. She'd lost blood.

"I'm sorry I wasn't here." Raleigh could barely speak over the lump forming in her throat.

Thalia didn't appear angry. "You left us. But it must have been for a good reason. I told mom. She…."

"It's all right." Patrick moved over a seat so Raleigh could sit.

Raleigh sat and steadied herself. "You know how I can feel people?"

Thalia nodded. "I'm not going to walk again, that's what you've come to tell me."

"We're here to help," Tau said. "The inflammation is pushing on nerves, but if we can decrease it and repair the damage, then maybe you will."

"It's true, but the pressure must be taken off, faster than the anti-inflammatories are doing it, or the paralysis might persist." Rho didn't mince his words. The three brothers stood in a line along Thalia's feet.

Raleigh took her sisters fingers in hers. "These men are like me. They can sense people, and we can also do something called influencing. That means that we can control what's happening in your body."

"What?" Patrick's eyes were wide. "Surely…."

"With enough Lucidin and receptors," Rho said. "And we can help Thalia."

"Is that all right?" Raleigh looked into her sister's eyes. "Will you let us try?" Raleigh wasn't ready for this test. There were years of schooling and experiences that were supposed to lead to such a difficult case. None of that mattered, she stood ready, despite her lack of experience.

Rho turned to Tau. "You're the most skilled at the endocrine system, and the cytokines are likely the problem. Would you show us what to do?"

Tau didn't hesitate. "Yes. Raleigh, can you feel the source of the inflammation? The way the cells are… well, like angry in response to the trauma?"

"Yes."

"We're going to work at quieting them down." Tau went over to the head of the bed, grabbing a chair and positioned himself across from Raleigh. "It's going to be a long process. Most of the cells are damaged beyond repair. What we're trying to do makes it so the neighboring ones don't overreact."

It wasn't an easy task. Raleigh's mind couldn't directly communicate with the cells. She had to interact with her sister's mind instead. From there Thalia's mind had to relay the request, and the traumatized cells were inclined to not listen. Simply put, it was hard. Raleigh influenced, encouraging the mind to pull back on the inflammation, but it wasn't an easy battle to fight. "Thalia, do you feel any different?"

"Tingling, in my feet, but I can't move them."

"It's going to be a process," Rho asserted. "You won't overcome it today."

"I'll work on the concussion." Tau leaned over Thalia. "And let's see if we can't get rid of some of that nausea."

Tau and Raleigh hovered over Thalia, deep in concentration. The minutes ticked by in silence, the ambient noises from the ward drifting in.

"You should know, Mom is pissed at you." Thalia coughed a bit on the words. "My stomach feels better. I feel better, light as air."

"Tau's messing with your endorphins." Raleigh shot a glance across to Tau. "She has pain meds."

"My method is better."

"You can affect pain?" Patrick stepped over hesitantly.

"Yes." Tau paused. "How much do you want us to tell him?"

"He knows enough," Rho said.

Raleigh's heart broke a little. Patrick had known all her secrets since she was young. "It's not my place to tell."

Tau turned to Rho. "We've told him this much. Uncle Patrick is one of Raleigh's closest confidants."

"And what am I?" Thalia said.

Tau smiled down at her. "A rebellious little sister, from what I've heard."

"God you're gorgeous," Thalia said. "Absolutely beautiful."

Raleigh squinted across the way. "Tau, pull back on those endorphins. I don't want her to say something she'll regret."

Thalia laughed and closed her eyes. "Just don't tell my boyfriend. Uncle Patrick, when is he coming?"

"Your boyfriend?" Over the last few months Raleigh would have given anything to tell her sister about Rho and Tau. Now she realized that she'd missed out on hearing about her sisters first flirtation with love.

Thalia managed a smirk despite the tubes running around her mouth. "Alec Quick, the kid whose pants fell down, but please don't remind him when he gets here."

Patrick checked his watch. "And I'm sure he'll get here soon. How long do you think this will take?"

The tingling Thalia described was promising, but it would be an uphill battle to reverse the damage caused by the crash.

"I can't say," Tau said. "But we've gotten a good start. We'll take turns calming the cells now, and then in a few hours, we'll work on the nerve connections. This is going to go slow." His face was set, his message clear. Don't lose hope.

Patrick's phone buzzed, and he pulled it from his pocket inspecting the text. "Raleigh, your mom is going to be here in a half hour. Have you thought about what you're going to say to her about where you've been and what's happened to you?"

"What makes you think something happened to me?" Raleigh asked and casted her eyes down to the floor.

Thalia interrupted. "Are you making me sleepy?"

"No, that's the drugs," Tau said. "Go to sleep."

"Don't let my mom murder her," Thalia whispered as she shut her eyes.

Kappa cleared his throat. "Raleigh, take Rho and Tau and explain things to your uncle. I'll stay here with your sister and work on the inflammation, we've got a good jump on it. Tonight we'll work on the nerves."

Raleigh grasped her sister's hand. Now that she'd made it here, she didn't want to leave her, but Kappa was right. They would need to explain things, and she wanted Patrick to be on her side for when she confronted her mom. Reluctantly she stood.

Rho paused and then turned to Patrick. "Do you have someplace private we can talk?"

CHAPTER
02

PATRICK TOOK THEM over to a secluded part of the cafeteria. They walked past the empty tables, the sounds of the kitchen preparing for dinner clanged through the vacant space. Outside the winter sun began its descent behind the mountains. The streetlights would be on soon.

Raleigh pulled out one of the plastic chairs and sat. Tau and Rho took the seats on either side, leaving Patrick to stare across the middle of the table at her.

"Your mother thinks you ran away to be with some guy," Patrick said without accusation, his eyes darting between Rho and Tau. "But it isn't like that, is it?"

"No. Lucidin, or Lucid as it's commonly called, is more complex than I realized." Raleigh had no intentions of lying to her uncle.

"The influencing." Patrick leaned back in his seat, rubbing his hand along his jaw, the potential of what they'd done in Thalia's room no doubt swirling through his head.

Rho turned to Raleigh. "And you want him to know everything?" Raleigh nodded. "I can't tell him my story without telling him yours, too."

"Then I'll tell both." Rho paused, and when he spoke, he chose his words slowly. It started with their origins, of Grant and Able in the earlier years. It continued through to his escape from the island. Months ago he'd given her this same speech, but he told it better now, without hesitation or shame. Then he started in on Belgium and how he met Raleigh. "She saved my life."

Rho's hand reached across the table, his fingers weaving with hers. He was stronger now, but she would never forget the weakness in him at their first meeting. She'd never forget their first words, him, hoping to get her out of whatever jail they'd been imprisoned in. Being the leader had made Rho come off as cool, but now, as he turned to her she saw who he was before he took up the mantel of guiding his brothers. For a brief moment she could picture how he would be if everything was resolved, the joking carefree boy who'd walked with her around Paris and made an oath to run away with her.

She'd kissed him once, and he'd rejected her, but now that she thought back over the months, she realized that she'd pushed him away first. Rho picked back up the story of how Tau and Mu were captured by Grant and Able and how Raleigh had gone undercover.

Patrick exhaled. "I had wondered why your views on Grant and Able had changed. Your mother was so obsessed with finding a treatment, she fought Belgium, but she didn't think twice about sending you to Arizona."

Raleigh interrupted before Rho could continue. "Grant and Able aren't bad. What they're doing with Lucid, it's the same thing I did to Thalia upstairs. Honestly, I almost stayed with them."

Rho's fingers tightened at the omission, and now Tau picked up the story. He told Patrick about the Receps and their addiction. He explained how Raleigh had rescued him. Then he and Raleigh took turns filling Patrick in on the story of the synthetic.

Patrick chewed on his bottom lip as the story unfolded. He pounded his fist against the table. Anger and helplessness heating his blood. "And that's why you look so frail? I had no idea it was that bad. Your mother, she made it sound like you had no real reason for leaving. Of course I knew that wasn't the case, but everything you told me, it's far worse than what I'd expected. I'm guessing you won't stay here long."

"Not with Sigma still out there. There are things we still have to figure out." Raleigh sat back in her chair and looked down at her hands.

Patrick turned to both Tau and Rho. "And you'll go with her? You're here now to make sure that she is safe?"

Tau interjected. "Don't make it sound too altruistic. Raleigh has saved me on more than one occasion. She's strong enough to have her own back."

"Sometimes I feel like we're simply along for the ride," Rho muttered. "We stand together, she is one of us."

Patrick exhaled. "I'm happy for that. But…."

"Uncle Patrick, I know you'd hide me away, but this is happening with or without me. Sides will be taken, and if we're to win…."

Patrick held up his hand. "I won't tell you what to do. It's clear from what you demonstrated up there that you have a path before you that I can't imagine. Have any of you wondered what would happen if your secret got out?"

Rho lowered his head. "I'm sure people would study us, the lab experiments that we are."

"I'd die first," Tau said.

Patrick shook his head. "Being Designed, although fascinating, isn't what I was talking about. If Lucid becomes an everyday thing, it will stratify society. Think of what you've told me of the Receps, whose receptor volume matters, now toss in the population as a whole. Think of how quickly people are willing to divide themselves. And this gives power to the victors. Obviously the medical advances can't be discounted…."

"There will never be enough Lucid," Raleigh told him. "That was the issue Grant and Able ran into. Sure, people can separate themselves into tiers based on Receptor volume, but at the end of the day it isn't going to matter. Not unless a synthetic is devised."

"I'm almost glad to hear it." Patrick pulled his phone from his pocket. "Your parents will be by soon. I think the fewer details you can give them the better. Your father thinks your leaving is in rebellion to the tight rein they kept you on, play off that angle."

Raleigh crinkled her nose. "And my mother thinks there's a guy. Honestly, maybe Thalia would be so flighty, but not me."

Patrick again snuck a glance at Rho and Tau. "Regardless, now you've brought three of them. It isn't going to help your case. Just remember that right now your mother is emotionally fragile with Thalia being injured. Try to humor her."

Thalia. The thought of her sister upstairs brought on another wave of sadness. What if Thalia had died? What if she'd never seen her sister again? The handful of days she'd been home over the summer she'd fussed over her own problems. "I should have been here for Thalia."

Patrick stared directly into her eyes. "Your sister will be fine. Despite what your mother thinks, you didn't abandon your family. If anything, your absence has been to ensure their safety."

Raleigh slid her seat back from the table, its metal legs scratching against the linoleum floor. "She's not going to like Tau and Rho."

Rho laughed. "Most people find me charming."

Her face warmed as she considered the comment. She remembered the effect he had on her when they first met. That was the first time he asked her to run away with him, after only knowing her for a day. Something had built between them in those early interactions, something that made her search the room for him. Her mother wouldn't have such an intense response, but it was true that Rho was effortlessly likable.

"If she thinks you're the reason Raleigh is no longer at home, then she won't." Patrick began typing something into his cell. "I'm texting my wife, Shannon, and telling her that you're staying with us." Then rose from his seat.

"Thanks," Raleigh said.

"No problem. Now, your mom should be to Thalia's room any moment, and I'm not sure how we're going to explain Kappa being left up there alone. Let's head her off at the pass. It would be better if you met up at home rather than here."

Patrick was no fool, he anticipated that there would be a blowup when Beth saw her daughter again. There were better places to have their argument than the hospital room.

The four of them left Thalia with a promise that they would be back later that night to work on the inflammation and nerves. For now they would go back to Raleigh's house. She would stay with Patrick, but there was a conversation she needed to have with her mother first.

———

RALEIGH UNLOCKED THE door to her house, pushing it open and stumbling in the dark to find the front light. Two sets of boots, Thalia and Lana's, sat piled by the door, evidence that her older sister was home from college. "Hello!" Raleigh shouted up the dark stairwell. No answer. The smell of oranges and cinnamon flakes hung in the air, a reminder that Raleigh had missed Christmas for the first time. "Everyone must be at the hospital."

Kappa turned to Rho. "We need to make calls, everyone will want to know we're all right. I'll take Gamma, and why don't you call Collin and Trevor?"

Rho agreed. He pointed to her Dad's office. "You mind if we use the study?"

Raleigh nodded, and Rho and Kappa ducked into the office.

Raleigh went to the kitchen with Tau. "I'll put together something for us to eat." It was the kind of statement her mother would make, under the assumption that a person should never have guests without offering up some kind of food or drink.

Tau sat down on the stool at the kitchen island, her morning breakfast seat, and his arms spread across the marble countertop. Her eyes went to the entry, all the sounds of the house tended to echo into the kitchen. When Rho and Kappa returned she would hear them before she saw them.

"My sister." Raleigh stepped closer to Tau.

He stood up and wrapped his arms around her. "She'll be fine."

"If I was here...."

"She would still have gotten into an accident. We'll heal her, don't worry."

Raleigh tucked herself tightly against his chest, his chin turning so he could watch the entry.

Then his arms loosened.

"Don't. Don't pull away." Raleigh gripped him tighter. In the bunker she learned to crave the comfort that came with Tau's embrace. She desired him not simply because of infatuation but for something more. Here, with him, it was as if nothing could touch them. The beat of his heart picked up with hers. They were both barricading, but it didn't matter, their bodies knew one another on a different level.

"Raleigh." Tau kissed the top of her head. It was just a peck, his lips flickering against the top of her head for but a moment, but he remained close, taking in a deep breath of her before stepping back. "I can't do this to Rho."

"Can't do what to Rho?"

"Hook up with you behind his back. He assigned me to take care of you in Italy, and I betrayed him. I've seen the way he looks at you, he's in love with you."

"I haven't seen that." It didn't matter how Rho looked at her, not when she longed to be lost in Tau's eyes.

"And you could be in love with him."

"I'm not. I'm in love with you."

Tau flinched, his face twisted as though her words had stabbed him. She wanted him to snap out of it, to remember what they had, to feel like she did. That they'd survive any awfulness together.

"I won't hurt Rho by being with you. I've stepped between the two of you, I've distracted you. I'm sorry for that. The two of you are meant to be together, and I muddled things."

"Rho didn't want me."

"That's because you're both strong, and he's not used to being shown up. But together you'll be great. You'll push him to be a better leader, and he'll help ground you, because for all the power we have, we still can't fly."

"But I'm good with you, we have something great. Remember the bunker?"

"I survived that because of you. But it wasn't a natural situation, it was a survival one."

"That's the only time you could be with me?"

Tau exhaled loud and frustrated. Raleigh could relate. She

wanted to shake him right now. He said, "I can't have a romantic relationship with you. You're meant to be with Rho."

"Just because I'm not with you doesn't mean I'll be with him. I get a say in all this."

"Of course you do, but if you don't end up with Rho it would be a mistake. I'll always care about you, and we'll always be friends. Please, don't be mad at me, I'm doing the right thing."

Raleigh's heart splintered, a pain filling her chest before radiating down her back. When Rho had rejected her he'd said it was the wrong time. Now Tau left her because she was the wrong person.

"You're stronger than you think," he said quietly.

She hated how people were constantly telling her that. What if she didn't want to be strong? Vulnerability, insignificance, and delicacy ran across her skin. She wanted to scream at him, to change his mind, but it was made. "If this is what you want."

"I do. I want you to be happy. And although it might not feel like it now, this will be what leads to your happiness in the end."

Raleigh stood there, recalling how perfect it had been lying beside him night after night in bed. She looked at his lips, the rip in her chest expanding, making her lungs struggle to take a breath.

Kappa and Rho had finished their conversations and returned from the study. Wiping her eyes, she went over to the fridge and wrapped her hand around the stainless steel handle. Her reflection came back blurry in the door—so this was what her face looked like when she was broken. Could Tau be right? Was she only with him because of the bunker? Doubt tasted metallic on her tongue. Her attraction to Rho had always been strong, was Tau nothing more than a distraction?

As if on cue, Rho moved up behind her. "Your sister will be fine."

She turned. The tears in her eyes falling in round drops. A sob escaped her lips, her heart's plea to save it as it broke. Rho wrapped his arms around her, not unlike how Tau had done a moment before. She peeked around Rho to see his expression. Was his heart imploding too? No, he offered up a small smile. Encouragement.

She pulled away, running the back of her wrist under her eyes to dry her tears. She should be crying about Thalia. Collecting herself, she had no time to focus on Tau. Her family would be visiting Thalia for at least an hour, and when they returned she'd have to give them answers on where she'd been the last few months. There would be an argument, she'd been gone too long for her mother to see past her leaving. The thought of going up against her mother sapped her remaining energy.

Tau and Kappa slipped out of the room leaving Raleigh standing there, staring out the window over the sink. Frost clouded the edges of the glass, and even in the dim evening light she could see the first few snowflakes falling. In the bunker she'd dreamt of home, but now it was a cold, unwelcoming place. Rho stared at her. She didn't know what to say. There were so many emotions weighing her down she could barely breath. Thalia, Tau, the unexpected trip home, each one a brick added to the others.

"My mother is going to be angry at me when she comes home. What do I tell her? She won't be supportive like Patrick."

Rho shook his head. "We'll handle your parents. Why don't we bake a tart? Did Maggie ever teach you that simple one with custard?"

"Yes."

"We'll make it for them, they'll be hungry and tired after seeing Thalia."

"I should think up arguments."

"When I'm worked up and upset I'm not any good at arguing. When I've had time to think, and can calm down, that's when I can discuss things rationally. And it might just be a discussion. It might not be an argument."

"You don't know my mother."

Rho opened the drawers alongside the stove, finding the one with aprons and handing her one. "Can't hurt to have something to do with your hands."

Raleigh tugged the looped neck of the apron over her head and tucked her hair into a ponytail. Rho handed her the eggs, and she grabbed the whisk.

CHAPTER
03

AN HOUR LATER, Raleigh finished cleaning the last bits of flour off the counter before brushing a strand of hair from her face as she bent down to peer in the oven door. The corners of the pastry had browned to a beautiful golden color. It'd be done soon, and the kitchen smelt like Maggie's bakery back in Belgium. Back when her days were a droll routine.

Rho crouched down so he could see in, as well. "What are you thinking?"

Raleigh stood. "How boring my days were before you."

"That could have passed for a compliment if I didn't know how you'd spent those days." He exhaled leaning back.

Raleigh reached out her arm, her fingers tentatively touching his wrist for a moment. "What are you thinking?"

"That you've saved my life, made it infinitely better, and all I've done is placed you in worse and worse situations."

"The last one was my choice."

"That doesn't mean that it hurt any less." They stood now, not far apart, and he turned so they were closer. "And what do we do now? Things have stalled out with Sigma, Grant and Able, and the Modified. We're waiting, but it could be for a while."

"We don't have to hide." The fact that they stood in her childhood kitchen was evidence of what she said. A few months ago she wouldn't have ever come back home. The threat Sigma held hung in the distance like angry rainclouds, the storm would be weathered worse by Grant and Able. And if they were victorious? Sigma would have to die. And it might be by her hand. She still recalled the sensation of driving the knife into his arm. She could be haunted by her actions without regretting them.

"That isn't the same as what we should do? What do you want, Raleigh?"

Raleigh craned her neck slightly, so close that his breath slid the words across her cheek. His hands traveled to her hips, his eyes questioning if the small gesture was acceptable. Through her shirt and apron she could feel the pressure of his fingertips, and her skin prickled blissfully against them. Her eyes studied his. Was Tau just a distraction? He was right, she liked Rho.

They stood close now, all she had to do was lean in a little further and they'd be kissing. And committed. And forever. Because things with Rho already felt written in stone, and any action was written with a chisel.

The mudroom door opened, and Raleigh jumped, Rho pulling her closer. Turning himself towards the door, an instinct born of years on the run. A mindset she shared, her fingers clutched his upper arms, not fighting as he drew her in closer.

There wasn't a synthetic thug or Recep on the other side. Instead it was her mother, father, and older sister, Lana. Sad faces on all three, faces that morphed into shock upon seeing Raleigh.

Snow and cold hung on them. The draft fighting with the heat coming from the oven.

Raleigh pushed off from Rho, who stepped back, falling into his casual stance. Raleigh held her mother's eyes and watched a multitude of emotions cross her mother's face.

"Raleigh," her father said sweeping around his wife and wrapping Raleigh into a tight hug. "We've been so worried about you."

"I'm fine."

Tau and Kappa came in from the other room, and Raleigh gave them a worried look over her shoulder. "Mom, Dad, these are my friends, Kappa, Tau, and Rho."

"Where have you been!" her mother shouted.

Lana winced beside her. "Mom, maybe this isn't the best time."

"Don't tell me not to lose my temper." Beth moved two quick steps towards her daughter. "Raleigh, you missed Christmas. Months have passed, and you didn't call. I assumed that you were dead. Now you've shown up and act as though nothing has happened."

Kappa stepped forward, his green eyes kind and his hands open. "Mrs. Groves, we've come to see Raleigh's sister, not to upset you."

Beth's exaggerated hand movement brushed away Kappa's words. "And who are you to tell me what should and shouldn't upset me? Raleigh left us." She pointed at Rho. "Is this the boy? Is this the one that you left us for?"

"I didn't leave you over a boy." Raleigh's cheeks flamed, from embarrassment, anger, or both. "I left because I had to."

"I know you felt stifled. I know you wanted to go to college. We had to get you better first. I didn't think you'd run off with some boy!" Beth's voice shook through the small room. "And he's not even a boy, how old are you?"

"Twenty-two." Rho didn't deny being with Raleigh.

Beth turned to her lawyer husband. "Isn't that illegal? Statutory rape?"

Raleigh erupted before her father could assure her mother no. "I'm eighteen. And we're not even dating. I left because I had to."

"You left your treatment in Arizona. I know, I spoke to Agatha, and she told me that you'd left on your own accord."

"You called Agatha?"

"What else was I supposed to do? All you told me was that you couldn't talk to me anymore, that we'd be better off if we forgot you existed. Where else was I to go?"

Raleigh repressed her anger towards her mother. She needed to stay rational. Of course she'd call Agatha. Of course she wouldn't have respected Raleigh's request that they forget about her. It didn't change the situation, she couldn't poke around things. "Lucidin, the hormone in my system, is part of a very complex world. A world I'm a part of, and it isn't always safe."

"More of your delusions. That Agatha woman, she encouraged your delusions about feeling other people's bodies."

Rho cleared his throat. "That isn't a delusion. Lucidin allows people to sense and influence one another."

"So you're encouraging her fantasies too!" Beth whirled on Rho. "Is that how you coaxed her away from us? You brainwashed her."

"Your daughter makes all her own decisions. If you know her at all, then you know that she does nothing that she doesn't want to do." Rho turned to Theo. "You must know that about her."

"She's stubborn," Lana said.

"Driven," Rho corrected.

The front doorbell rang, and Theo gave Raleigh a worried glance before dashing into the hall to open it. Patrick's voice echoed through the house. Raleigh noted that her mother seemed more upset, the muscles in her arms tensing, not eased by her brother.

"Patrick, we are in the middle of a family discussion," Beth said.

"I wanted to come and tell you that Thalia is improving. The inflammation has gone down significantly, but we still need to pull it down further."

Beth put a hand to her forehead. "Yes, the doctors said that."

Raleigh felt the weakness that radiated through her mom. The anger masked her weariness. It was likely she hasn't slept at all last night, and the concern for Thalia gnawed on her. Kappa must have sensed it too, because he grabbed a chair from the kitchen nook and brought it over. "Sit down Mrs. Groves. This is all very upsetting, but I can assure you that all of us have come to help."

Patrick rang his hands. "Raleigh, I wondered if I could speak to you and the guys for a moment."

"You knew she was here?" Beth's face hardened. "You knew my daughter was back and you said nothing?"

"I knew you would be mad, and we don't have time for that. The key now is to get Thalia better."

"Raleigh isn't a doctor."

"But she can heal. You know that." Patrick stood up to his sister. "We need to go back to the hospital."

Beth clutched her head in her hands. "It's delusion. You're all feeding into these fantasies she has."

Kappa turned to Rho and Raleigh. "I think Raleigh is going to have to prove it."

"I've sensed her hundreds of times, she doesn't want to believe," Raleigh told him.

"Influence," Kappa said quietly. "If you want I can give her a demonstration, but it would mean more if you did."

Influence her mother? Raleigh didn't want to. The denial that her mother had built up protected her. If she influenced, her mother wouldn't have to worry about her sanity, but she'd glimpse the truth. She'd see how strong Raleigh was, she'd understand the stakes. Even without the details she'd understand the gravity of the situation. "It will only upset her."

Rho put a hand on Raleigh's shoulder. "You don't have to."

Kappa held firm. "Tau, back me up?"

Tau stepped forward. "You said you wanted her to know." He spoke of her daydreams in the bunker, when she picked apart all the things she would have done differently aloud in their coffin underground. When she thought she was going to die she wished her mother would have known. Her perspective shifted when death didn't hold her so closely.

"Mom, I'm going to make you stand and walk into the living room." Raleigh stopped just short of asking for permission.

Beth lifted one eyebrow. "What?" She began to ask as Raleigh made her stand up and walk towards the living room. Her legs moved like planks, the motion unnatural, like a marionette with a new puppeteer.

For good measure, Raleigh did the same to her father and Lana.

"What the hell?" Lana said. "I'm not trying to do this."

"I'm making you. It's the Lucidin in my system. It allows my mind to sense what's happening in your body and control it." She sat them down in the living room and then stood in front of them. "Do you understand?" Not a fair question. "Do you see now that things are complex?"

Her mother didn't say anything. Just sat with her mouth open. Her father shook his head. "It's unbelievable."

Raleigh said, "And we've come to help Thalia. Rho, Kappa, and Tau, they're like me. They make Lucidin, and they can influence. We're pulling down the inflammation in her spine. I have to go. We're staying with Patrick tonight. I'm going to stay as long as I need to in order to help Thalia."

Her mother went to stand, but Raleigh kept her seated. "Don't you dare…." her mother threatened, and Raleigh froze her mouth.

Raleigh ripped off the apron and shoved her feet into her shoes before storming out with the Designed. That couldn't have gone much worse.

Patrick followed after them, his eyes on the front door as it shut. "How long is she going to be stuck like that?"

Raleigh didn't turn back as she walked to the car. "Distance plays a part. I'll let her go once we're on the road."

C H A P T E R
04

RALEIGH STOMPED OUT of the car up to the hospital. Flour hung on the tips of her hair, and anger flared hot on her cheeks. Patrick kept opening his mouth and then shutting it. No doubt he wanted to depart some elder wisdom, but what was to be said to a girl who had just frozen her mother and stormed out of the house?

"Do you, uh... want to talk about it before you see your sister?" Rho asked.

"What is there to talk about? How would you feel if your mother acted like that!" As she spoke she reached the front doors. They slid open, but she didn't enter. Instead she took a deep breath and turned to Rho.

His brow troubled with emotion. "I didn't have a mother, so I can't pretend to know."

Raleigh now felt less like kicking her mother and more like kicking herself. "I'm so stupid. I shouldn't have said anything."

"It's all right," said Kappa. "I'm not sure you have it easier or harder with a mom like that. Did she listen to anything you said? It was infuriating."

Rho grabbed her hand and stepped into the lobby. "I'm sure she loves you, and it's not like any of this is easy. Some of my brothers were disowned when their parents figured out what we could do."

"That's horrible," Patrick interrupted. "The whole thing. None of you boys were given a decent chance." He spoke as if Rho and the others were still young. To him they were. She'd wondered if he'd take them all out for ice cream later. Despite the cold she could really use the comfort.

"It's over now. We can't dwell on it." Tau moved to the elevator. "And some of us had good childhoods, with decent parents. Things didn't fall apart until we ended up meeting everyone else."

"But you got some brothers out of it." Kappa grinned and socked Tau in the shoulder.

"I had brothers. But it was a relief meeting other people who could sense." His eyes flicked to Raleigh. She hoped he'd never call her a sister. A kindred soul yes, but of the three only Kappa had a brotherly relationship with her.

Raleigh stretched her neck and rolled her shoulders. The only member of her family that she should be considering right now was Thalia.

The hospital was experiencing its last push of visitors. Unlike earlier, people lined up for the elevator. Raleigh had to squeeze between the guys and Uncle Patrick to find a spot. The other riders stood tense with concern. She took a deep breath and didn't let it out until they stepped onto Thalia's floor.

This time she passed the nurses' desk without hesitation, and with a quick knock she entered her sister's room. Thalia still lay with her hair matted to her pale face but internally was stronger. Raleigh went over to her, taking the chair nearest her sister.

Tau pumped a spritz of hand sanitizer onto his fingers before entering. He joined Raleigh at the head of the bed. He smiled down at Thalia. "Your toes are tingling."

"Yeah, they have been since you left."

Tau's smile widened. "You'll get better. Do you mind if I work on pulling down the inflammation?"

"Sure, can you help with my pain, too?"

"You're not in as much pain," Raleigh said.

"Shh, Raleigh, let your boyfriend do that trick he did earlier."

Raleigh's spine stiffened at the boyfriend comment. She was in the habit of always wearing her barricade, and thankfully she'd made sure it was up after fighting with her mother. The others wouldn't feel the response her sister's words had. Did she do such a poor job of hiding her feelings about Tau? Did her sister know?

Tau didn't address the comment. "You're not in very much pain. But if you need it in the future, I can."

"He's not my boyfriend." The words barely slipped out over the bitter taste that had filled Raleigh's mouth. No one, not even Thalia, seemed to have heard them.

Rho stepped closer too. "Should we take this in shifts? Raleigh, do you want another crack at it?"

"She's frazzled from that thing with her mother." Kappa pulled out a chair. "I'll work on it with Tau for now."

Raleigh studied her sister as Kappa and Tau influenced her. The changes they made were subtle, barely perceptible even by someone as adept at sensing as Raleigh. Thalia squirmed a bit in her bed. Now that the initial shock of influencing had worn off, she could better think about the ramifications.

Raleigh wrapped her hand around her sister's, careful not to dislodge any of the lines that linked Thalia to the medicine overhead. The dull hum of the machines echoed across the small room. The tubing reminded Raleigh of her own port. Extractions had become a necessary part of Raleigh's life, but she hated the smell of the plastic and the static the machines produced in the air. She resented her reliance on a machine, and for a moment wished she could tell her sister that she understood how she felt.

Thalia closed her eyes, and Raleigh tightened her grip on her sister's hand. For now, she wouldn't say much. Everyone relaxed into their seats. The healing process drew their attention, the world outside of this room melted away from Raleigh. Inside her ears Raleigh could hear her sister's heartbeat. The nauseating medicine Thalia had taken had them each pressing a hand to their own stomachs. Those minutes were filled with unity and passed uninterrupted and quickly over the next hour.

It took Raleigh a moment to register Lana's voice. She pulled out of her trance, her eyes focusing on Thalia's before she turned to find her older sister in the doorway.

"We need to talk," Lana repeated.

Raleigh pulled her hand out of Thalia's. "This isn't the place."

"Then let's find one. Mom's in hysterics. Dad convinced her not to come here but only because I agreed to come instead."

Raleigh started to stand, and Thalia grabbed at her wrist. Her weak grasp wouldn't be enough to hold Raleigh, who stopped despite being able to break free.

"Don't. You've been gone too long, and I've been worried. Whatever you're going to tell Lana you should be telling me." Thalia pressed her lips together. Of the three sisters Thalia and Raleigh had been the closest. Lana often took on an annoyingly maternal role. Thalia was right, she should know any information first.

The vitals monitor behind Thalia's head registered a weak pulse, reminding Raleigh that her sister was in no place to receive bad news. And these days that was the only kind she seemed to have. "I can't put my burdens on you right now. We can talk later."

Thalia tried to sit, and Tau placed a hand on her shoulder. "You're doing better, but you're a ways off from leaving this bed. Raleigh will talk to both of you. We've done what we can for now."

"I could use a coffee," Kappa said from the back of the room. "Rho, come on show me where the cafeteria is?"

Tau stood and pushed his chair back to the wall. "I'll go too."

Patrick moved over to the doorway with them. "If you three need me, I'll be at the nurse's station."

With that, the three sisters were left in peace. Raleigh couldn't help noticing how much she'd switched places with Thalia. Now she was the one with the secrets and rebellion, and her sister was sick. Raleigh sat back down in the chair nearest Thalia, and Lana took the one Tau had vacated. Lana leaned back, flipping her silky brown hair over her shoulder and out of her eyes so she could glare at Raleigh.

Raleigh didn't know where to start or how much to say. Uncle Patrick could understand the whole story, but here she would have to omit or reframe much of what had happened to make it more palatable to her sisters. Lana's thin nose had always been a bit brown, she'd suck up to their parents any way she could. No doubt anything that Raleigh said now would be relayed over to them later tonight. Did she tell part of it now and part of it later when she had a moment alone with Thalia? The answer was no, her sister had her own set of worries, and Raleigh didn't want her dangerous world to encroach on her family's. The less they knew the better.

Raleigh started with the good. "The people I stayed with in Arizona, Grant and Able, they have a team of healers that help people the way we just did with you Thalia."

"And how exactly are you helping her?" Lana tilted her head towards the bed.

"My friends, the ones I've brought, are like me. They can sense illness, and they can influence like me as well. We're working on getting Thalia's legs to work."

Lana's mouth flapped open at the mention of sensing. Early going Lana had believed Raleigh's claims of feeling illness in people, a belief that she'd grown out of the same way a person loses faith in most childhood magic. When Raleigh's ability didn't fit into how the world worked, she swept the notion away. Lana had always taken strongly after their mother.

Raleigh didn't want to discuss yet again if sensing was real. "You know that I can sense and influence. That's why I froze you all at home." Sensing they could ignore or explain away, but influencing was an entirely different thing.

The heartbeats on the monitor picked up as Thalia's ears perked. "Really, you froze them? That's what you were doing just now at home, before you came here? Wow, I bet that freaked her out."

"I didn't plan on it. I was going to bring it up gradually, but you know how unreasonable Mom can be."

"Freaked out doesn't cover it. After you left she ranted for a good thirty minutes about how you're some kind of monster now." Lana spoke harshly, not trying to save Raleigh's feelings.

Raleigh's heart sank. How could her mother think that of her? Even worse, parts of the statement were true. In October she'd killed that kidnapper with no more than a thought. Her kind of power could corrupt anyone, but in her heart she believed that she hadn't been ruined, not yet. "She's so mad at me. I didn't have any other option than freezing her, I had to prove that I wasn't making any of this up. I'm not delusional, despite what she thinks."

"She's angry you left, and when you do come back we find you making out in the kitchen." Lana lifted one eyebrow. "Has that boy brainwashed you into leaving?"

"What? No. And I didn't make out with him in the kitchen. You all just see what you want to see."

"You looked really friendly."

"That's because we're friends. Look I'm not talking about Rho right now. If you want me to tell you where I've been, you can't accuse me of lying."

Lana shifted further back, looking down at Raleigh as she lifted her chin. "Then don't lie."

"Fine. I wouldn't exactly protest if Rho and I started dating. But we're not. I promise you. There isn't anything there."

"Yet." Thalia gave a small smile. "Although I think you should date the one that did that pain trick."

"She can't date any of them, they are all older than me! She's only eighteen, and they have to be in their mid-twenties." Lana clung to her notions of dating, which could be a bit antiquated at times. She still went out on formal dates, where the guys paid and she painted her face with an extra layer of makeup.

Raleigh said, "They are twenty-two."

"But they're brothers?" Thalia asked. "How does that work?"

Raleigh's back jaw clenched, how did she explain them without telling the whole truth? They all had the artificial likeness about them. "They're cousins, but they call each other brothers. Anyhow, I met them through Grant and Able."

"Who are these great healers who you left?" Lana's sarcasm bit more than her honesty.

Raleigh let out a long breath. "Yes. Because the thing is there isn't enough of the drug that I make, Lucidin. Both of you remember when Dr. Orman came last summer and told me that I made it."

"They tested us for receptors, because they said it would help them understand your disease," Thalia said. "Neither of us have any."

"That's right. It's not always genetic. Anyhow, Lucidin is in short supply, and Grant and Able didn't have enough to keep their healers stocked."

Lana seemed bored with Raleigh's explanation. "So you left them? Wouldn't they need you more?"

"Yes, but I couldn't keep up with the demand, and they made a version of Lucidin in the lab, a synthetic. But it doesn't work as well, and it makes people very edgy. It's not good for them. I didn't like that they were giving it to healers, so I left."

Lana squinted her eyes. "You spent every waking moment in this hospital with Uncle Patrick, and you left a group of healers, who were going to send you to college at no charge, because you didn't like that they were giving their healers a synthetic drug?"

"It's really nasty," Raleigh said. "It destroys people's lives. I tried to explain to them, but they didn't listen. I had to go."

"And you broke ties with us just to hurt Mom?" Lana accused.

Raleigh flinched. How could her sister think that of her?

Thalia chimed in. "It really hurt her that you left. All you said was that we'd be better off, but we really haven't been. Mom's been anxious and angry. We thought about hiring a private investigator, but Dad said that if you wanted to leave we couldn't force you to stay."

"That and it was too much money after all your medical bills," Lana added.

Raleigh slouched in her seat. The medical bills were something she would never be able to repay her family for. Lucidin had cost them so much. How did she explain to her sisters the level of danger she was in without showing too much of her hand? "It wasn't safe. There are people that are after me for my Lucidin. I didn't want them to come after you to get to me."

"That's crazy. Now you think people are chasing you? Have you thought about seeing someone?" Lana's face was both annoyed and sympathetic, an odd combination that only her sister could master. "You indulge in these fantasies." Her sister repeated the words their mother often said to Raleigh, just as stubborn to not believe.

"They aren't fantasies. I was in very real danger."

"So are we in danger now that you're back?" Lana said. "Or are these evil people conveniently not chasing you right now?"

Lana was so frustrating. Raleigh mulled over the right answer and kept her calm. "There is danger, but some of it has gone away, but even now I can only stay long enough to make sure Thalia's okay."

Thalia shook her head. "Don't disappear again."

"I'll keep in better touch this time."

"Don't leave." Thalia reached out her hand, the IV lines swaying above with her movement.

Lana didn't ask her to stay. "It might be good. Mom needs to cool off. That thing you did back at home, she's scared of you. You're not the Raleigh we knew."

The last sentence rang true. Raleigh could barely see her old self in the person she'd become. "I've changed a lot over the last few months."

"The new you seems way cooler." Thalia smiled, and the oxygen lines to her nose moved as she did. Then she took in a deep breath, her body sinking further into the white-sheeted mattress.

Thalia was too frail to hear more or to talk any longer. Raleigh said, "I'll come back when everything is safe."

"Do you promise?" Thalia asked.

"Yes." In the event that Raleigh didn't succeed, she'd be dead. Those were the stakes in her world, it was one of survival, and she had no illusions of her safety. Sigma had taken Quinn, and struck the first blow, there were only so many ways things could end.

Lana didn't show much emotion about Raleigh leaving. Maybe because after freezing her family everyone realized Raleigh no longer fully belonged. "Next time try not to be making out with any boys when we come home. And give us a heads up."

Raleigh nodded, making a silent oath to herself that there would be a next time. She wouldn't be able to clean things up with her mother this trip. There wasn't time to work through all their problems. After Sigma that would become her next goal.

C H A P T E R
05

FOUR DAYS LATER, Raleigh sat at the counter in her uncle's kitchen staring into her bowl of breakfast. She traced a spoon through her cereal, not very hungry to eat it.

"Thalia will be going home in a week or two. The doctors say that she's going to make a full recovery, in time. They're calling it a miracle." Patrick interrupted her thoughts. He grabbed up his coffee cup and walked to her patch of counter. After taking a long sip of coffee he stood waiting for her to speak if she wanted. Apart from the conversation about the Designed the first day, she'd ignored talking about anything too deep.

The very notion of her mother made her temper flare. Patrick had helped her navigate avoiding her family for the most part at the hospital, never once forcing her to talk about how she felt. Now, he waited for her to talk but remained patient.

"I guess if Thalia's returning to her life there's no excuse for me not to go back to mine," Raleigh said.

"You're welcome to stay here as long as you need."

Raleigh dropped the spoon into the bowl, causing the remaining milk to ripple. "That's nice, but the longer I'm here the more strained your relationship with my mom will become."

"She'll be thankful that I didn't turn you away one day. She'll be happy that I kept my head when she behaved rashly."

"Maybe someone else would feel that way, but I'm not so sure about my mom. My disease has troubled her for years, and now she's realizing that it was me that she feared all along."

"I've always said that you're more than your disease. And that is still the case."

"It's a pretty defining characteristic." Raleigh didn't mean to throw herself a pity party, not when her uncle had been so kind to take her and the guys in during their stay. "We need to be getting back anyways."

"Where are you going to go?"

She almost mentioned Chicago but then stopped.

"I shouldn't have asked, you probably can't tell me. I understand that you need to keep your whereabouts secret," said Patrick.

"No, it's not that. I'm not entirely sure what we're going to do next. Grant and Able are going to help us locate the rogue Designed, but as far as I know they don't have any leads yet."

"And you think it's wise to go after these violent men?"

No, it wasn't wise. "We're the only ones who can stop them."

"And after the threat of the rogue Designed are gone will you pursue your dreams of becoming a doctor?"

"You've always wanted to see me in a lab coat." Raleigh hoped to make this conversation lighter. Patrick didn't interrogate her, but the questions were heavy and ones that she wasn't ready to fully consider.

Patrick smiled. "Don't fool yourself, it's your dream. But if you chose something else, I'll support you whole-heartedly."

"I don't know if I'll ever openly be able to use my abilities as a healer. What we did with Thalia has potential, but it will never be mainstream. The problem is that there isn't enough Lucidin. With the exception of me, the only people who've made it have been built to do so. No one is going to be quick to make up more Designed after Sigma."

"But more Modified?"

Raleigh pushed her bowl to the side and rested her forearms on the countertop. The stool she sat on was high, and as recently as last year she had been sitting here swinging her feet, chatting about medical mysteries. Now her feet rested on the bar, unmoving, as she thought.

"It's immoral to make both but more so with the Modified."

"It sounds like the Designed have had a pretty rough go of it. All of them have been exploited, and from what your friend Rho said, some of them have nearly been killed."

"That's true, but they can defend themselves. The Modified are like cats that have been declawed. They'll be chased, and they lack the resources to fight back."

Patrick nodded his head. "I wonder too how people would treat you and the Designed if they knew. All of you are nothing short of amazing, but you're right, it's a frightening amount of power. You can heal people, but you could just as easily use it to harm."

"Some of them have." Raleigh desperately wanted to tell her uncle about the man she'd killed in Chicago during Gamma's kidnapping attempt. Rho had glossed over how they'd been found out by the synthetic, prompting them to work on dismantling the trade. But, he hadn't brought up the specifics. Either because he wanted to let Raleigh decide who should know, or he considered her actions necessary in her defense, something she needed no explanation for.

"Yes, and if your mother is quick to demonize you, others will be too." Patrick's eyes locked onto hers. "You must be very careful, those few bad Designed aren't your only problem."

Raleigh hadn't given much consideration as to what the general public would make of her. Ending the synthetic had been her main goal. Now that it was conquered, a fresh host of problems came at her. She rubbed the bridge of her nose. For each problem she solved another seemed to be waiting to take its place.

Raleigh sighed. "And even if we get enough Lucid, there is the problem that half the population can use it while the other can't. Some of the people who bought the black market stuff were athletes, so they could get an edge."

"It would have an effect on sports to be sure. It would have an effect on everything. If it was widely available, then only those with Receptors would be made doctors. For all the book learning I've done, and all the patients I've seen, I will never understand the disease I've encountered on your level," he admitted.

"It's as though half the population would have an advantage over the other in countless ways." Raleigh grimaced, thinking about the Receps. "And from there, the top six percent can influence, they'd be at the top of the heap."

"The distribution of power would be different. Wealth is something that stratifies the population, but theoretically anyone can change their status for the better."

Raleigh added, "Or for the worse."

"Yes. But part of the discourse in our society is that the system is poverty and one that's hard to break free of. It's a case of the haves and have nots. And, with Lucid those divides would be stark and unmoving. The hierarchy of society would be completely toppled."

"I wonder if Grant and Able considered all this. For the most part they seem happy to have just a few healers." Raleigh pictured the small glimpses she'd gotten of their facility in New York. "When they talked of expanding into healthcare… all these problems were a long way off."

"It's careless, all of it."

Raleigh's stomach twisted. "Funny, after seeing Thalia I've never wanted to be a doctor more."

"And you'll be a good doctor. I'm just saying that perhaps it's for the best that the world doesn't know about you. Maybe it's a good thing that Lucid is in short supply."

"It's not black and white."

"That's for sure. I just want to make sure that you don't run headlong into training people on how to use it before you consider some of the ethical issues."

"I won't." Raleigh wondered if her problems would ever be something so theoretical. Did Grant and Able think about things like this? They, like her, were focused on survival. When placed in survival mode it was easy to focus on saving herself, and a few others, rather than the consideration of hypothetical victims down the road.

Patrick rapped his fingers on the countertop across from her. "I almost forgot, Tim Moore wants you to visit with him before you go. He's been anxious to get a hold of you for a couple of months now."

"Dr. Moore? It isn't one of his patients, is it?" Surely a cancer patient wouldn't have been able to wait the ten months that she'd been gone.

"No, it has to do with Lucidin, but it isn't that. Stop by his house before you go?"

Before she went. It was clear that it was time to be moving on again. "I guess that means I should try to see him today."

"Give him a call, I'm not sure of his schedule. And don't forget Raleigh, you'll always be welcome here."

Here, but not her home. How different would her life be if she was her uncle's child and not her mother's? A question that she would never know the answer to. There was no point in ruminating about something that could never be. "Thanks. Look out for my family, will you?"

"I always do." Patrick said with a smile.

Their conversation came to an end as Kappa entered the kitchen. Raleigh slid the box of cereal in his direction. Patrick gave her a head nod and a small greeting to Kappa before leaving.

"It sounded like you guys were discussing something serious, I hope I didn't interrupt. Was it something about your mom?" Kappa asked pouring milk into his bowl.

"Not my mom, the ethics surrounding Lucidin."

"A happy topic, then." He smiled as he sat down next to her.

"We should be leaving soon, and my uncle wants me to check in with one of his friends before we go."

"I don't think Rho or Tau will fight you about going, none of us like to stay put anywhere for too long," Kappa said.

The handful of days they'd spent in Colorado had been short, but they'd given her a lot to think about. "We'll make plans to leave sooner rather than later then."

C H A P T E R
06

LATER THAT DAY, Raleigh didn't yet have any plane tickets to leave home, but she did have an appointment with Dr. Moore. Unlike in the past, where they met up in the hospital or at Patrick's, this time he'd invited her over to his house. It was no secret that his schedule was packed, he was the kind of man that never seemed to stop working, but when he finally did, he unwound by playing sports. She preferred to meet with him without the Designed and walked the four blocks from her uncle's house to his alone.

She arrived at a two-story cream house with blue trim. The short brown lawn was neat, and the cars sat in the driveway, not the street. Metal artwork littered the flowerbeds, hinting at the personality of the family inside.

The only other time she'd been here it had been in the winter, at a holiday party. She imagined that in the summer most of that sporting equipment would be sprawled across the grass. During the party she'd spent the whole first hour trying to think up something to say to Keith, Dr. Moore's son. She'd spent the second hour kicking herself for how stupid she'd sounded when she had spoken. It hadn't endeared her to the place. Their relationship had existed in the hospital, and the personal feeling of the house made her walk slowly up to the front steps.

When she reached the front door, she removed a glove and pressed her finger to the cold doorbell. Inside, chimes echoed, and she fought down any of the nerves in her stomach. She'd spoken to Dr. Moore hundreds of times, the place wouldn't matter. Likely he had something routine to discuss.

As the door open she mustered up a smile. It faltered when Keith, his son, stood on the other side. Despite being thirty years younger, Keith felt the same way physically as his father. Both fit and strong, with muscles that ached from the sports they played. It hadn't occurred to her that the younger of the two would answer.

"Raleigh, good to see you." Keith gave her the smile that caused her stomach to drop.

Raleigh stood frozen in the doorway. Usually she had a script prepared for when she spoke to Keith, so she didn't trip over her tongue. "Your father invited me over."

Nodding Keith stepped back. "Yes, he said you'd be coming. He's missed you since you've been gone. Come on in. Mom insists we take our shoes off in the front hall."

Raleigh slipped out of hers, placing them neatly in line with the others. The foyer smelt like dirt and hockey equipment, and she noticed cleats and skates piled in a corner with running shoes.

"Is now a bad time? Should I come back later?" Raleigh didn't know how long Dr. Moore would be out and didn't really want to hang around unwanted.

"He said he'd be on his way soon and that I should entertain you. Do you want any water or tea? Sorry, my parents don't keep soda or juice in the house." She could feel the cold on his bare feet as he walked across the gray tiles.

"Water would be fine."

"I haven't seen you around much. Usually Dad has a lot of stories about how you've helped him at the hospital, but he said that you've been gone. Are you home from college for winter break?"

Raleigh put her hands into her pockets. He didn't know that much about her. "I didn't go to college."

Keith's eyebrows shot up. "Dad was so excited that you'd be going to university. He's got grand plans about you joining him in oncology someday."

"It's not in the cards right now. What about you? Are you planning on following in his footsteps?"

"No, you've taken the pressure off me. I was never leaning that way, up until a few years ago he'd insisted. But then then you came along, and it was Raleigh this and Raleigh that. You've been the apprentice he's always wanted."

For the first time Raleigh began to see her relationship with Dr. Moore through the lens Keith must have. A peer who his father spent time molding into his protege. "I didn't mean to step on your toes."

"Oh, no." He flashed her a wide smile. The kind that slid up one side of his mouth. A grin that she'd described in great detail in more than one diary over the years. "You didn't. I've always wanted to go into finance, so it was nice to have you to distract him while I found other interests."

"He's very proud of you."

"I know, and he's proud of you, too."

Keith filled their glasses with water and handed one to her. The cool water was warmer than her icy winter hands. She took a small sip, not sure where the conversation would go.

"Now Dad just hopes I'll marry a doctor, ideally you. I'm sure you've been a victim of his attempts to play match maker. I'm mortified to think of all the times he's probably hinted that we should be a couple."

"He may have mentioned it once or twice." Raleigh gulped down a sip. "You never seemed interested." The brazen words tripped right out of her mouth. This was why she needed a script when talking with Keith Moore.

Keith's smile grew, and he stepped closer, faint amusement hanging in his voice. "I figured that once you found out I wasn't as smart as my father all bets would be off. That, and you always shied away from me in school."

"I did." Raleigh admitted. "It's taken me a long time to get over the embarrassment of blacking out."

"Really? You were one of the bravest people at school. You've always been who you are, unapologetically."

"I never had a choice."

"Not true. You could have stayed home, you could have taken the bus. Instead you wore that reflective jacket and cycled around. That took guts. I wasn't comfortable enough in my skin, and I didn't have anything to contend with."

She drank another sip of her water unsure of what to say. "Something tells me that you would have found the courage if you needed to."

"So, have I blown my chance? Would it be weird if I took you out while you're back home?"

Raleigh's stomach flipped. In all the countless daydreams she'd had about Keith asking her out she'd managed to say something cool. And the answer in all the scenarios was a resounding yes. She believed what she told Tau, she didn't have to end up with him or his brothers.

But it wasn't meant to be. She'd never bring anyone into her dangerous world so naively. "I don't think we should."

"Don't look so apologetic, I should have gotten up the guts in high school."

The distant sound of a door shutting hailed the arrival of Keith's father. He strode into the kitchen with a pile of mail in one hand and his gloves in the other. "It's cold out there." He absently put the mail down. Then he ruffled Keith's hair with his frozen fingers. "Thanks for covering for me."

"No problem." Keith started for the stairs. "It was good to see you, Raleigh."

Dr. Moore flicked his eyes between the two of them. No doubt curious about the conversation they'd had. If he suspected anything about his son asking her out he didn't say. Instead he waited for Keith's footsteps to be heard overhead and then become accompanied by a reverberating sound of a bass guitar. Their secrets would stay unheard to Keith's ears.

"How have you been? Are you still being treated? Patrick said things fell through with Grant and Able."

Raleigh nodded. "Fell through and then improved." She couldn't say too much, most of the story wasn't hers to tell. "Lucidin is a lot more complicated than I thought it would be."

"Most things in life are."

"Uncle Patrick said you wanted to talk to me?"

Dr. Moore pulled out one of three chairs that sat around the table in the kitchen nook. He motioned for her to sit before taking the one nearest it. "I've invited you here because Sabine wasn't my only lead. She was the most promising, the one offering to do lab work, and the one who got back to me fastest. But since you've left I've been contacted by another. Someone else who works with Lucidin, or at least I think they do."

"Someone other than Grant and Able?" No one had mentioned a rival group of researchers. The idea hadn't occurred to her.

He shook his head. "Related to Grant and Able in a way. I think they might be the tribe of people who they originally did their research on. Do you remember that article I showed you at Patrick's birthday?"

"I remember." Her uncle's fiftieth birthday party had been the night that her whole world had changed. That was the first time that she'd learned of people like her. Even if she didn't remember the article he'd told her about at the party, she recalled that Grant and Able still spoke about the tribe. Their elusive inducer, something that they tried in vain to recreate in a lab, was based on what the tribe used.

"They're the ones that speak to the spirit to help cure illness. You've moved on from simply sensing to helping."

"Influencing. I didn't realize Patrick told you."

Dr. Moore shook his head quickly. "Patrick didn't say a word. Thalia's recovery has spoken for itself, and all I know is that you've had a hand in it. You don't have to tell me more than you're ready for. I only bring it up because they help treat people."

"Did they describe the process in which they heal people? Anything about using a medicinal drink?" That was the most significant part of the original tribe, but she didn't say why.

"I didn't think to ask. The doctor in the town nearby that I've spoken with, Dr. Alexiou, he says the pilgrims come, and they help them. He said that they don't touch them, just pray or something nearby. It may very well be the placebo, but he thinks they're too successful for it to be attributed only to that. Unfortunately, many of the pilgrims' illnesses return once they leave."

"That could be right. Chronic disease may need continual treatment. I'm not really there yet." Raleigh didn't want to tell him too much, especially because she'd yet to really use her skill on anyone other than Thalia. "Grant and Able is looking into using Lucidin for healing, but they've hit a snag, there isn't enough to go around, among other things."

He sat back in his seat, his feet shifting beneath him uncomfortably. True to his word he didn't ask her anything. Instead he chose his words carefully. The lines of his face relaxed again. "As you said, it's complicated I'm sure. Dr. Alexiou asked if they'd be willing to see you as a pilgrim, and they'd agreed. They only see a handful of people at a time. Apparently back in their heyday they saw hundreds, but they've pulled back now. It was hard to get you in, but it's happened."

"Dr. Alexiou isn't one of their healers, is he?"

"No. He lives in the town nearby and helps set up pilgrims. The townsfolk no longer work directly with the people, that's one of the reasons they've seen less."

"And where are they located?"

"They're in Greece."

"Greece?" With a surname like Alexiou the country shouldn't have come as such a surprise. But it contradicted the notion of a tribe that she'd conjured up when hearing the initial stories. She pictured rustic people from South America or Africa. "Are you sure this is the tribe?"

"Like I said, I'm not for certain that it's the same group or that they're using Lucidin at all. They could be religious healers and it might be the placebo effect that they are trading in, but it might be worth checking out."

"Yeah, great, give me the information. I've got to push off from Colorado, anyhow."

"Still have the issues with your mother?"

"Yeah, things haven't improved."

Again he showed restraint and didn't pry. "Raleigh, don't let your family get you down. You're going to be a great doctor someday, and if you ever find yourself in Denver, I would very much like to work with you."

"You too, Dr. Moore. You've always been an inspiration."

"Patrick mentioned that you're staying with him, I'll get the information about Dr. Alexiou tonight."

"That's great."

Raleigh stood up and gave him an awkward handshake. They weren't close enough to hug, but shaking hands was too formal. As she went over to the door and slid into her shoes all she could think about was the inducer. Grant and Able always said its discovery would be a game changer, and this could be one step closer to getting it.

CHAPTER
07

THE WINTER AIR stung Raleigh's cheeks as she walked from Dr. Moore's house to Patrick's. Her steps were long and steady, and her attention remained half on the conversation she'd just had and half on navigating the icy patches of the sidewalk. If an inducer could be found it would mean a steady supply of Lucidin, and that meant that more people could use it to heal.

She rounded the corner, and Patrick's house came into view. The warning he'd given her earlier about Lucidin's place in society hit her as hard as the cold wind. Maybe the world wasn't meant to have it. But the Receps at least, needed it. Adam and Gabe had been trapped by Lucid addiction for too long. The larger ramifications would have to wait. They'd need an army to fight Sigma. Since she didn't want the Receps to take Lucidin, finding the inducer seemed like the only alternative. She went up to the house.

Entering through the door, the smell of cold lingered on her as she shrugged out of her coat and walked into the living room.

The conversation the Designed and Patrick engaged in ceased the moment she arrived.

"What did Tim want?" Patrick asked.

"He thinks that he's located the original tribe. They're in Greece, and they heal people."

Rho stood up from his seat, his brow furrowing. "I thought that Grant and Able said they only sensed."

"It might only be sensing. It sounds like the people who see them improve, but the doctors in the area have been quick to attribute it to the placebo effect. They used to have a lot of visitors, but now they don't have as many. Doctor Moore put my name down on a waitlist months ago. They'd be willing to see me for my blackouts."

Patrick said, "But you're no longer sick. What would be the point of going? Their genetic information is in these three men already. From what I've seen of your abilities, you don't need them to teach you how to use Lucidin."

Kappa interrupted before Raleigh could speak. "They had an inducer. A drink that made people increase their own Lucid production. Most people make little to none, even if they have receptors. This solved that."

Raleigh said, "The Designed and me are the only people that have ever made enough naturally to use it all the time. These people found a way to temporarily make their bodies create it."

"To have the inducer would be a game changer," Tau said.

"Yeah, Grant and Able have been working on it since they met the tribe, to no avail." Raleigh imagined the lab that she'd seen when she lived in Arizona. It had been devoted to the task, and the people working there had been frustrated. The inducer research had all but stagnated.

Kappa ran an uneasy hand through his blonde hair, his face dipping into a frown. "And the reason that Grant and Able are so behind is because the tribe didn't share a shred of information about how to make the drink."

They probably wouldn't share it with her. The realization hit her like a ton of bricks. But she wouldn't give up, not when she'd just seen a glimmer of hope. "G and A were more focused on figuring out Lucidin. They might not have been paying close enough attention to the drink. A lot was happening. Their primary goals were to learn the genetics and devise a synthetic."

Kappa's face remained skeptical. "True enough, but remember they left on bad terms. Poor enough terms that they've never told a soul about the whereabouts of the tribe. If they thought that you could get information, I have no doubt they would've sent you already."

For the first time the inducer seemed within reach. She couldn't let it slip away so quickly. Raleigh gave Kappa a pleading look. "But it would be amazing, wouldn't it?"

"It's not like I like to be the bearer of bad news," Kappa whispered. "I'm just being realistic."

Rho let out a long sigh. "Raleigh, can I have a word with you in the other room?"

Disappointed, she passed by Kappa and the others. She followed Rho into her uncle's library. Books wedged tightly together inside the tall bookcases. It smelt of peppermint. A cup of cold tea sat next to the computer on the corner desk. He shut the heavy door to keep their conversation private.

Raleigh turned to Rho, her reasons for why they should go to Greece bouncing around her head. She'd have to make a sturdy argument, and her desperation for finding the truth for the inducer wasn't the best place to start.

"Rho. I think that I should follow up and take the appointment." She stood up straight, her voice unwavering.

He stepped closer to her and put a hand on her shoulder. His fingers warmed her cold skin through her cotton shirt. "Of course you want to go. If this is the original tribe, and we could somehow get the inducer, it would change everything. We'd no longer be hunted, Grant and Able, and whoever else we gave it to, would have enough to satisfy as many healers as they wanted."

"You think it's too dangerous."

He moved his hand down her arm, sliding it across her forearm and eventually taking her hand. "Of all the things you've suggested doing, from going undercover at G and A to bringing down the synthetic, it's the most rational of all."

"But you still don't want me to do it?"

"It's not about what I want. I've made that mistake one too many times with you. I know you're going to leave no matter what I say. And I hate waiting for you to come back, worrying that you won't. Last time I should have been with you."

"Then you would have ended up in the bunker."

"I was in my own hell while you were there." His blue eyes stared at her intensely. He'd suffered when he'd thought her dead. His hand tightened around hers. "This time I want to go along."

"But your brothers need you to help devise a plan to get Sigma."

"We're at a standstill until we get more information on where Sigma is. I don't see any problem with us checking this out for a few days. Why not see if there's anything there?"

Relief burbled up in her chest. She wouldn't have to fight Rho on this. He'd go along with her. "You think the Sigma problem can wait?"

"Grant and Able have far better resources than us. They're more likely to find him. I'd say going is better than sitting around."

"Great! Then we'll buy the tickets. Do you think that we should use false passports? Should we get Trevor on it? Dr. Moore said he would send over the information tonight. But Athens has got to be the main airport in Greece, we can probably start looking at flights."

"I think Kappa will want to come. And Tau too. Let's see who wants to go."

Raleigh squeezed Rho's hand before opening the door to the library and telling them that they'd decided that it would be worth checking out the group in Greece.

Tau didn't appear at all surprised, but Kappa didn't change his attitude on it and said, "You should call Agatha and find out exactly why they haven't contacted the tribe in the last thirty years, despite how urgently they've needed that inducer. And we should remember that if they don't like G and A then they're not going to like us."

"They don't need to know about you. We don't have to show any of our hand." She'd gone undercover at G and A and with the synthetic. Rho was right. They'd squared off against far worse.

Rho didn't dismiss Kappa's plan. "We should call Agatha. We'll have to let them know where we are in case something with Sigma comes up. And it might not be a bad idea to know what exactly went sour so we don't set ourselves up for failure."

"Then let's call her right now. Do we have her number?"

Patrick surprised them. "I have it. She gave it to us once you left, she said if we had any leads about your whereabouts we should call."

Grant and Able had their hands on everything. Raleigh pushed past her annoyance that they'd contacted Patrick and asked, "Can we use your phone Uncle Patrick, I'd like to give her a call."

Patrick located the number on his phone and extended it to Raleigh. She stared at Agatha's name. So far, she'd seen and spoken to Grant and Able solely through Gabe. The last time she'd seen Agatha was when she'd broken out Mu and Tau. The intense moment had solidified her betrayal. Could she set all that aside so easily?

Raleigh stepped towards the library a second time. "I'm going to take this in private. I didn't leave things on good terms, and I don't know how she'll take me calling now."

"Remember that Adam said that even when they were hunting us they were under orders not to hurt you," Tau said.

Another turning point in her life. The evening Gabe captured her and Tau she refused to have Adam help her escape without him. It had been the moment Tau figured out they were on the same team, and from that friendship so much evolved. How she wished he would bolster her now as he'd done then, but he remained sitting on the couch.

"Do you want me to talk to her with you?" Rho offered.

"Yeah." Raleigh stepped back so Rho could shut the door. "All right, here we go." She pushed the call button.

"It'll be fine," Rho said as the phone rang.

She turned to look at him. Agatha had chosen his coloring to be the same as a little boy she'd known growing up. With his long lashes and easy smile, Raleigh wanted to reach out and touch his face. What did Agatha think of him now?

"This is Agatha Grant." As always, Agatha held professionalism in her voice. Before, the formality made her trust-inspiring. Now it just made her distant.

"Agatha, this is Raleigh Groves. And Rho is here, too."

A pause crackled across the phone. *"Raleigh? Is everything all right? Gabe told me that you were checking in on your sister."*

"Everything is fine, my sister is fine." Raleigh planned to extend pleasantries and avoid the discussion of that fateful night where she'd escaped with Rho, but it weighed too heavy on her to think about anything else. "I'm sorry about how things played out at the benefactor dinner."

Another long pause, and when Agatha spoke her voice was

deeper and raw. *"I understand why you did what you did. You'd told me on more than one occasion that you feared the Receps were addicted. Since that time I've faced the problem head on."*

"And?"

"And it's the same one that you grappled with. The potential of Lucidin is limitless in medicine. The benefit immeasurable. But, it does cost the user, I'm willing to say that now. Natural Lucidin is better, but it still carries with it the potential to cause addiction."

"But you're still training Receps."

"Yes. The benefits outweigh the risks. Now, with Sigma capturing our Modified, we are forced to protect ourselves, and the playing field is not even. Is that why you wanted to speak to me? To discuss the Modified?"

Raleigh wished she had something on that topic to say. "Dale is safe."

"I'm thankful for that."

"I've called because I met up with one of my old physician friends. He's arranged an appointment for me to meet with a group of people in Greece who we believe use Lucidin. We think they might be the original tribe that your dad studied."

Agatha inhaled sharply. Clearly she hadn't expected this. *"What?"*

"Yes, he found a group of people in Greece that 'speak to the sprit' of the ailing person. They work on healing them. Could it be them, could they be influencing?"

"Raleigh, the original tribe, they aren't interested in Lucidin. They won't want to talk to you. We didn't end things on good terms. They were livid with us exploring Lucidin. To them it is a divinely given gift, they refused to acknowledge it any other way. We broke ties, and there is a reason that we've been forced to research the inducer without them."

Rho reached out for the phone. Raleigh handed it to him. He pressed the speakerphone. "Agatha, this is Rho. Are they dangerous?" Raleigh turned and scrunched her nose. There was no way these people had anything on Grant and Able or the synthetic dealers. Rho put up a hand. "I'm not saying that we won't go, I'm just saying that it might be nice to know what to expect."

"*They weren't dangerous.*" Agatha paused. "*No more than anyone who chooses faith in the presence of science.*"

Raleigh stomach twisted. "It isn't really faith though. Faith is a belief in something you can't see. A person can experience Lucid. So it's more of a belief in magic instead of science."

"A mistake that many people have made for centuries," Rho said. "What is magic but something that we've yet to understand the explanation for?"

Agatha broke through their musings. "*These people, they think they've been touched by some divine being. They said that messing with who could use Lucidin would bring a curse upon us.*"

The Designed. A curse for messing with something that shouldn't have been explored. Grant and Able describe things as missteps, the Designed, the synthetic trade, they were the cost of doing something amazing. Maybe Agatha was more like the tribe than she realized. She'd put her faith in Lucidin, believing strongly that the setbacks would be worth it in the end. Raleigh wanted to think about it unbiased, but with both the drama of the Designed and her harrowing experience in the bunker, she struggled to see it untainted.

"But, the tribe could be in Greece? And they could be influencing?" Rho repeated the original question. "The word tribe had me considering someplace more remote."

"*They are nomads. Exiled from their home centuries ago for being witches. They are a tribe of people, and yes, they have settled there. I would caution you that if you go it is likely the same group. You, Rho, should be very careful. I don't think they would be happy to meet one of our creations.*"

"Did they know that you made people with the genetics you took?" Raleigh asked.

"No," Agatha said.

"So they have no way of knowing about our interest in Lucidin or that we even know about it unless we say," Raleigh reasoned. "And they still have the inducer. We need to go and check it out."

"They won't tell you about it. The inducer affects the mind in more than just Lucidin production. It's akin to a religious experience for them. I would caution you. Your time would be better spent in a lab than in their presence."

"Thanks, we'll take that into consideration," Rho said. "Thanks so much for your time, Agatha."

"Wait! Don't hang up just yet. I'm going to have Gabe meet with you in Athens and provide backup. I'm not sure how well these people will receive you. Adam's been concerned about you, Raleigh, since you were trapped. He'll want to go along as well. Let them go, too. They can help if you get in over your head."

"It's a simple tribe of people. Do you really think that they could do anything to us?" Raleigh asked.

"They've been working with Lucidin for centuries, any advantages that you'd normally have you won't with them. I'd feel better if Gabe is close enough to help you out this time. We're supposed to be on the same team now, remember?"

"All right. He can be nearby but not directly involved. I don't want any hint that you're involved in this," Raleigh said.

Agatha paused as if wanting to say more. She settled on a farewell. *"I'll let him know. Take care, Raleigh."*

"You, too, Agatha," Raleigh said and then the line went dead.

"Do you think she only wants the inducer?" Rho asked.

"She knows that I'd give it to her to help aid the Receps. No, I think that she's frightened of the tribe, and I think that she can't beat Sigma without us. Like she said, we're supposed to be on the same team."

"Then Gabe and Adam can come along, but let's not involve them anymore than we have to."

Raleigh stared at the phone. She didn't know enough about the tribe to know the danger, but a group of healers couldn't be that bad. And Agatha was wrong, their advantage was that the tribe wouldn't know that Raleigh could use Lucidin, she'd have the element of surprise on her side if things went south.

CHAPTER
08

AGAIN RALEIGH FOUND herself in one of the black airport terminal seats. She'd flown from Colorado to Pennsylvania, and now she had a connection for an overnight flight to Greece. They'd arrive in the morning. Over the last day she'd said goodbye to her family, the parts that still spoke to her, packed up her bags, and headed out.

The rough carpet beneath her feet was the kind that masked stains and muffled noises. Kappa, Rho, and Tau sat around a pile of cards, all of them paying more attention to their game than the large planes that passed by the window.

A gray sky promised a bumpy flight. Red delays marked the nearby arrivals and departure boards. A storm was barreling its way up from the south, and Raleigh desperately wanted to leave before it hit. Flying was bad enough when you didn't add lightning into the mix.

Her nose crinkled against the smell of too many people crammed into too small of a space for too long of a time. Even though it was late afternoon, the aroma of coffee drifted through the air, heightening her senses even more than usual.

"Are you worried about the flight or what we're going to do when we get there?" Tau glanced up from the cards long enough to catch her eyes and with it her answer.

"More the flight than anything else."

"Don't get your hopes up too high about the inducer." Kappa tossed down a card and took up the pile. "We should discuss what we're going to tell them about your disease."

"I'm going to tell them that I faint and no one knows why. They should have no reason to suspect the truth. I obviously won't be barricading, but I've never sensed Lucid in one of you. Can you sense it in me?"

"No. The first time I met you I had no idea that you had any of it in your system." Kappa rubbed the back of his neck.

Rho nodded. "I can tell when Collin takes it, but then it's more because he stops fidgeting."

"And you can tell when someone has taken too much and they over-control parts of their body," Tau added. "But once again it's the effect of Lucid you can sense, not the actual hormone. So you should be fine."

"I'll wear long sleeves so they won't see the bandages." Once again her port had been removed, this time by Patrick. "If they see the scars, I'll tell them that that it was a failed attempt at a treatment."

Tau shifted uneasily in his seat. "If you faint around them, all bets will be off. I'm not sure how'd we'd explain that."

They all tossed their cards down onto the dark gray carpet and Kappa snatched them up. He began shuffling the cards his eyes on Tau. "Why do you say that?"

"When she faints, she amplifies the sensations around her. But they only happen every few days."

Raleigh said, "And even then they only last for a few seconds, I'm out afterward for around five to fifteen minutes. But I only exaggerate the other's sensations during the overload."

"Maybe you should have left in your port." Kappa dealt out the cards again.

"No. It would be too hard to explain." Rho's eyes darted around the terminal. Most of the people were frustrated by the changing flights, they weren't eavesdropping on a conversation that out of context made little to no sense. "If they do figure out that she makes Lucid, she can feign ignorance. If she's got a port, they'll wonder who's been taking it out of her. That's a bunch of questions that lead back to Grant and Able and us."

"So what's our story?" Tau asked. "We're to be three friends who are worried about her wellbeing?"

Rho said, "Yes. We don't need to have an elaborate cover like you all did with the synthetic. We're not hoping to infiltrate them, we'll keep it simple, it will be easier to stick to the script if it's not too detailed."

"I guess it's a plan." Kappa picked back up his hand as their plane pulled into the gate. A few minutes later a stream of people exited, and the information on the board showed that they'd be boarding soon, after the grime of the last flight had been tidied up. Soon enough they'd be on their way.

THE DISADVANTAGE TO buying plane tickets the day before was that none of their seats were remotely close together. Raleigh sat in the middle of the plane, aisles on either side of her set of seats and beyond them more seats and a window. From here she caught only glimpses of the sky and had to rely on the feeling of the plane to know when they'd sliced through the clouds to calmer air above. The man to her right drifted off the moment he buckled his seatbelt, and the girl to her left played on her phone, her large university sweater falling over her thin hands.

Raleigh hadn't had a phone in a year and rarely missed it now. But a distraction would have been nice. Unlike other overseas flights she'd been on, this one didn't have individual televisions, only a screen a few rows up. With little to do, she considered the girl, who might be going abroad for the semester. Would Raleigh have done that in College? The questions of what might have been stacked up in her mind. For the first time in days the worried thoughts of Thalia and the excited expectations of the inducer weren't occupying her mind.

"Excuse me?" Kappa's voice said, grabbing her attention.

Raleigh's eyes darted to the seatbelt sign. How long had it been off? And what was Kappa doing back here now? She opened her mouth to ask but found that his words hadn't been directed to her. Instead he'd spoken to the college student that Raleigh had been trying to put herself in the shoes of.

"Yeah?" The girl sounded annoyed as she drew her attention from her phone to Kappa. The slight impatience was replaced with a smile at the sight of him. Raleigh sensed her mouth dry ever so slightly. A clear sign of nerves, apparently she thought Kappa was cute.

He laid on the charm thick. "I'm sorry for bothering you. But could I swap seats with you so I can sit with my friend? I'm a few rows up and nearer a window."

The girl glanced around her seat. The backpack she'd stowed under the one in front of her was easy enough to move. "All right."

"I really appreciate that." Kappa's smile grew wider, a dimple appearing on the right side.

Had the scientist developed that dimple? It didn't exactly fit with the whole flawless skin thing they had going. Was that an odd anomaly? If it was, it certainly helped now, the girl practically fell over herself getting out of the seat. The only thing that could have made it worse was if she were to giggle.

As she stood up, Kappa leaned close to her as he pointed out his former seat. She gave him one last smile and headed in the direction that he'd pointed. Then Kappa slid into her seat sitting down beside Raleigh.

"You flirted with her."

"I wanted the seat. And it wasn't really flirting."

"Yeah, but she only switched with you because she thinks you're cute."

"Cute isn't the word for it. And once again, that's out of my control. And please, Rho's constantly using the same tricks on you."

"I haven't been fooled."

"Not lately. Which I give you credit for, but that's the reason I wanted to talk to you now, when he's not around."

Raleigh'd hoped he'd realized how anxious she'd been about flying and that he'd come back to reassure her that the plane wouldn't crash. "I don't want to talk about my dating life with you."

"And normally I would say that it's none of my business, but he's going along with whatever you say to get on your good side. That effects all of us."

Raleigh snorted. "That isn't Rho. If anything he's stubborn. We discussed going to Greece. It was actually his idea."

"You're kidding yourself. The moment you walked in that door, I could see the excitement on your face. You'd have to be an idiot to not guess that you wanted to go. Rho is anything but stupid."

"We should go, we've faced a lot worse, and the payoff could be huge."

"I'm not disagreeing with you. I brought up the drawbacks only because that was Rho's job, and he's not doing it."

The plane hit a bump, and her stomach dropped. Her hand grabbed the armrest as the turbulence jostled the plane. Kappa didn't appear bothered, and he didn't mention the ride, keeping his face serious.

"He's never gone along with me before," she said.

"I've known him all my life. In that orphanage we were the only family each other had. I'd never call him a pushover, but he's not following his gut now. He likes you."

Raleigh huffed turning away. "I'm not in a relationship with him."

"But you will be soon. Look, he said that dating would discredit you, but that isn't the case, all of us think you're great."

"Then why are you interrogating me?"

"Because he was devastated when you went missing. When he found out that you were in a bunker underground, I half expected him to dig up all of Europe. It was bad, he was a wreck. He said that he wished he would have gone undercover with you."

Rho himself had said that he would rather have been trapped than not knowing her whereabouts. "I'm sure he was worried, but I don't think that he would agree with me to get on my good side."

"You came back from the bunker, and the chemistry between you two had fizzled. Tell me that wasn't because of how he pushes back on you."

She shifted in her seat, the bumps making her clutch the armrest harder. Tau had been the reason. But the fewer people who knew of that the better. Tau considered their relationship a slight to Rho, would Kappa? None of it mattered, Tau had been clear. "I had a lot on my mind after the bunker."

"And now you and Rho are falling back into step, and he's going to do whatever he has to do to keep you by his side. Even if that means walking into an awful situation." Kappa held up his hands. "I'm not saying that this is. But the great thing about you is that you're a risk-taker, and the good thing about Rho is that he assumes the worst-case scenario. Together you're good at balancing out the group, which is why you're great leading together. But if he's not following his real desires, then the whole dynamic of our group will fall apart."

"So you don't want me to date him?" Maybe Rho'd been right about his brothers disapproving, maybe that was what this really was about. They had a limited dating pool, and Kappa could be jealous that Rho had someone.

"Date him or don't. The point is, pay attention, encourage him to speak his mind."

Raleigh stared forward to the front of the plane. Rho sat up there somewhere. What Kappa accused him of wasn't fair. "Fine. I don't think it's necessary, but fine."

"Great, that's all I ask." Kappa turned forward as well. "So tell me about this Adam kid. He's a friend of yours?"

"Yeah." Adam she could discuss. Anything was better than analyzing her relationship with Rho. She took up explaining the Receps and their addiction.

CHAPTER
09

ATHENS, UNLIKE DENVER, wasn't trapped under the icy hand of winter. People here wore lighter coats, and as they left the airport, they encountered sleet rather than snow. Despite the warmer weather, Raleigh sunk down in her coat trying to fight back the chill that ran down her back. She'd not seen Gabe since the team had rescued her from the bunker, and it had been longer since she'd seen Adam. Somehow their already complicated relationships had intensified.

Tau stepped closer, and she fought the well-trained butterflies that wished to skip across her spine.

"What's wrong?" Tau asked.

Raleigh'd been barricading, and she hoped that only Tau would be able to read the apprehension on her face. "Things are weird with Gabe and Adam."

"Weird because you're worried that they'll betray us?"

"No, because I screwed them over. That, and they're addicted to our Lucid. Adam hasn't always been like this."

"I know. The Receps got a raw deal, but hopefully the tribe has solved that."

Another expectation that the tribe might not be able to live up to. But still, they must have some of the answers. They'd lived for millennia with Lucidin as a critical part of their culture. Grant and Able must have missed an important piece of the puzzle, if after only a generation they were ripping apart at the seams.

The wide windows of the café reflected Raleigh's face back to her, and through that translucent image, on the other side of the glass, were Gabe and Adam. Now or never. She lifted her chin from the warmth of the coat, let the cold steel her, and then entered.

At this hour people were beginning their days. With breakfast being served, most of the tables were occupied by people speaking energetically. She passed by imagining the stories that unfolded. The unfamiliar syllables of Greek scrolled across the chalkboard menu were nonsensical to her. In the air the aroma of coffee and bread mingled with herbs and spices that tickled her nose.

Gabe and Adam's small table had an uncomfortable number of chairs clustered around it. Both rose as they approached. Raleigh stuck out her hand to Gabe who shook it formally while nodding to the Designed. If Grant and Able were going to betray them and attempt to take Rho, this would be the moment to do it. Raleigh waited, standing between the Designed and Grant and Able. Positioned directly behind her was Rho, his breath crossing her shoulder by her ear. Nothing unexpected, there were no hidden Receps waiting to shoot them with inhibitor.

"Rho." Gabe put out his hand. "It's good to meet you. I know neither of us ever anticipated we'd have this truce, but here we are."

Rho's arm reached around Raleigh to shake Gabe's hand. Raleigh wanted to reissue her warning to Gabe, to say that if anything happened to Rho… she couldn't think about it. Gabe was correct, the decisions that they'd made, that she'd made, had led them here.

Gabe motioned for them to sit. "The tribe is about an hour drive from Athens."

Everyone clustered around the table, with Adam, Tau, and Kappa in the seats slightly removed. It surprised no one that the people who would be having this conversation were Raleigh, Rho, and Gabe.

"My uncle and Dr. Moore got me an appointment with their healers." Raleigh lifted the edge of her coat cuff. Her shirtsleeve made it so the fabric bunched well below her port. "I took out the tubing."

Gabe nodded. "That's for the best. Agatha and Oliver said that things ended poorly with the tribe. The tribesmen aren't stupid. They figured out why Grant and Able had been so keen to learn their genetics."

Kappa swore lightly.

Rho cleared his throat, drowning out the expletive. "Agatha said they don't know about us."

Gabe crinkled his nose. "No, but they know that the information was going to be used to enhance people."

"So they don't know people were created from scratch to use it," Raleigh reiterated. She turned to observe Rho. The artificial beauty that was a hallmark of the Designed was impossible to ignore. At least it was for her. Once you learned what a Designed looked like you could pick out the others. But the tribe wouldn't have had a rundown on what had been done to the make the guys, only that they had their genetics altered. That could easily mean that they would appear like everyone else.

"As Designed you stand out," Gabe said to Rho. "And if they learn you make Lucidin…."

"They won't." Rho interrupted before Gabe could predict the outcome. Gabe had guessed what they'd all come to the conclusion about at the airport, these people would probably be hostile if they knew about the Designed.

Raleigh said, "They aren't going to barricade or influence. They're saying that they are friends of mine, along to make sure that I do all right."

Gabe sat back in his chair. "Adam and I could accompany Raleigh. I understand why you don't want to send her in alone. But your existence will be an affront to these people if they find you out."

"No way. We're going in with her." Rho's tone left no room for argument.

Raleigh put a hand on Rho's shoulder, and he relaxed under her touch. "Gabe, that's thoughtful. But both you and Adam are twitchy. It's the addiction." She put up her hand before he could speak. "I know you think that we exaggerate the effects of Lucidin on you. But, the truth is that you and Adam both seem off to me. If the Designed don't influence or barricade there should be no evidence of the Lucidin in their systems. Yours is clearly affected by it."

Adam interrupted. "If you all would give us more Lucid, we wouldn't be like this."

Gabe shot him a warning look. "We didn't come here to beg for Lucidin."

"Great, because we've agreed you're not getting any," Rho said. Her wishes spoken by his lips. Or maybe Rho was fine with some Receps getting Lucid, just not these two.

Gabe nodded with his words. He evidently hadn't expected the Lucidin. "The tribe is located on an island. They don't invite outsiders to stay, so all patients like Raleigh stay in the town across the water."

Raleigh hadn't realized that the tribe was on an island. The physician who Dr. Moore had coordinated her appointment with had arranged a hotel and said that she would be brought to see the healers. In that way she knew that the tribe remained separate and that she wouldn't be staying with them. However, this was the first time that she'd heard of a physical separation between the tribe and the doctors who'd arranged her stay. "I didn't realize they were that isolated."

Gabe said, "They are very isolated. Grant and Able were invited to the island, but they won't extend the same offer to you. The village houses pilgrims who come to see the tribe, but over the years the tribe has seen fewer and fewer people."

"Why is that if they're healing people?" Raleigh imagined all the miracles that Lucidin could accomplish. She'd figure the line to see the healers would be out the door.

"They put a religious bent on it. They don't touch or do anything obvious to heal the sick. Most people attribute their recoveries to God. As medicine has offered up more and more answers their soul speaking hasn't been able to compete. People still see them to be sure, and people donate money to their religious cause, but they don't have the draw they once had."

"So you'll stay here in Athens?" Rho asked.

"Yes, we don't want too large of a presence. Her having three companions for a visit is already a lot. We won't draw unnecessary attention." Gabe shot Adam a look as he spoke. From the way Adam squirmed it was clear he wanted to be more involved.

Rho stood. "Thanks for that. We'll let you know if we get in over our head, and we'll keep you informed if we find the inducer."

Gabe rose and shook Rho's hand one last time. "You have my number. Let us know if you need us."

THEY TRADED THE hubbub of Athens for the rolling hills and serene countryside. Eventually they rambled into the village where Dr. Alexiou lived. Houses greeted them on the outskirts, their quaint structures and bright doors hinting at the culture within. Further into town the houses became apartments, and the commercial industry went from blue collar to white. It wasn't terribly different than the smaller towns around Liège. They wound through the roads, their car's GPS eventually leading them to Dr. Alexiou's.

A breeze whipped by Raleigh as she stepped out of the car, leaving the taste of salt on her lips. The short street lined with offices sat on a hill, and the wind tumbled down it as though in a tunnel. Turning, she tucked her hair behind her ear and faced the sea. An island hung in the distance, and a city rose up from its rocky cliffs. Medieval compared to the more modern city, a reminder that Europe had far more history than the United States. Could this be the island of the tribe?

They walked up the short set of stairs to the door where a shiny metal plaque read Dr. Alexiou. This had to be him. Kappa knocked on the door, and a moment later a middle-aged man opened it. He had a neatly trimmed beard and happy eyes that roved over the four of them, ending on Raleigh. "You must be Miss Groves. I'm Dr. Alexiou, please come in."

Raleigh and the others filed into the front hall. Hints of domestic life peeked out in the worn rug and the tattered umbrellas in the coat rack. In Belgium many residences sat over stores and offices, and it wouldn't have surprised her to find that this was not only his office but home as well. A change to the sterile square buildings back in the States that housed many different medical practices all at once.

"Please have a seat, you must be tired after your flight." Dr. Alexiou walked them over to a small seating area. Magazines, both medical and pop culture splayed across the coffee table, and seats lined the room breaking the illusion that it was a den and hinting at its dual purpose as being a waiting room.

They took the chairs, and Raleigh half expected him to offer her tea. "Thanks for seeing me." She didn't know how much Dr. Moore had told him about her, obviously he would know about the blackouts but probably little else.

"It is no problem to me. I've been in contact with your friend Dr. Moore for quite a few months. Most of the medical professional I discuss the Docents with think I'm crazy. Your Dr. Moore has been very open-minded."

"Is that the name of the healers that you've arranged for me to see?" Raleigh asked.

"It's what they call themselves. They see themselves as teachers and stewards."

"And do they ever see any of your patients here?" Everything around them hinted that Dr. Alexiou was a traditional doctor, but he may have combined his western medicine with their abilities. Not unlike the way Dr. Moore had her come in to meet the occasional difficult case.

Dr. Alexiou shook his head. "No. They live on the island that you can see from the village. They used to invite people there, but they closed their doors around thirty years ago. Now pilgrims, like yourself, are boated across and seen. They used to see hundreds of people, but they've pulled back. As modern medicine has gained traction, their unorthodox methods have fallen out of favor."

"What are these different methods?" Rho kept his voice light and free of judgment.

Despite Rho's lack of skepticism, Dr. Alexiou shifted in his seat, pausing before he answered. "They treat the soul." He held up a hand. "I'm not a religious man myself. But a lot of their patients have seen improvements. It may be the placebo effect, it may be that these people's problems were all imagined."

"Raleigh's problems aren't imagined," Tau said. "She blacks out."

"Quite right, many of the people are truly sick. All I know is that people get better, at least in the short term."

"So they're faith healers?" For a fleeting moment she considered that maybe this wasn't the tribe. Perhaps it was a coincidence, Greece wasn't a tiny country. They could be the original tribe or a group of charlatans.

Alexiou's brow furrowed at the reference. "No, if you're talking about the religious leaders who put on shows where they heal people. If anything, it's the opposite. They sit with the ill. Like I said, their methods are different from the type of medicine I practice. That's part of the reason they've had fewer pilgrims, trying to heal the soul is different from our advanced understanding of the body. Some of the people who visit them are disappointed."

"How so?" Raleigh asked.

"Little is done during their sessions. They take you to a room, and you sit. There isn't any talking about symptoms, or emotions, it's just sitting. Nothing fancy. People are often angry that they've made the trip for so little. Hopefully you will keep an open mind and not go in expecting too much."

Raleigh's skin grew warm. If a person was to use Lucidin, it wouldn't appear to be anything special to an outsider. Anyone who'd passed by Thalia's hospital bed would have assumed they were all sitting around her deep in thought. "How does it work?" The words came out of her mouth barely over a whisper.

"I don't know the particulars, only that the soul is helped.

Something happens during these sessions. Tomorrow, you'll see if they can help you at all."

"Thank you for setting this up." Rho extended his hand.

"It is nothing. You'll be staying at the hotel across the water from the island. They'll arrange the visitation tomorrow with the boatman. The Docents don't work directly with the doctors, they use the hotel and the boatman as their go-between."

They extended their thanks to Dr. Alexiou one last time before leaving his office and heading back out to the car.

"They heal by sitting around." Raleigh repeated under her breath.

Rho nodded. "Yes, it's promising. Let's find that hotel."

CHAPTER

10

THE HOTEL THAT Dr. Alexiou mentioned sat on the edge of town nearest the water. From the front stoop Raleigh got a good view of the island. It stood near enough that she could see some of the pillars of the old town and the high stone wall but far enough away that she could discern little else. Overhead, birds sailed on white feather wings, dipping into the choppy water. Raleigh didn't trust water, and the sight of the unpredictable sea made her stomach fill with a sense of foreboding.

Rho followed her line of sight. "We should go inside and get your boat trip arranged."

What, if anything, did the island mean to the Designed? They'd been trapped once on an island, even though it wasn't this one. Rho had nearly died plunging into the sea when he found his freedom from the synthetic. Did dreams of saltwater haunt him like the nightmares of being buried alive plagued her?

They went into the hotel. The reception area was small, a room that could fit little more than the desk and a coat stand. On one side was a staircase with tattered red carpet, and to the other a larger room was filled with tables. An old woman sat staring out of the window in the dining room, a glossy expression on her face. The way she stood indicated that she wasn't a guest, that this was her home, and that even though Dr. Alexiou had described it as a hotel, it was more akin to a bed and breakfast.

The man at the reception desk looked up from his work. "Do you have a reservation?" Behind him there was a wall adorned with thirty hooks. Dangling from most of them were heavy metal keys each tagged with a plastic metal number.

"Yes, I'm Raleigh Groves. I should have two rooms reserved."

"That's right. Two rooms with two twin beds apiece." The man scanned the Designed but didn't comment further on the sleeping arrangements.

"I'm also supposed to see if you can arrange a boatman to take me across to the island," Raleigh said.

"The Docents are expecting you, and you can go across tomorrow morning. Your name will be on the boatman's list. The boat leaves at ten a.m, on the pier across the street. There are a few other pilgrims crossing, it should be easy to find."

At his words the old woman turned and tossed up her arms. She moved in an erratic, hurried fashion in their direction. Her white hair made a halo around her head, contrasting with the black of her pupils, which were large and frightening. "Cursed. Don't go. Cursed. *Witches!*"

There had been time to move, but Raleigh had been so shocked by the ranting that she'd stayed stationary. The woman's arthritic hands reached out, grasping Raleigh by shoulder. The long nails dug into Raleigh's jacket.

"Let go." Raleigh could have stopped her. The woman was

weak. She was so frail that she worried any forceful movement might hurt the elderly woman.

"*Witches!*"

Swiftly, the receptionist went behind the woman and detached the old woman's hands from Raleigh's arms. The woman's fingers still curled in the air as the receptionist walked her back a few feet. "She's old and believes things about the Docents." He shouted into the adjoining room, "Phoebe!"

A pregnant woman appeared in the neighboring room, one hand on her belly as she rounded the table nearest the entrance. She clenched her teeth in response to the pain in her back and then let out a breath before addressing the old woman in soft, rapid Greek. With a hand on the elderly woman's narrow shoulder, she soothed her while tugging her back towards the dining room window.

Recovering quickly, as though this wasn't the first time the old woman had clawed his guests, the receptionist walked towards them with a smile. "Your rooms are up this way." He started up the steps and motioned for them to follow.

Kappa followed on the receptionist's heels. "What the hell was that about?"

The receptionist said, "The Docents don't believe in God. Some people, like my mother, believe them to be witches. She's an old woman whose age is hurting her mind. Please ignore her."

As Raleigh climbed the steps, apprehension twisted in her. How common was this opinion of the Docents? Evil and wicked? No one had ever equated Raleigh's skills to witchcraft, but they had been compared to miracles. It might not take much to sway it across the mystic line that separated the two.

They reached the two simple rooms, and Rho caught her eye as the receptionist handed them the keys. She couldn't room with Rho, not when their relationship teetered close to dating, and she hadn't yet decided that's what she wanted. Her heart craved Tau, and she fought the urge to turn to him. She couldn't room with him, not if she couldn't curl up beside him during the night if the terror of the darkness became too daunting. "Kappa, share with me?"

She opened the door, and Kappa threw his bag on one of two open beds. The small room had very little else, they'd be sharing a bathroom at the end of the hall. The door shut, and she put her bag on the open bed.

"Not Rho, huh?" Kappa said.

"We're not discussing my relationship with Rho again."

"Fair enough. Do you want to discuss that woman in the lobby?"

Raleigh put her hands on her hips and stretched her spine. No, she didn't really want to talk about it. "You, of all people, should understand how people can see those who use Lucidin as evil."

Kappa gave a small laugh. "True again. Come on, let's go find some food with the others."

They would need to eat, and Raleigh usually liked exploring new towns. But after the long flight, the meeting with Gabe, and the frantic old woman downstairs, she was ready to sleep. She gave the thin bed a longing glance before following Kappa out, promising herself that she would make it an early night.

RALEIGH WOKE TO pitch black. Sweat clung to her neck and plastered her hair against her cheek. Half-awake she moved her arm out to find Tau. Gone, she was alone. Was she back in the bunker? Tossing off the blankets, the cold air sobered her mind. The fear ebbed as her memory of the night before beat back the haze of her jet lag. She was in Greece. The knot in her chest loosened. Across the way Kappa breathed lightly. Lying back down she hoped to return to sleep, but in the dark the room was suffocating. What she needed now was to see the sky.

Padding over to the window she separated the wooden blinds and found a dark night. Clouds drizzled down blotting out the stars and gave the streetlights halos. The scene wasn't enough to calm her nerves. She drew on her coat and left the room.

She passed the main lobby and stepped out into the night. There was a time, not even a year ago, that she would've been cautious going out in the dark. She'd taken enough self-defense classes to know that women weren't safe enough in the world to venture out at all times of the day. A luxury her male companions probably never had to deal with. But, now her Lucid provided her protection, and she didn't fear anything that lurked in the night.

The fresh air shocked the last of the drowsiness from her system. Finally she could breathe. The air was cold, but her lungs relaxed enough to actually use it. No bunker, she was free. In the distance, the town of the Docents waited. Water separated their town from the one she was in now, and in the dark, the black expanse appeared more like an abyss. She allowed the night to envelop her a while longer before stepping back inside.

"You're up." Phoebe, the woman who'd soothed the older woman this afternoon, intercepted her before Raleigh could make it up the steps. The robe Phoebe wore barely tied around her belly. "I heard the door open and wondered who would be out at this time of night."

"I didn't mean to wake you."

"Don't be silly, it wasn't you. This baby is keeping me up."

Raleigh sensed the child, who had dropped. He'd be born within the next few weeks. His legs were strong, and his size took a toll on his mother. Her heartburn probably was what kept her from sleeping.

Raleigh didn't mean to worry her. "I'll get back to bed."

"Stay, talk with me a moment." Phoebe motioned to the small dining room off the entrance. Mismatched chairs circled scraped up tables. Raleigh pulled out one of the seats and sat while Phoebe lumbered into the one beside her.

After situating herself, Phoebe took a deep breath and then focused on Raleigh. "That woman this afternoon, who grabbed you, she is my grandmother."

"Oh." Raleigh didn't know what to say. The minor interaction she'd had with the woman had been less than pleasant. "I'm sorry if I caused her stress."

"No, don't apologize. We house pilgrims because we are close to the docks, and she's always had a problem with it."

"Because she believes the Docents are witches?"

"I don't know how much research you've done."

For all she knew about Lucid she knew little about the Docents. "My doctor spoke to one in your village, he said that they might be able to help me. I have a disease that no one understands."

Phoebe broke eye contact and inhaled slowly. Her lungs, uncomfortably constricted in her chest, didn't fully expand due to the baby. "The people who live on that island are a cult. They believe that we are all connected to a Universal Soul and that God doesn't exist."

"And that's what makes them witches?"

"That's the issue my grandmother takes with them. A long time ago they welcomed people onto their island. The townsfolk there were fanatic about their Docents, their religious leaders, practically worshiping them."

"And you saw this?"

"No, but she did."

"What's your opinion of them?"

Phoebe whispered, "I'm not as religious as my grandmother. If they simply wished to practice their own beliefs I would have no problem with it. But, I do worry that they take advantage of people like you."

"The sick?"

"Yes. They won't charge you a fee, but they do accept alms. Back before my time they made a fortune seeing people, preying on the desperation of the ill. Many of them claimed to be healed. But when they left a lot went back to being sick."

Phoebe's words complemented what Dr. Alexiou said. "But they got better, at least for a bit."

"The people are hopeless, and they offer them hope. Then they collect alms. How ethical does that sound?"

"It doesn't sound incredibly different than a lot of other religions I've seen."

"The separation and the fanaticism?" Phoebe held up her hands. "I'm sorry that you are one of the people who was sick enough to come. I just didn't want you to be taken advantage of."

Raleigh would get less information if she defended the tribe. She switched tactics. "Thank you for telling me. Why do you think the healing works? Any ideas?"

"They say placebo effect. But a lot of the doctors don't agree with that. They think it's more. Some scientists visited. A while ago, a year or two before I was born. They tried to figure out if there was any explanation for what they did."

How old was this woman? Probably near thirty. Raleigh's ears perked up. Could she be talking about Grant and Able? "What did the scientists say?"

"Nothing. They were driven off the island. Shortly afterward the Docents closed the docks. Now they only let one boatman take people across. It's been that way for the last three decades."

"Why were the scientists driven away?"

"Obviously because they were about to uncover them as liars. Officially the Docents said that it was a sin to try and find a scientific reason for the majesty of what they did. But I'm guessing they didn't want to be exposed."

If it was Grant and Able, they must have been turned out shortly after they discovered Lucidin. Maybe the tribe didn't like the scientific explanation, or maybe they saw that once their secrets had been understood they could be exploited.

"Will you see them tomorrow?" Phoebe asked.

"I've come too far to go back now. But thanks. This conversation has opened my eyes. I will keep in mind what you have said."

Phoebe smiled and hoisted herself from the seat. "I hope you find relief from your illness someday." She squeezed Raleigh's hand and then headed towards the stairwell.

Raleigh mulled over what had been said and then followed. Slowly the complex story of the tribe's relationship with G and A came into focus. She didn't know if it helped her at all, except to say that she had to be very careful. Under no circumstance could she let slip what she knew about Lucid or what she could do.

CHAPTER
11

THE PROW OF the boat cut through the water as it headed towards Raleigh and the others. They stood together, Raleigh and Rho out front with Kappa and Tau a step behind. Underfoot, the slick wooden planks of the dock gleamed with a mist of water. She ignored the spray of the sea as the wind tumbled past. Soon enough the boat would see them across, and she'd meet the Docents at last.

They weren't the only pilgrims on the dock. Further back, a man with Parkinson's wore a heavy slicker. The tremor of his arms shook against the thick overcoat, and his wife clutched his hand, stabilizing him. Raleigh caught her eye, finding long lines of worry etched into her face. Proof that illness touched the lives of not only the sick but those around them. Raleigh's thoughts threatened to go to her mother, and she looked away from the couple.

Farther down the dock, sitting on the lone bench, was another woman accompanied by a female companion. This pilgrim had fatigue tormenting her muscles. It was the kind of weakness that begged a person back to bed. Raleigh couldn't suss out what exactly was wrong, and she didn't dare ask Tau with the elderly couple so nearby.

Of the three she appeared to be the heartiest. Would the Docents think that she'd made it up? Her skin bore the scars of past falls. Not all illnesses were continual, some were episodic, and surely they'd have attended to people who, like her, were fine most of the time.

The other boats tied to the dock thudded a disjointed, macabre rhythm that reminded her of her dislike of water. One of the many things she loved about her home state of Colorado was that it was landlocked and that she'd successfully avoided boats since her illness began.

"You're nervous," Rho whispered into her ear. They'd agreed that barricading had the chance of thwarting their cover, and all of them stood now open to interpretation from the others.

"It's not the Docents," Raleigh told him.

"What then?"

"The boat." And failure. But she only told him of the one. "I don't swim."

"You don't know how to swim?"

"I know how, I just don't do it."

"Why not?"

Tau spoke up. "It's the blackouts. It isn't safe."

Rho grimaced, as if he should have been able to figure it out himself. "Don't worry, I'm a strong swimmer. If we go down, I'll get you to land."

She had no doubt about that. If he'd survived the near draining and leap into cliffside waters, she assumed this wouldn't faze him. "Thanks, but let's hope it doesn't come to that."

An attendant skirted around them to aid the boat in mooring

to the dock. The captain eyed Raleigh and the other passengers and pointed to a set of life jackets. The attendant handed them around. She grabbed one and slid her arms through the rough orange vest. It sat heavy on her, her coat cumbersome beneath it. With the straps tugged taut she could barely breathe. Or maybe it was the wind whipping away her next breath.

The midsized boat had a center console for the captain. As they stepped on, she saw the controls through a dingy window. Their seats were at the front of the boat. Nets were folded and hung, and the place reeked of fish. She guessed that it was used for fishing when it didn't take pilgrims across. It took a while to get the older man onto the boat, but soon they were all sitting at the bow. With little fanfare the captain undocked, and with an ominous jolt they cut back into the open water.

Kappa tilted his head in the direction of the other pilgrims. "They've done this before. The other patients are familiar with the boatman."

Raleigh remained too focused on the water and the disconcerting sway of the boat to add her two cents. Instead she gripped her seat and shielded her eyes against the salty air as the boat pressed on. The motion and fish odor combined made her nauseous. The island hung in the distance. Through the mist the stone city rose, spiraling up on the small island, gray and cold, like the sky behind it and the waters around. In her head she counted down from one hundred, a trick to calm her nerves. The trip was long enough that she had to repeat the task a couple of times.

They didn't dock at the front of the island, instead they circled around to a smaller pier. At the end of the short dock stood the tall wall and narrow walkway. "This isn't the main entrance," she told the captain.

He gave her a smile that betrayed that he didn't know what she said but was trying to be polite. He motioned for them to head up the stone walkway.

"You can't go into big city. Here is for the sick." The woman companion of the fatigued patient spoke in halting English.

They had no choice but to enter the island here, and Raleigh and the others got out and left their lifejackets aboard the boat for the return trip.

From the dock all they could see was the stone face of the high wall. A dirt path that spanned ten feet wound up around the side, a thin rail wall that kept its walkers from a fall into the water. From here she could see the ribbon of road steeply incline before turning abruptly into the side of the stone. There must be some kind of inlet there, but at this angle she couldn't make it out.

Not risking the fall, she reached her hand out to the cold stones of the wall. She wasn't the only one who gave pause. The fatigued woman gripped her companion but gathered herself after a moment. Despite the weariness of her nerves, she was happy with an eager look in her eyes. Kappa was right, this wasn't her first session. Raleigh knew what hope looked like, especially after it had been drowned out by uncertainty, and this woman had it on her face.

Together the pilgrims and their escorts ascended the inclined path. The stones made it so that they were not given any hint of the city inside. Raleigh longed to know more of the residents, of the Docents, but it was clear that the pilgrims weren't allowed to truly enter. So close, but for all her mind tricks she couldn't pass through solid wall.

Eventually they reached the turn off. The road split here, the main part entering a corridor built into the side of the wall, the other a thinner path that lead to heavy set of doors. It was clear that they were meant to enter the corridor, and they did, finding shelter from the wind.

A wood desk with an attendant waited inside along with a series of benches. Peering deeper into the space Raleigh discovered a short hallway with small alcoves built deeper into the space.

The wife of the Parkinson's couple found her husband a seat before walking over to the woman at the lone desk. There she scrawled something into the book before finding her way back to her seat. The fatigued woman, with the help of her companion, also went to the book, signed, and then sat down.

Raleigh stepped forward, aware of her shoes echoing across the room. Concrete and stone were too similar for her liking, and she repressed images of the bunker as she made her way to the register.

"Are you Raleigh Groves?" the receptionist asked.

"Yes."

"Please sign in. And sign in your caretakers as well." The woman turned the heavy book to face Raleigh. Her name sat written in print with a spot beside it for her signature. Quickly Raleigh scribbled her name and then wrote in the one letter symbols for each of the guys. Their being in Greece played into their hands. Or maybe naming the boys Greek symbols had been a bit tongue-and-cheek all those years ago at Grant and Able. A roadmap of sorts to lead them back to their origins someday.

"Thank you," the woman said. "Please have a seat."

Raleigh found an open bench, and the Designed filled in around her. The simple room gave little hint of what was to come. The walls were bare, with the exception of lights. The now modern bulbs haloed sooty walls that had once been stained by a real flame. An earthy aroma of dirt, flowers, and lavender lingered in the stale air.

The receptionist hadn't asked about Raleigh's symptoms. There had been no triage, no medical history, and no background of any kind. Weren't they interested in their patients? Without her voicing her illness they wouldn't have a clue. She possessed nothing as telling as the man's shaky hands or the woman's withered body.

"Raleigh." The woman called out her name again. "Our Docent is ready to meet with you. Please go one room over. Your caretakers can stay here."

"They can't go with me?" Raleigh asked.

"No, they won't be needed now. Please, one room over."

Rho went to stand, but Raleigh put her hand on his shoulder. Then faced all three. "I won't be that far. I should be close enough that you can assist me if I have an episode." Or if she had a problem he would be near enough to sense her.

"That's right." Rho caught her meaning and reluctantly stayed. Tau and Kappa nodded their head at his words, in a pinch they would be there too.

Raleigh padded down the hall noting that this place bared no resemblance to a traditional doctor's office. The room didn't have a door, only an archway. Thin fabric curtains were pulled open, not even trying to give the illusion that they might provide privacy. A bench, like the ones in the entry room, sat in the middle. The room closed off in the back rough and unpolished almost like a cave. It comforted her, she would've been more put off by concrete. At least without a door she couldn't be locked in, but the small space left little reassurance beyond that.

The minutes passed slowly, and she waited. Her solitude broke when a tall, blonde man arrived. His indigo tunic reached down to his knees and cream linen pants hung loosely beneath. The shirt and pants, like the cushions, were hand sewn. As he moved towards her each of his steps fell soft, muffled by his leather soled slippers.

"I'm Anders. One of the Docents. I've come here to help."

Raleigh stood and shook his hand. "Thank you."

"Please sit." He offered and then sat down beside her.

"I suffer from blackouts."

He held up his hand. "I'm going to listen to your soul, it speaks of our physical ailments."

With that he centered himself beside her on the bench. Raleigh crossed her legs and drew her shoulders in. There was no doubt in her mind that he sensed her now, and she didn't feel guilty about returning the favor. He was young, like her, and strong. Like most people his age there was nothing notable about him, no serious problems. He wasn't stressed or worried, to him this ritual was a worn routine.

After five minutes he opened his eyes. "Your body is weak, you've been through a lot, and it is tired. Nothing that a few hearty meals and walking couldn't improve."

"I'm perfectly fine until I have an episode. Then I black out and lose consciousness."

"You only suffer in these temporary moments?"

"Yes, but I have them every few days."

Anders considered this. "Then you shall stay on the mainland nearby until you have one and come to us shortly after. Any effects it has on your body should still be there. Hopefully then your soul shall tell what's upsetting it." He pulled a piece of paper from his pocket and a small charcoal pencil. "I'm giving you a note to provide the boatman. Usually he comes across daily, this will see to it that you can travel outside of that visit. Do you have any forewarning? Any lights or visual cues?"

"No, it's not a migraine or seizure." Raleigh took the thick paper note and folded it. She wondered if medical terminology would offend him.

Anders gave a small smile. "We don't diagnose here. We ease. Now, since I've found nothing specifically wrong I can perform a traditional healing, meant for all, including the healthy."

"Sure. Thanks."

"Close your eyes and concentrate on your physical being." He pressed one of his palms to her forehead and took her nearest hand in his.

She held very still, letting his hands warm her. The oddness of the situation made her heart trip in her chest, but it slowed. Not on its own accord. Unmistakably he influenced her now. If he were a Recep, that would place him at least in the 94th percentile. Did he make enough Lucid to accomplish this on his own? If not, had he taken the inducer?

Calm filled her, her body relaxing into the cushions beneath. The tranquility mirrored the same sensation as standing alone on a mountain trail. The world was bigger than her, and she was content to be a tree in land covered in forests. Together they sat in silence, the serenity making the handful of minutes stretch out across her mental clock. Then it was over, and he pulled his hand from her forehead.

Together they remained, silent, and Raleigh slowly came out of the mental trance he'd placed on her. She opened her eyes, her pupils focusing on his light iris. His coloring wasn't what she'd expect in someone hailing from the Mediterranean, which figured, these people had migrated from a distant land.

Anders stood and bowed slightly at the waist. "I hope you find the peace you seek."

This man had sensed and influenced her. Did he know about Lucidin or the relationship his people had with Grant and Able? He was too young to have been here at the time, maybe a year older than the Designed. He was someone like her, a natural. Even with the Designed she often encountered a sense of isolation and loneliness in what she could do. Like her, he'd built his life around Lucidin. She wanted to be a healer, which he was, only he'd replaced the science with mysticism.

Raleigh said none of this, instead settling on a simple thank you and farewell. Then he left. She stayed sitting a moment longer before heading to the front desk and the Designed.

"How'd it go?" Rho asked casually when he saw her.

The way Kappa's mouth turned down in the corners meant he understood that she'd been influenced. He would have felt it, they hadn't been sitting far from her.

"It went well. He found nothing wrong." Tomorrow she'd be welcomed back with the other pilgrims, but she didn't tell them about her hand-written permission slip. Their grimacing faces gave her the impression that they didn't want her to come back at all.

Rho scooted on the bench leaving a spot between Kappa and him for her to sit. "We're to wait here until the others have finished their session."

"They were taken just after you," Tau told her. "There is more than one Docent working at a time."

Stretching out her mind she could feel the other patients being influenced as she had. Questions flooded her. How did they address Parkinson's? Usually medications were needed. She wondered how successful the Docents methods were. If she could stay longer, she could learn so much. As it was, she was in no position to inquire about any of it. Maybe they'd made the wrong decision, maybe they should have been upfront with the Docents and explained who they were and asked for help.

The other patients returned to the room and their caregivers. Everyone followed the path back down to the boat. They slid their life vests back over their heads. The pleasant calm Anders had instilled remained with her on the return voyage. Once again they found themselves on the villages dock. The time spent on the island so short that it left them with a day to fill.

"Do you think anyone gets to go into the main part of the island?" She wondered.

"We asked the receptionist. She said no," Tau said. "Only their townsfolk are allowed in the town. What you experienced today might be as far as we get."

Raleigh squinted across the water to the island. "We have more to learn. Let's not give up yet."

C H A P T E R
12

THE DOCENT VISIT taught them nothing that they didn't already know. The return pass Anders gave her sat light in her pocket but heavy on her conscience. Her fingers skimmed it now, running along the course edges and rolling over the uneven texture of pulpy paper.

"What do we do now?" she asked.

Kappa rubbed his hands and drew his attention away from the water. "Go home. From what Dr. Alexiou said, and what we've seen there, I don't think we're going to step foot on the actual island. Getting the inducer doesn't seem likely."

"What? But we just got here." She couldn't argue that it wasn't a lost cause.

"We could feel out what the people in this town know." Tau considered staring up the main alleyway into the village. "We've really only spoken to Dr. Alexiou."

"And that crazy woman who told us they were witches," Kappa tacked on.

Rho studied Raleigh's face. "We can spend a few more days. They might not be able to grow everything they need to make the inducer on the island. There's a chance they might import some of its ingredients. Let's talk to the grocers."

"And the doctors, some of the older ones, might have been invited onto the island before they closed it off," Raleigh said.

Tau took a step towards the far part of town. "We'll separate and meet back here in a few hours. I'll take the eastern part."

"I'll take this stretch." Raleigh faced the main road.

"I'll go with you," Rho offered.

Raleigh shook her head. "No. We'll cover a lot more ground if we separate."

Rho didn't back down. "It could be dangerous, if that old woman is any indication, people are pretty heated."

"She can take care of herself," Tau said.

Rho's eyebrows shot up. "Of course she can. I didn't mean to imply that she couldn't."

"Then let her go on her own." Kappa grimaced. "I'll take the west. Meet you back here."

Raleigh didn't give Rho a chance to change his mind and gave both him and Tau a short wave before taking off on the center roads. This way they'd divide the city into quarters.

Raleigh spent the next two hours desperate to learn something about the Docents that she already didn't. The grocers said that once a month the people came by to replenish their food stock. They bought flour, sugar, and other staples. Nothing unique that had to be specially ordered or stocked. Either the inducer could be made with ingredients found in any standard grocery store, or the answers didn't lie there.

It was harder to speak to doctors about it. Unlike the grocers, they required appointments that she didn't have. It looked like

Alexiou would be the only doctor that they spoke to. Same went for scientists, she didn't run into anyone who hinted they'd specialized in biology.

It was difficult starting up conversations. Her handful of Spanish, French, and smattering of Italian, didn't help in the least. Rho had been correct, a lot of people clammed up when talking about the Docents. Those that said anything were eager to paint them in a poor light.

She was the first to arrive back at the meeting spot, and she kicked a stray rock into the curb. They'd found the tribe, they'd seen how they could influence, but now they were stymied. Rho could be charming, and if anyone could tease out secrets it would be him, but she had the sinking feeling that there were no secrets to be found. The Docents had done an effective job of isolating themselves.

"I take it that you learned nothing?" Tau walked up from behind, startling her out of her thoughts.

Kappa and Rho weren't anywhere to be seen. She wanted to confess her frustration and have him ease it all away as only he could. But their relationship had shifted, and she didn't want to crave his conversation and reassurance as much as she did. Not when he didn't need her the same way.

"I learned nothing. Except that they closed off around the time that Grant and Able came. Do you think they were upset to learn a scientific reason?" Raleigh asked.

"I'm not sure. I would think it would bolster their arguments. Most of the people here think it's the placebo at work, or worse, black magic."

"Yeah, the Docents could prove both wrong with Lucidin."

"I don't think they care about what the villagers here, or the rest of the world for that matter, think. They pick up some cloth from the fabric store." Tau stared off towards the island. "They're very self-sufficient, but that island can't provide everything. They've got a lot of money left over from when they took in a lot of pilgrims. And people say some wealthy believers still donate. They're well taken care of financially, and they don't need much."

"So there's no reason for them to rejoin with the mainland."

"No." Tau stepped closer to her and dropped his voice. "How are you feeling about it?"

His words resonated deep in her stomach—how badly she wanted to pull him close. "I don't want to go back to the States."

"I don't think we're going to accomplish much else here. I know how important the inducer is. This thing with Sigma is going to come to a head. After it's addressed, I'll set up a lab with you. We'll figure it out."

Tau made it sound too simple, their clandestine interaction with Sigma would probably be fatal for some of them. A grim reality that she wasn't going to point out if she didn't have to. "Grant and Able haven't been able to figure it out."

"We're smarter than their scientists."

"Maybe you are. I've met them, they're pretty brilliant."

"But not as driven as you." He lifted his hand, as if to touch her shoulder, and then brought it back. Could he not stand to touch her? "If it comes to it, we can come back here if we don't make any progress. We're not giving up on the inducer, we're just putting it aside until we can delve into it."

The frustrated pressure in her chest loosened. He'd alleviated part of it. She trusted that he would help her figure it out. "It would be helpful if we got the inducer before we went up against Sigma."

"More and more I'm learning to live without the things I want." He stepped away as Rho and Kappa appeared on the street.

Did he mean her? If he felt any pain about their breakup, he'd been skilled enough to mask it. None of it showed in his body when she sensed him, and his face held the practiced emotionless stare that had aggravated her early on. Back when she couldn't get away from him fast enough. How quickly her fickle heart had changed. Maybe, just maybe, it could turn back to Rho.

Kappa stepped forward, his hands stuffed deep in his pockets. "We found nothing we didn't already know."

"We were thinking that we ought to push off." Rho watched her face as he spoke. Luckily, Tau wasn't the only one who'd developed a good poker face. "Kappa can get tickets for the day after tomorrow."

"All right." She agreed, but it sickened her to go without more answers. Her finger ran over the piece of paper in her pocket. How could they be within reach but so distant at the same time?

They returned to the hotel, and Kappa told the receptionist that this would be their last night. Tomorrow they would go to Athens and tell Gabe and Adam that they'd had no luck. No one said it, but they'd also have to start giving them Lucid. The two men were close to breaking under the strain of addiction. They'd offer a temporary solution for a permanent problem.

AGAIN SHE AWOKE in the middle of the night. Nightmares of the bunker were quick to take advantage of the dark room and her sleepy mind. Sweat stuck her nightgown to her back. She repeated to herself that everything would be fine.

Only this time she didn't believe the words. Things weren't going be fine. Not for Adam, and not for Gabe. They couldn't wait years to get the inducer. She'd had to see the Docents before they left. Maybe she'd tell them that she knew about Lucid. They'd rejected Grant and Able, and they'd undoubtably shun the Designed.

But she wasn't Designed. For once that would be her advantage. Yes, they were brilliant and attractive, but she had her strengths too. She was authentic, and she'd carried the weight of her abilities. The Docents were kindred, they'd pick up on it. Quickly she dressed her hand on the pass Anders gave her. Checking to make sure Kappa was asleep, she exited the room.

She slipped out of the hotel into the street. The wind howled around her, chilling her ears and plastering her loose hair to her cheek. Angry storm clouds blotted out the sky, making it seem later than 11:30. Her feet broke the puddles that formed in the street as she dashed in the direction of the docks. The boatman's house still had its light on. She rapped on the door with her gloved hand, adding to the chorus of the wind banging on the windows.

A moment later she sensed the boatman on the other side, he unbolted the locks, and gave her an annoyed look. He asked her something in Greek, and she responded by handing him the paper.

He read the note his face furrowing as his eyes lifted to the watery passage. She turned too, wondering how bad the crossing would be. Thunder clapped overhead and lightning cut through the darkness illuminating their path for a moment.

The storm licked the water, spraying salt in the air and leaving the small channel choppy with waves. Raleigh's heart rose up in her throat at the prospect of traversing them. The calm boat ride earlier had been overwhelming on its own.

The boatman paused, then stepped inside leaving her alone in the cold. What was he doing? Was this his way of saying to get lost? Then the door opened, and he grabbed his coat off a nearby hook. He held up his hand like a phone to his ear, he'd called the Docents. His large hand, covered in thick worker gloves, pointed to the boats. That was all he conveyed as he strode towards the pier.

Raleigh followed in step behind him. The boats clapped furiously against the dock. With each angry hit the wood planks reverberated. She grasped her coat, trying to hold on to any courage she had left.

He pointed to a smaller craft with a propeller. She gulped. Surely he wouldn't want something this small. What if they capsized? Her eyes remained transfixed on the craft as he handed her an orange life vest. Was Tau right? Was this a lost cause? What if she died on the way over, and what if it was all for nothing?

The boatman got in. If the weather scared him it didn't show on his windburned face. His pulse kept an even, yet elevated rhythm. All she had to do was go onto the boat, and he'd take her across. Nothing was expected of her, but she still hesitated.

Grant and Able had been searching for the inducer for the last thirty years. If she made it across she could have the inducer much sooner than that. Now was the only time to go, tomorrow they'd talk her out of it, and they'd leave. Stepping down she reminded herself that she'd been through worse than this. The wailing winds screamed into her ears trying to convince her that her reassurances were no more than lies.

The boat moved erratically under her feet when they touched the metallic bottom. Swaying, she gripped the side of the small craft, her fingers finding the side wet and slick. Water sprayed onto her face and wetted her hair, but her hand remained tight on the side rather than sweep it back.

With a sturdy tug the motor hummed, and diesel filled the air. The boatman untied the craft from the dock, and they set off. The waves lifted them, and her stomach sank. The distance wasn't far, but the boat struggled to make any headway. Between the life vest and her fear she could barely breathe.

Halfway across. In the distance she could see someone waiting for her on the dock of the island. Her hair whipped against her face as she turned to see the shore they'd left from. Rho stood on the edge of the pier, Tau and Kappa a short distance behind him. They'd realized that she'd gone.

Her mind sensed Rho with a stark clarity. The tension in his shoulders, the painful pinch of worry between his brows. Kappa stood anxious, his heart hammering, and Tau remained calm. She sensed the boatman, his hands gripping the throttle so tightly his palms ached. On the shore she sensed the Docent that stood waiting, his body young and healthy. Anders. There were more people in the village, just on the other side of the wall that hid the town from prying eyes like hers.

The humanity swirled around her stronger than the wind. The pain and joy of them crashing into her harder than the boat hitting the white crested waves. They roared in her ears drawing out the screaming of the wind and the steady hum of the motor. She was going to black out. There was no stopping it, the most she could do was pitch forward rather than back into the water.

CHAPTER
13

THE SALTY WATER chilled her cheeks and harkened her back from the oblivion. Her fingers clawed the stiff life jacket as her eyes opened. She'd been on the water, and she'd blacked out. One of her legs kicked out, hitting wooden planks rather than the metal underbelly of the boat.

"You're all right." Anders bent over her. "You're all right."

"The water." She gulped, amazed that the water hadn't become her grave. The boatman stood backlit by the moon, the waves crashing behind him on the dock. They must have made it across.

"You fainted, as you said you did," Anders said.

Raleigh turned to him. When she blacked out her mind sensed everyone and relayed that information to anyone with enough Lucidin in their system to listen. It had been what saved her from the bunker, but now it may have given too much away. She'd only hoped to meet with Anders one more time, to learn a little more about his people. It hadn't been her intent to reveal the extent of what she could do.

As the gravity of her situation seeped in, the boatman spoke a few feet away. Raleigh didn't understand him, but Anders did. They exchanged words for a few minutes, and then the boatman climbed back into his boat. Was he heading back already without her? She didn't dare stop him, the last thing she wanted to do was be on the water right now.

"That's my ride back," she said to Anders as the boat pulled back from the dock, preparing to start the hazardous return.

Anders stared unflinchingly into her eyes. "You'll be welcomed here. When you were on that boat, before you fainted, your soul called to mine. It told me things about you, and about the people on shore, and even myself here on the island. Surely you understand that something happened."

There was no point in denying it. "Yes, before I black out I can feel people."

"Our souls once all communicated to one another, we are all connected as one, but our bodies, they separate us. That is what we do here, the Docents, we connect to the Universal Soul. That is how we treat the pilgrims."

"Yes, I know, I came to you because I'm sick."

Anders shook his head. "You are not. You came because the Universal Soul is strong here, and after what happened on that boat, it is clear that it is strong within you as well. We're connected."

Raleigh didn't know what to say, his confident words left little room to argue. She pressed a hand to the dock, and Anders helped lift her to standing.

"Come, we should get away from the water, you're cold, and we need to get you warm." He helped her remove her life jacket, revealing dryer patches of her coat where the orange padding had been.

He was right though, besides those areas, the rest of her was drenched. The water from the bottom of the boat had soaked into her jeans, and she shook against the cold. The dock lay exposed to the wind and storm, and with the boatman gone she'd run out of options.

"Getting warm would be good."

Anders walked with her. His body half shielding her from the elements as he took sideways steps up the path. It was as though he expected her to disappear before his eyes. He only turned away when they reached the curve in the road before the reception area that she'd visited that morning.

"Not that way. There aren't any sleeping accommodations. We'll go into the city." He led her a few steps beyond the entrance and took a set of heavy metal keys from his pocket. At the end of the narrow walk was a door, and he slid the key into its large metal lock. When he turned the key, tumblers fell into place ending with a resounding thunk.

On the other side of that door lay the city and its people. It had been her intent only to speak with Anders one more time, and now she would be experiencing the culture first-hand. But was she ready for what lay ahead?

He opened the door but stopped her before she could enter. The significance of what he did wasn't lost on either of them. "We haven't had a visitor in my lifetime. Pilgrims aren't permitted past this point. But since your soul has argued for you to stay, I shall let you enter. Please, be respectful. Our beliefs will likely be unusual to you."

"I understand."

He ushered her through. They passed through a tunnel, a cave through the formidable wall. On the other side they exited onto a street. She wrapped her cold fingers together, thankful that the wind was thwarted by the buildings across the way.

Houses and businesses lined the street. They were built close together, having settled into each other like a set of crooked teeth in an overcrowded mouth. The lights in their windows were out, but she didn't have to squint to see, overhead lamps lit the way in a shocking white. Solar panels sat atop the lights, a modern nod in a place that was so old and remote.

Anders lifted his arm and pointed to the right, inclined part of the road. "This street goes along the wall, and at the end it curves into the Docent dormitories. Nearby are apartments where guests used to stay. It's been a long while, but there should be a bed there you can use to get some rest."

Raleigh observed the streets as they walked. The gray stones, bricks, and wood made the town appear monotone in the dark. But hints of personality broke through. Misshapen metal bells hung on garlands over doorways. They chimed a disconnected song that made goosebumps crawl up her arm with each change, like a too wide smile that hints at mania rather than joy.

Raleigh sensed her before she saw her. The woman walked down the path, the muscles of her legs taking longer than comfortable strides. She appeared at the far end of her street, her nearly white hair haloing her face as it drifted down to her waist. Soon she'd made her way over to them, and Anders bowed his head.

She put a palm to his forehead, and he raised his eyes to look at hers. "What has happened?" she asked.

"This is Raleigh, a pilgrim, who suffered from failing spells."

"It's your soul that called to mine, that woke me up from my sleep?" she implored Raleigh, her eyes curious but not accusing.

"I didn't mean to wake you." Instinct told Raleigh that this woman held authority—with her chin raised and her voice so assured.

"Do not apologize. You must have a strong connection to the Universal Soul."

"I thought I would find a place for her to sleep," Anders told the woman. "She's freezing."

The woman nodded her head. "Of course. My name is Thora. I'm a Sapient, a leader of the Docents, and I welcome you as my guest to the island."

The leader. How quickly she'd tumbled into the center of this universe. There was no going back, and she didn't dare guess at the course of events that she'd started rolling when she blacked out on the boat. She gulped down her apprehension, this could be a good thing. Hadn't it been the goal to learn about these people? Surely this promised more insight than what the normal pilgrims received. "Thank you. I'm very tired."

Thora and Anders led her up the path that curved into the center of town. Above, the streetlights cast shadows, and the rain from the storm left the stone walk slick and glossy. The chill from the sea iced her skin, and her breath came out in rattled white plumes. Questions about the Docents begged to be asked. But with her nerves frayed, and her body freezing, it was the thought of a warm bed that pushed them aside to be dealt with later.

The street dead-ended in a courtyard. The round space had buildings all around. Some were tall, with many windows, another short with a mighty dome. A temple or shrine, she wouldn't be surprised to find a religion here, not when the people across the way spoke of a cult, and when Thora mentioned a soul. But the iconography that decorated the space wasn't the ones applied to the religions she knew. Again, a topic for tomorrow.

"I shall see you again in the morning," Thora said. "Anders see to it that she's warm for the night.

Andres bowed to Thora and then opened a door to one of the narrower buildings in the courtyard. Raleigh stepped inside, instantly glad to be out of the sleet. Anders flicked on a switch, and a set of lights overhead hummed. "We used to have visitors here, a long time ago. It's a little outdated. But it should be all right for tonight."

Up they went to the first landing where they stopped. The hallway wasn't dirty or cluttered, but the air had the musty dryness of disuse. The old bulbs overhead left yellow hues on the walls illuminating outlines of former furniture now nothing more than ghostly impressions on walls.

He pressed open a door. Inside a bed sat piled with blankets. That was all she needed.

"In the closet there should be some clothes. In the morning come downstairs and go into the main building, I will meet you there."

"Thanks."

Anders paused at the doorway, as though he wanted to say more. Then he gave her a small smile and departed. Alone in the old building it would have been easy to let the foreboding set it. The wooden door had no lock. She didn't sense anyone else on the floor. As she kicked off her wet boots she gathered her courage— she wasn't defenseless. Tomorrow she would get her bearings and learn all she could about the inducer.

CHAPTER
14

THE TANGERINE HUES of sunrise woke Raleigh. She'd pulled the comforter up high around her face hoping to conserve as much warmth as possible. As she blinked against those early rays, the smell of salt reminded her of the night before. A few gray clouds still dotted the sky, not enough to churn the sea like the night before. Her stomach grumbled, and her mind went to food.

Now, in the stark light of day her action came into focus. Without intending to she'd propelled herself directly into the heart of this culture. Kappa would be livid. They'd discussed how the tribe shouldn't know about what they could do and that they might guess that they were products of Grant and Able's immoral science. But she wasn't like the Designed and doubted anyone would ever suspect her of being created in a lab. Eventually she got out of bed, still wearing the tunic and pants that she'd pulled on the night before.

She went down the steps and pushed open the door to a much brighter courtyard than the one she'd seen the night before. Following Ander's directions she went into the adjoining building. Inside she found a hallway with three doors. The far one to the right appeared to lead into the domed section of the building, a set of double doors were directly in front of her, and to the left the smell of food and spices tickled her nose, telling her that she'd found the right place. She followed the aroma and found Anders sitting on a bench just outside the open doors near the end of the hall.

Anders drew his attention from the book he read placing in a page marker and closing it when he saw her. "You're hungry."

Raleigh rubbed her hand over her stomach. There was no point in lying. "Yes. I'm not used to people knowing such things." Even around the Designed she barricaded.

"Our bodies converse all the time." Anders stood and motioned to the open doors. "Communication is important, we are built to understand what is going on in one another. Even those who cannot hear the Soul. Think of how many emotions can be shown on the face. Many times you know a person's mood without them saying a word."

Raleigh couldn't disagree. "Of course, people have poker faces."

"I suppose so." Anders gave her a wan smile. "Breakfast is in the Docents dining hall. It's early, so we should find a table easily."

Raleigh expected it to be like Grant and Able's cafeteria in Arizona. Instead it was a large dining room with eight wooden tables that could accommodate thirty people a piece. Wood benches lined them, looking uncomfortable if functional.

"Sit here, and I will get you some porridge." Anders motioned to the end of the nearest table. There were people on the other end, but they still had their space.

Raleigh sat down and tried her best to ignore the stares of the fellow eaters. Children kicked each other one table over, and their parents sat with their heads knitted together in close conversation.

Not everyone seemed fascinated by her, but enough eyes sneaked glances in her direction to make her feel uncomfortable.

Anders returned and set down a large bowl of oatmeal. Nuts and dried fruit were scattered across the top. When she pulled the wooden spoon from the meal many of the oats clumped onto it. It was the kind of breakfast that "stuck to your ribs," as her mother would say.

Raleigh took a taste finding it flavorful but not sweet. Her father usually added brown sugar to hers growing up, and she missed him now. "Thank you," she said before taking another bite.

"What part of America are you from?" Anders took a hearty helping of his breakfast, trying to keep the conversation light, but she could feel the flutter of excitement in his chest.

"Colorado."

"And can anyone in your family hear souls?"

"No. Only me."

"I'm making you uncomfortable?"

Raleigh shook her head. "I'm not used to talking about it openly. Most people think I'm crazy when I bring it up."

"You bring it up?"

"If someone is sick, I usually let them know."

Anders nodded his head. "Yes, the sick often yell so loud they can't be ignored. We were endowed this gift so we could help the ill."

Raleigh didn't agree with him that it was a gift, but surely helping the sick was the best thing to do. She pictured the army Grant and Able had built and the weaponized version of Lucid Sigma used. A child from another table pointed at her, and his mother swatted down his hand.

"They're all watching me." She tore her eyes away from the boy.

"We never have outsiders. Our texts say that people from all over can have the ability to hear and speak to souls, but only in history books have we seen any examples, now here you are in the flesh."

"And that's why you've allowed me to stay?"

"Surely you can't think it is a coincidence that you're here."

Heat rose up across her spine. Of course it wasn't a coincidence. But she didn't dare say the real reason, and his wide eyes suggests he knew nothing. "I guess I think it's good luck but not completely out there. I'm sick, and you treat the ill."

"Your soul wished to come back. How else do you explain it?"

Her soul, it was better than him thinking of Grant and Able. The tunic itched the back of her neck as she rubbed the collar. "I don't believe in fate." She hated destiny, all it did was perpetuate impossible expectations.

"It isn't just fate." Anders put down his spoon and traced a large circle with his index finger on the table. "At one point all human consciousness was connected. All souls spoke to one another, heard one another. It was a utopia, because we all shared each other's joys and comprehended one another's pain. But people retreated into themselves, severed from the Universal Soul. Over centuries people lost the ability to connect to one another. Our people have retained that understanding."

"But that doesn't mean I'm fated…."

"You've tapped into the Universal Soul. We have, too. Our people and you, we swim in the same ocean of existence. The tides brought you here, for like magnets we are drawn to North, to togetherness, to that being we all once were."

A religion based on Lucidin. And in such a religion those who had were nothing short of gods. The problem with fate was that it mocked reason. And if he discovered who she was, and why she'd really come here, how well would he listen to her reasons for coming? Her eyes stared at her food, the bit she'd eaten solidifying in her stomach. "Those aren't my beliefs."

Anders stared in her eyes. "This isn't some obscure cult. I know that's what outsiders think, but it isn't true. We don't require belief to further our dogma. We are proof that the Universal Soul lives on. You've experienced it, whether you believe it or not, it has happened."

Raleigh shifted in her chair. She'd never had strong religious beliefs herself, but she'd had friends who had faith. This wasn't like that, these people deliberately separated themselves. Now they believed that she'd come back, that she was meant to be there. His convictions didn't set well with her. She repressed any apprehension his fanatical words evoked. Grant and Able had warned her that they had extreme views. What mattered was the inducer, and she could see past their eerie views to get it.

His face softened. "During our Convocation you will understand more."

Was the Convocation the ritual Grant and Able discussed. "What's that?"

"When we listen and speak to the souls of our people. It follows breakfast and is an important part of the day. It's my favorite, and you'll grow to love it."

How many of these Convocations did they expect her to attend? He acted like she was here to stay, when really she was only here long enough to learn what she needed. "How long am I welcomed here?"

"For as long as you live, now that you've returned."

"I can't go home?"

He opened up his hands, the sleeves of his tunic falling away. "No. Of course you can leave. We don't force anyone to be here. To live here, within these walls, is a privilege. Our customs might be strange to you, but our way of life is a peaceful one. You're misunderstanding."

Raleigh's shoulders relaxed. Was she letting the fear of the unknown get the better of her? Anders was many things, but he was not an addict. He wasn't governed by the insatiable yearning for Lucid that plagued the Receps. Their tenets were off-putting, but she couldn't deny that they found a way to live with Lucidin, to thrive, and to heal the ill. Those things she desperately wanted for herself and wouldn't undervalue now, despite that alarm bells still rang in her head.

"My friends are back on shore. I have to let them know that I'm all right, they'll be worried about me."

He let out a sigh. "Of course we'll tell them that you made it across all right and that you've found your place here."

The Designed would be even more put off by the Docent's dogma than her. It had been a risk coming across on her own, and hopefully it would be one that paid off. The Convocation seemed like the best place to start.

C H A P T E R
15

WITH BREAKFAST FINISHED and the bowls put away, it was time for the Convocation. Hopefully, this is what she'd come all this way for. Rho and the others would be upset about her coming across, and she needed to learn *something* that would redeem her.

The Docents walked from the dining area down the hall to the far door that lead to the domed room. Raleigh watched them leave but waited on Anders before she followed. She kept her steps measured. She didn't want to come off as too eager.

A calmness lingered in the halls, a quiet brought on by mindfulness and concentration. By contrast, on the other side of the building she sensed the townsfolk. They stood with early morning haste, excited to start the day. They waited in droves to attend the Convocation. This was the heart of the city, and the people were like oxygen-starved blood cells.

"What exactly happens at the Convocation?" asked Raleigh. Ander's words about the Universal Soul left a lot of questions.

"It's hard to explain, but you'll understand once you participate. The Docents sit in the middle, but since you haven't taken that commitment you'll sit with the rest of the townsfolk."

On cue they stepped through the door into the domed space, finding themselves at the top of a steep aisle. It led down into a deep room that echoed up noise. It resembled an arena or theater in the round. Other doors opened onto aisles, but ones across the way, behind which were the townsfolk, remained closed.

The stone benches that circled out from the center stage could accommodate hundreds. The space was on par with a lecture hall, not a church. "How many townsfolk are there?"

"Most people make it to three to five Convocations a week, we have between four and six hundred people a day."

"How many people live here?"

"Roughly a thousand. Come, we'll go down so I can take my place with the other Docents." As they descended, Anders pulled a purple scarf from his pant pocket and wrapped it around his neck.

"What's that for?" she asked.

"It's our way of signaling that we can hear the Universal Soul."

"So anyone with a purple bandana is a Docent?"

"Anyone with a scarf or this." He pulled down the corner of his shirt. There a tattoo peeked out. It looked like a circle of trees all connected at the roots or nerves finding their way to one synapse. It didn't look like any of the tattoos Thalia's friends had sported. Its puffy white skin had the glossy shimmer of a scar.

"What is that?"

"The symbol is etched into our skin."

Raleigh tripped over her feet, regaining her balance. They branded their Docents like cattle.

Anders brow furrowed. "I promise you it was my choice, a way to show that my body is simply that, a body. Our pain can unite us as much as joy. When I had the symbols cut into my skin everyone shared my agony, before they took it away. Here is your seat, up near the front."

Raleigh sat down and shifted her weight against the cold stone surface of the bench. The air tasted stale. She sat alone in the audience, the townsfolk were yet to enter, and the Docents took their seats. She caught Anders with a question before he could leave her. "What if these people don't want me here?"

He paused, turning back to her. "They will not harm you. You're a guest of the Sapient and Docents."

"And that will be enough?" Could thirty years of isolation be broken so simply?

He stared directly in her eyes. "Trust us."

Anders bowed to her and continued on to the center of the room where a raised platform waited. The Docents sat on simple wooden chairs, their purple sashes cuffed around wrists and tucked in pockets. Anders took up a seat, amongst the others. From her vantage she counted maybe fifty, all sitting quietly. Their bodies were serene, their muscles at ease, a stark difference from the Receps. They used Lucid, but it didn't destroy them. Her eyes studied their untroubled faces until she was distracted by a deep cup passed along the rows. They took long sips before passing it on.

Worries of the Receps and their addiction now was overshadowed. Her eyes followed the path of the unremarkable metal chalice. Could this be the inducer? Oliver Able had said that they passed around a drink before they sensed. Leaning closer her ears perked up straining to hear the liquid sloshing against the sides.

The mood of the room changed when the doors opened, and the commotion of the townsfolk rumbled down the aisles. Quickly people found their seats. Unlike the composed Docents these people chattered like a flock of birds on a pond. Raleigh pulled her gaze from the Docents and adverted her eyes down, only lifting her head to move out of the way of the attendees scooting by.

Many of the people were healthier than a normal cross-section of population. They were thin for the most part, likely because food on the island wouldn't be in abundance if they had to grow most of it. Their ages ranged from a few months to nearly a century old, with every stage of life between. There were hundreds of them. It amazed her that the people collected this way daily.

They studied her, but not in the evaluative way the Docents did. She didn't know if it was worth trying to introduce herself. The voices around her spoke in Greek, but the cadence was different than what she'd heard in the other parts of the country. They returned her curiosity. It occurred to her that Anders was probably one of the few people who had daily interactions with anyone outside of the town.

Soon enough the rows of benches were full, and she sat with strangers on either side. Their voices had quieted, but they still spoke, exchanging greetings and other tidings of the early day. The din lessened, and the people looked towards the center. Raleigh followed their gaze.

Thora and an elderly man rose from their seats in the center of the Docents. Upon seeing her rise, the crowd hushed. After waiting for their silence Thora spoke. She used the same commanding voice she'd used the night before when speaking to Anders, the only difference was this time her words were exclusively in Greek. The meaning wasn't lost on Raleigh. Thora announced some kind of welcome and then started the ritual.

The Docents' faces became slack, and with open eyes they lifted their faces to the sky. The people around her mimicked the gesture. Some of their mouths hung open, others rocked slightly. Seeing that number of people copy one another unsettled her.

Despite the alarm bells ringing in her head, her pounding heart slowed. It struggled to move faster, to alert Raleigh to the potential dangers of things unknown, but instead it crawled slower. It was the same false comfort provided by Anders the day before. A calm created not by an untroubled mind but by influencing.

Like the day before she didn't barricade and gave into the experience that the Docents wished to create. The warm caress of endorphins radiated from her brain, down her spine, and into her fingers and toes. Dopamine wiped away her worries and beckoned her to accept them further.

Tau had once told her that they were but products of their neurotransmitters, and now, with the Docents controlling hers, they held a power over her and the rest of the people in the room. A power that she let them have, basking in her contentment.

She sensed the people near her and then the townsfolk farther to the back. Their hearts beat in time to hers, with certain allowances made for the old and young. They too gave in to the influencing, their muscles slack and their minds ensnared by the elation the Docents provided. Together they breathed in unison. Raleigh sensed their blood running freely through their veins as well as she knew her own.

This was the Universal Soul Anders spoke of. In that minute they all sat connected. There were so many villagers and Docents, but they shared something. Like a grove of aspen trees she'd seen on her mountain hikes. They stood apart, but their roots wound together out of sight.

Time became fuzzy and inconsequential. The present required all her attention, and her body ceased to be hers. It belonged to this greater group. She handed over her individuality, relishing the destruction of the barriers that had separated her from this sense of oneness for so long. The reassuring embrace of togetherness held her tight, and she let it hold her. Minutes passed, but she didn't track them.

Then her skin prickled against the cold air of the room. Her ears once again began to notice the commotion of the crowd. The rhythm her heart resumed was uniquely her own. Again, she became aware of her individuality, of herself. The endorphins still remained, but they didn't drown out the world. The isolation doused her like a bucket of cold water. How long had she been sitting here? It worried her how quickly she'd dropped her defenses and given herself over to the feeling of inclusion.

No wonder these people believed that everyone was connected by one soul. Even Raleigh, who understood the mechanism for how'd they done it, had been captivated by the experience the Docents had provided. Maybe they were a cult, all scrambling towards the ecstasy that they'd held for a handful of minutes. Was this what humanity was meant to experience? She'd never asked why Lucidin existed. Could this connection be the reason? How easy it would be to slip across the line that separated these philosophical questions into a deep-seated belief.

The people streamed out of the arena, their movements softer and their voices calm. To them this was merely part of the daily routine. Raleigh watched Anders wind his way through the Docents. Thora followed behind him as he approached Raleigh, who fought back the last of the haze caused by the Convocation. A question sat in Thora's eyes. Raleigh would have to decide to go or stay.

Leaving was the safest thing to do. To stay was to risk being discovered. But it also gave her a shot at the inducer. Last night she'd dashed into the situation. Now her steps were guarded. She had more time to think about the direction she headed, but the momentum of last night still propelled her on.

"What did you think of the Convocation?" Thora asked her.

It had evoked strong emotion. Raleigh wouldn't have to lie and say it hadn't affected her. "I've never felt so connected to so many people. It was wonderful."

"This is the connection you've always felt, the one you demonstrated last night. Do you see now that we are like you, that the Docents are the keepers of the Universal Soul?" Thora put a hand up to Raleigh's forehead. Her fingers hovered over Raleigh, not quite touching, but close enough that she could feel their warmth.

"Yes. I see that you are like me."

"Then you shall stay?" Thora said. "Because your soul has brought you here. We shall make you a Docent."

The false contentment the Convocation had produced left Raleigh abruptly. Her muscles in her legs tensed. A guest was already a large offer, but this was something more serious. "A Docent? I couldn't possibly."

Thora held up her hand. "You already engage with the Soul, you are already a Docent. We are simply giving you the title to describe the relationship that exists."

"Can I stay longer without becoming a Docent?"

Thora's brow furrowed. "As I said, you already are, it's a formality. But no, to stay you would have to officially take the title."

"And then I could never leave?"

The creases in Thora's forehead deepened. "No one is ever kept here against their will, it is an honor to stay." Then her wrinkles smoothed. "But you're worried about you friends on the mainland? Of your family and life abroad. We shall send word to them that you are all right. Family is important."

"I didn't tell my friends I was coming across last night."

"Then we shall send word to them."

"It's a mistake." The words of warning wavered out of the small elderly man that had stood with Thora at the beginning of the Convocation. "She is not one of us."

Thora turned to the man. "Ivar, you should meet Raleigh. She's the one who spoke to us so loudly last night."

The man inched forward, his back bowed heavily over his cane. His eyes scanned Raleigh. A lifetime of wrinkles weighted down the already unhappy frown on his thin lips. "She is like us, but that doesn't make her one of us."

Thora eyed him. "I believe she should stay. And most of the other Docents feel the same. This thirty-year isolation has done nothing but decrease our resources and the number of pilgrims to whom we attend. I will not have it deny us someone who is meant to be here as well."

Ivar's body shifted over his cane as his mouth filled with saliva, preparing for an argument. Then his heart swelled in his chest uncomfortably. He coughed on the pain it caused. A lifetime of cardiac problems left him with an enlarged heart. His fighter's spirit now struggled with a dying body. He didn't have much left in him, and with his limited energy he would have to choose his battles wisely.

Thora sensed it too. "You need rest, Ivar. We'll discuss this later in private."

His hand tightened on his cane, but he didn't refuse the help of two Docents that rushed over to aid him. The three retreated, and Raleigh once again stood with Thora and Anders.

"Ivar is from a different time," Thora said. "He is a Sapient, like myself, and his opinions hold a lot of weight, but he's grown more suspicious with age, and soon his position will be handed over. Do not listen to his rantings, he fears for the people, because he knows that soon they will have to manage without him."

"Will you stay?" Anders asked.

Raleigh considered the cup and the inducer. This had been the reason that they'd come to Greece in the first place. Yes, she could leave now but empty handed. She didn't want to be like Oliver Able, old and recounting tales of an inducer that she'd seen used but never discovered the true secrets of. She'd already crossed over some unforeseen line that separated these people from the world. The pieces were in place for her to get what she wanted, all she had to do was turn a deaf ear to the warning bells ringing in her head.

"Yes, I can stay."

Thora's warm smile was real, meaning that if nothing else, her offer of making Raleigh a Docent was authentic. "Then we shall go send word to your friends about your decision."

They would take it poorly. If only Raleigh could frame why she'd chosen to stay. She needed to convey to them that she'd seen the inducer being used, that the Docents were ready to accept her based on her ability alone, and that these people were creepy but likely harmless. "Can I send a personal letter?"

"Of course," Thora said.

Before anything else could be said a man ran up to them. His face was flushed from the exertion and the cold, and he took heaping breaths as he tried to steady himself. He bowed, trying to follow protocol, but his actions were quick and meaningless, he had something to say, and it couldn't wait. His words tumbled out between his heavy breaths. The only thing she understood was the panic that hedged what he said.

"Your friends, they are trying to break down the gate," Anders told Raleigh.

Thora straightened her shoulders. "Then we shall go and speak to them now."

CHAPTER
16

THORA LED ANDERS and Raleigh down the path to the pilgrim's part of the island. The street was more welcoming in the day, when the milky winter sunshine whispered most of the shadows away. But Raleigh had little chance to observe it. Thora's steps were fast, her tunic and wide legged pants bellowing out from her with each stride.

Anders kept an even pace with Raleigh, who tried to keep the worry from her face and her body. The Designed could intimidate as well as charm. Hopefully Rho wouldn't negate the offer of Docent that she'd accepted. He needed to keep his head, and she needed to stay calm herself.

As they neared the gate the pounding on the door echoed through the air. She sensed him, Kappa, and Tau on the other side. Thankfully, despite their anger none of them broke cover by barricading.

A wave of guilt tumbled over her. She'd come across the sea against their collective decision. The rage in their hearts was one that she'd earned.

Each pound on the thick wood door jolted her. Each thud a reminder that she'd left without telling. Now she'd have to convince them to let her stay, in front of Thora. Kappa would never go for it, but hopefully Rho and Tau would understand that this was their best chance at getting the inducer.

Raleigh covered her ears as they entered the small tunnel that cut a path through the wall to the door. Thora undid the heavy locks and the door swung open, clanging on its hinges. Rho rushed through it so quickly that he startled her. He swept her up into a tight embrace. "Are you all right?" His voice scratched out raw and worried.

"Yeah. Of course." But his emotion had caught her off guard. She'd predicted more anger than concern. The warmth of him for a moment reminded her of how alive he was.

He lowered her to the ground but didn't let go of her, not completely. Instead he drifted his hand down her arm and laced his right hand with her left. "You came across last night, we were worried you'd died in that storm."

"I'm fine." Raleigh tilted her head in Thora's direction. "They took me in."

Rho turned to Thora, his eyes traveled the length of her, no doubt trying to decide who she was. Some of the anxiety left his face, and he smiled, the charming one that made people trust him. "Thank you for housing her last night. We'll be on our way."

Raleigh didn't budge, keeping her and Rho planted on the village's side of the door. Tau and Kappa remained, waiting, on the pilgrims' side. She said, "I'm not ready to leave yet. These people, they're like me. You know how I can tell when people are sick?" Now she had to play the part for Thora's sake, to make it seem as though the Docents and their abilities were a surprise, hopefully Rho would catch on and play along.

Rho's eyes found hers. The agreement they'd made about not

telling the tribe about her abilities had gone out the window. She wanted to explain that she had no choice, from the shore he should have realized how large her episode was, and that it would have been impossible to keep her sensing a secret.

"I know that you have a very good gut feeling on things." Rho chose his words carefully, not making it sound like he too sensed or knew the details of what she did.

Raleigh tightened her hand in his. "These people, they can do it too, that's why they are able to help the ill."

Thora nodded. "It's why we've invited Raleigh to come stay with us. Her spirit connects to the world in the same way that ours does."

Rho stared at Thora for a moment his charm still intact. "I'm really not sure what to say. Kappa found tickets for us to fly home." He returned his attention to Raleigh, trying to discern what she meant without directly asking.

Kappa stayed on the pilgrims' side of the threshold. "Yeah, tickets for tomorrow, we'll spend tonight in Athens."

"I'm not ready to leave just yet." When she spoke Kappa's eyes grew wide. She had no way of explaining herself in front of Thora and Anders. Tau was the most likely to understand, but how could she convey to him that she needed to stay? Not only to learn about the inducer but to discover how the Docents had avoided the addiction problems of the Receps. Tau's blank face showed that he was working out why she didn't want to go and that she likely guessed the reason.

Rho drew her closer to both him and the exit, and she tugged against him. Now he trained his smile on her, letting it work its magic, but she could see worry in his eyes. "We can't leave you here, they are strangers."

"Then come and enter, and we will no longer be strangers to you." Thora waved for Kappa and Tau to join them. "It's been thirty some years since we've had guests, but Raleigh's soul has returned home. I invite you to stay for the week, while she gets settled. Then you can return back to your homes, knowing that she is in good hands."

Kappa's mouth formed a thin line. "That's very nice. But the tickets back are for tomorrow."

Tau interjected before Rho could pull Raleigh another step. "I think it's up to Raleigh." Now he had everyone's attention. "She's spent the night here, and if she feels that these people are kindred souls I believe her. If she wants to stay, to get to know them, then we shouldn't stop her. It's a generous offer that they have made." He stepped through the doorway and held out his hand to Thora. "Thank you."

Lifting her hand, Thora shook Tau's. "My name is Thora, and this is Anders."

"We go by our initials. I'm Tau, and that's Rho and Kappa."

"Wonderful. Anders will see that you are settled, now, if you'll excuse me, I have work that I must attend to." Thora's arm raised, her palm guiding around the circle, facing each of their foreheads in a blessing before she took her leave.

Anders put out an arm in the direction of the Docent building and the building Raleigh had stayed in the night before. "Please come this way."

They followed Anders. Rho hadn't let go of her hand. At first she'd considered it a statement to Thora and perhaps Anders. But neither of them had cared one way or the other. Anders's attention remained on leading them to their rooms and giving short descriptions of the village. Not once had he given more than a moment's consideration to Rho's proximity to Raleigh.

But she did. Rho's fingers laced hers so tightly that she'd deliberately have to untangle them to let go. There was something satisfying in the gesture, something comforting and sturdy. She caught sight of Tau behind her, but his attention was on the street and not her. Either because of his interest in the village or to not witness the affection or perhaps both.

The closeness meant that Raleigh could easily speak to Rho. "That's the temple where we had the Convocation this morning."

"What's the Convocation?"

Anders lifted his shoulder his chest filling with pride. "It is when all the members of our society connect to the Universal Soul. Tomorrow morning you'll be welcomed to join."

"Can't wait." Kappa's sarcasm caused Raleigh to frown.

Be nice Raleigh mouthed to him. The opportunity to tell the guys about Ivar's reluctance to them staying hadn't arisen.

When they reached the courtyard by the dormitories, they encountered a group of Docents who ceased their conversation and studied Raleigh and the others. How long would it take for them to get used to guests? Surely they wouldn't be so surprised by the end of the week, that's if Kappa didn't get them kicked out before then.

"It's been a very long time since we've had visitors, but this is where we used to house them." Anders opened the door to the apartment that he'd taken Raleigh to last night. Raleigh released Rho's hand and started up the stairs to her room.

The crammed stairwell didn't improve the mood. Kappa's shoulders tightened, he walked on the balls of his feet as if ready for a fight. "Are you hostile towards guests? Is that why you've banished them for so long?" Kappa asked. Raleigh put a hand on his shoulder. He was going to destroy the small amount of trust she'd amassed.

Anders let out a small chuckle. "I know that we're as odd to you as you are to us. People in the past have harmed us for our beliefs. We hoped the modern world would be more accepting, but alas, it is no better than the ancient one. While you're here, you'll be the only Americans a lot of the townsfolk have ever met. You can change their minds about outsiders or prove us right in thinking that you shouldn't be here."

Raleigh hadn't thought of it that way. She wanted to make a good impression and taking the inducer definitely wouldn't. Their instinct on keeping outsiders away rang truer than they realized.

Kappa clearly had focused on a different part of Anders's small speech. "Some of the people have never left the village?"

"That's correct." Anders turned down Raleigh's hall.

"By choice?" Tau kept the judgment from his voice.

"Of course. You might not understand it yet, but being here is a blessing." Anders sucked in a sharp breath and suddenly halted. Rho plowed into him, causing him to lurch forward, closer to whatever had shocked him.

Raleigh, behind the two, couldn't see over their shoulders to guess what in the hallway had caught their attention. Kappa, a head taller than her, had no such problem. "A blessing, huh?"

Anders moved forward, his moccasins slapping the wood floorboards harder than normal. He paused in front of Raleigh's room. He reached up and ran across the red lettering on her door.

GO HOME

Anders pulled his hand back, the tips of his fingers stained cherry red. "It's still wet." A frown bowed the corners of his mouth. "I'm sorry. This isn't the sentiment that most of us have."

"I know it isn't." Raleigh considered all the curious glances and Ivar's disapproval earlier. Surely that old man didn't have the strength to climb up the steps with a paint can in hand to commit such an act, plus it was too juvenile an action for a man his age.

"I'll get a bucket." Anders hurried down the hall leaving the four of them.

Kappa cleared his throat. "Am I going to be the only one to say it? That maybe we should do as it says and go home?"

Before Raleigh let her retort exit her mouth, she expanded her mind, sensing if anyone was in the area. The culprit might still be nearby, but she sensed no one. "Kappa, you don't understand at the Convo...."

"Don't talk about it in the hall." Rho moved closer to her, so close that his lips brushed the corner of her ear as he whispered. "We don't know if they can barricade. Let's go into the room."

Tau grasped the door handle and gave her the briefest of glances. In Italy they'd once entered her room to find an intruder, something they'd been prepared for, but it still had rattled them. He turned the handle, and they entered the small, desolate room.

Kappa brought up the rear, staring at the door for a moment before stepping inside and shutting it. "What are we doing here, Raleigh?" His face was red with anger.

"They had the inducer at the Convocation this morning."

"You're going to get us all killed." Kappa threw up his hand.

Tau shook his head. "If a bit of paint was going to scare you then you shouldn't have come along."

"I didn't *come along*. Raleigh made the choice to come across without consulting any of us. Is that how it's going to work now?"

"You should have told us you were headed out," Rho told her, but he didn't seem angry, more tired as though he'd been given too much time to think about it.

"I didn't know that you would say yes."

"And you're running the show now?" Kappa said. "I don't know if I even have to ask, of course you are. Rho jumps whenever you give the command."

Rho flinched. "Kappa, that's not fair."

"What's not fair is that we're trapped on this creepy island without having any sort of say."

"We can leave at any time," Raleigh insisted.

Kappa shook his head incredulously. "Really? Because Anders and Thora seem to think you're going to be here forever."

"That's because they believe this is my true home. They don't think it's chance that I'm here, they think that my soul drew me back. Look, this isn't helping my point. Are they creepy, yes. But that doesn't change the fact that they have the inducer. The sooner we get it we can leave. Let's not waste time arguing."

Anders's presence could be sensed from the top of the stairwell, and all four of them fell quiet at his arrival. Tau opened the door and stepped out into the hall. "Here, let me help you with that." He reached over and took the bucket.

Eventually the only evidence of the warning was a bucket of red water and a damp door. Anders patted Tau on the back. "Thank you. These four rooms are yours to have during your stay." He then peeked into the room where Raleigh and Rho stood. "Raleigh, your Docent initiation will be tonight."

Rho goggled at the notion. "A Docent, isn't that one of your holy men? She couldn't possibly take on that role."

Anders said, "It's a formality. Hearing souls makes her a Docent, all we need to do now is make it official. The dining room below will have food if you get hungry." He turned to Raleigh. "Do you remember where it is?"

"Yes." Raleigh gave him a short bow. Anders returned it, then lifted the bucket and left with it and the rags. Tau now stared into the room, his eyes meeting Raleigh's.

Kappa let out a loud exhale. "And you really think they'll let one of their Docents leave?"

He didn't wait for an answer and instead stomped into a neighboring room and slammed the door.

Raleigh didn't tell them that them staying was conditional upon her becoming a Docent. Anders made the process sound routine, and she wanted them to think of it as inconsequential.

"Tau, can you give me a minute alone with Raleigh?" Rho put his hand on the upper part of the door ready to shut it.

"Sure, let me know if you need anything. I'll take the room across the hall." Tau caught Raleigh's eye one last time before the door shut.

Raleigh let out a long breath. "All right, now that Kappa and Tau are gone, what is it that you have to say?"

"What makes you think I have some sort of speech?" He cocked his head to the side, considering.

"Because I can feel the emotion pounding through you. You're not as angry as Kappa, but maybe you're better at tempering it. Or maybe you're not as surprised."

"Oh, I was plenty surprised that you crossed that water all by yourself. I thought you were terrified of boats."

"Sometimes you have to push past your fears. We were going to leave, and I wasn't ready yet. Kappa and you can be mad for all I care, I don't regret it. I didn't come all the way over here to turn around at the first obstacle."

"Who said I was mad?"

Raleigh leaned back and squinted her eyes. "You're not angry?"

"Not about you leaving in the boat. I understand that you've been feeling helpless. I know that you made friends with the Receps at Grant and Able, and that their addiction is troubling to you. I'd be lying if I said that Collin didn't worry me."

"Good."

"But I would have liked to have been on the boat."

"Because you like nearly drowning in a storm?"

Rho stepped closer to her. "I know you're the type of person who jumps in with both feet. I'm not calling you irresponsible."

"But you think I'm reckless."

"I think that we didn't get much accomplished until you joined the team. You've encouraged us all not to be so stagnant. There are good and bad things about that. But the next time you run off I want you to take me with you."

"Would you have come?" She tried to replay the scenario last night with Rho slinking beside her in the shadows.

"We could have waited until the storm cleared. The point is, I want to do things together."

He stepped closer to her. It wasn't hard, there weren't many places to go in the minuscule room. She stared up into his gray eyes. Her legs weakened, and she became aware of small things, like the way she gulped. They'd been this close once before, with his fingers tangled in her hair, and she'd kissed him. Two months ago. How much had changed in eight weeks? Apparently not enough to calm the butterflies in her stomach.

He took her face in his hands gently. "I should have kissed you back two months ago."

"Then why don't you now?" Her heart was beating so fast the brazen statement barely made it out.

Rho kissed her, and she grabbed onto his shoulders so she could reach him better. Like before, his lips were soft yet firm, but this time he wanted her as much as she wanted him. The kiss was so long that she needed to break away to take a breath, but then she drew him back quickly, amazed that it was happening.

The lightheaded giddiness that filled her chest recognized the Lucid in his kiss. Tau. It was the same as kissing him. Only it wasn't, because when she kissed Tau the whole world melted away, and when she kissed Rho, Tau still took up too much of her head for that to happen. She pulled back, and Rho smiled at her.

Raleigh returned the grin. She needed to give up on Tau. But it wasn't just Tau that was a problem. Kappa said that Rho only agreed to things because he wanted to be with her. This small encounter fed into what he'd predicted. She said, "We shouldn't move too fast. Kappa is upset, and we should really calm him down."

Rho stepped back, letting his hands linger on her waist. "I don't think I'm going to be very good at that."

"You can't calm him down?"

"I think that I'm going to have a hard time keeping this smile from my face, and misery hates happiness. But you're right, we should at least try. Let's get Tau and him and find some lunch. Then we can figure out what this Docent initiation involves."

He leaned in, kissing her once quickly on the cheek. The impression of his lips remained as he headed out the door. The day had already been filled with too many emotions, and she guessed there would be more to come.

C H A P T E R
17

WITH A MEAL of white bean soup and bread sticking to her ribs, she stood in her room awaiting the Docent initiation. Her hand absently ran along her clavicle as she thought about the white scars on Anders's chest. Fitting that she could sense him on the other side of her door before he knocked. She walked over and opened it.

"It's time for your Docent initiation," he told her.

She straightened her shoulders, mustering up the courage to go. The last year had made her trust less, and she'd be vulnerable before a group of strangers. Still, now was the time, and she left her room without looking back. "Can I bring my friends with me?"

Anders turned towards the other doors in the hall, no doubt considering Rho and the others. "Our culture is very private."

"They'll respect that."

Anders gave her a sympathetic smile. "You're nervous, but you shouldn't be."

"Having them along would make me more comfortable."

Anders turned again towards the doors, and then he stood in silence, thinking. "We allow family members to attend. I think Thora would understand if you brought one of them. I'll let you invite one and meet you in the Docent's room, the doors right before the Convocation arena."

One was better than going alone. "All right. Do you need me to do anything before I come down?"

"No, we'll prepare you for the initiation there. I'll see you soon, don't take too long." Anders gave a small head bow and then went down the steps.

For a moment she stood in the hall listening to the sound of Anders shoes hitting the steps. They became fainter and eventually too remote to hear. In a minute she'd follow the same path. Even though she'd downplayed the initiation when talking to Rho, she understood it was no small thing. It held significance to them, and she wouldn't claim that it was meaningless. She knocked on Rho's door, and when he opened it, she saw both him and Kappa.

"It's time for the initiation," she said.

Kappa shook his head. "You really shouldn't do this."

"They said I could bring one of you."

Rho's shoulders relaxed. "That's a relief. Let me put my shoes on, and we can go."

The Docent scars would be a problem. Rho wouldn't stand idly by and let her get seared. He'd put the brakes on things and with influencing if he had to. He fussed over her too much to remain rational now.

"I was going to bring Tau."

Rho's face dropped. "Tau?"

"Yeah, he's better with neurotransmitters. Since they manipulated them during both the healing session and the Convocation, I think it's a fair bet that they'll do something with them this time. He's very skilled with endocrine stuff."

The emotion left Rho's face as he thought. Then he drew his shoulders up straight, the leader in him coming to the surface. "That's a good decision. He is in tune with that more than the rest of us." He walked across the hall and knocked on Tau's door.

Tau opened it. "What's up? Raleigh, are you going to go down to the Docent test?"

"Initiation. It's not a test," Raleigh clarified. It was stressful enough without considering it something she could fail.

"Raleigh gets to bring someone with her, and she's chosen you," Rho said. "You'll keep an eye on her? Stop it if things get out of hand. She may not be in a position to."

Tau left his room. "Of course. I won't let anything bad happen."

"Then we should head down." Raleigh headed towards the stairwell. Rho stepped closer to her and swept her up into an embrace. Her muscles tightened at the sudden movement and then she relaxed into his arms. This was their new normal now, and his support helped bolster her resolve. After a moment he let her go. "Be careful."

Raleigh nodded and continued on her way with Tau following after her. In the stairwell she turned to him. "The Docent initiation takes place in the room next to the Convocation arena. Anders pointed them out this morning." She continued on her way and eventually they exited the stairwell and stepped into the courtyard.

Now Tau stepped in line with her. "Why did you choose me?"

"Did you not want to come?"

He shook his head. "Of course. I'll always have your back. You said that you don't know anything about the Docent initiation, but that's not true, is it? Because you're nervous, and I've seen you go up against a room full of Lucid dealers with the same knot in your stomach. What about this don't you think is going to work out?"

The most frustrating, and best part of Tau, was his ability to understand her without any explanation. He pieced things together. Other people didn't know a puzzle was even there, and he already was half on his way to solving it. When applied to his interest in endocrinology the results were electric. Here, when it applied to her, it succeeded in exposing her.

"I think it's going to be unpleasant. Don't intervene. I'm not going to die from it. Anders promised it wouldn't hurt for long."

Tau grimaced. "So you're aware that pain will be involved?"

"I want the inducer." She played with a loose thread on the hem of her sleeve. A chill rustled past her, and she pulled the cuff down to cover her hands. "They're going to burn me."

Tau's eyes brows shot up. "What?"

"I'm not sure of its exact function in the ritual, but it goes to show something about how our bodies separate from who we really are. Anyhow, it might be unpleasant."

"*Might* be?"

"All right, it will be. What do you think we've been doing these past few months? I've got a lot more scars from that bunker." She rubbed the inside of her arm, the bumps of her former port itchy beneath her fingers. "None of us thought we would make it through this unscathed. A couple of physical scars are nothing."

"Except you can see them. Which means everyone will know."

The past months had changed her, the lines of her face harder than she remembered. At first she'd chalked it up to her near starvation, but now she saw that the changes ran deeper than that. "My sisters said that I'm unrecognizable. I didn't tell you all this so you can tell me how weird it is, I told you because I don't want you to stop it. Can you do that?"

"But you invited me along, which means that you know I have a point that I won't let things get past."

"A point much farther out than Rho's."

"He's not going to like that you didn't tell him that you knew about this going in."

She let out a sigh. "We'd both be better off if we stopped caring so much about what Rho thinks." They'd reached the doors to the Docent building. Inside the hallway diverged. One way led to the dining hall, the other the Convocation arena, while ahead lay the Docent room. Slowly she walked forward, stopping in the archway just before the door to stare at the metal handle worn from all the use. Then her attention crept down the hall. She'd been frightened earlier that day during the first gathering. "The Convocation was better than anything I would have expected."

"It felt pleasant. But from what you said it's using influencing to control people. The same way casinos use lights. Don't let it fool you."

"I'm saying that I'm probably scared when I shouldn't be." That was the emotion that gripped her. Not nerves but fear. "These people are revered. I doubt anything really bad will happen."

"Keep telling yourself that. But I'm only along in the event that something does."

"And to pay attention to what they're doing. Not only are you more likely to not interfere, but you're the best with neurotransmitters and hormones. Pay attention."

Raleigh wrapped her fingers around the cold door handle, and Tau's arm shot out, stopping her. "If you need my help at any time in there let me know. Squeeze my shoulder." He tightened the muscles over her scapula. Their signal of hope would now act as a siren if needed.

If it were Rho she would have told him not to underestimate her, but Tau didn't need that lecture. Finally, she gripped the handle and pulled the door open and entered. Inside fifty or so Docents waited. The large room had a domed ceiling, which added to its grandeur, but with so many people she had to repress the feeling of the walls closing in. She kept her chin level. They might sense she was scared, but she would not allow it to show. The first thing that caught her attention was a stone table in the middle of the octagonal room. A smoky smell tightened her lungs.

The Docents smiled at her, and those nearby reached out their hands to squeeze hers. The gesture moved her through the crowd. Usually they wore small purple scarves, but this time they wore long lilac tunics that reached down to their knees.

Halfway to the table Thora intercepted her, and the Docents moved back, creating a clearing around the two women. Thora lifted her hand and let her long fingers hover over Raleigh's forehead. "I welcome you, Raleigh, to unite with the Universal Soul."

"Thank you." Raleigh made sure all the Docents, not just Thora, could hear. Ivar stood near the table, his face a mask of concern. Anders waited closer, and beside him stood a girl not much older than Raleigh. The girl had her nose scrunched, as though she'd bitten into something bitter or smelt something foul.

"I shall take you to the side chamber so you can dress." Thora put a delicate hand on Raleigh's shoulder, and the Docents parted to allow them passage to a small room. They entered and found it scarcely larger than a closet.

With the door shut, Thora's voice filled the whole space. "Disrobe, and we'll put you in these." She pointed to a folded pile of linens on the only bench in the room.

Raleigh stripped off her layers but remained unclothed for only a moment. Thora handed her a pair of underwear and a short skirt that hit mid-calf. Raleigh's torso remained naked, and she rubbed her arms to fight off the chill. "I get a top, don't I?"

She'd seen part of Anders's scar and didn't know if she could stand before all those people naked.

"Of course." Thora unwound a length of cloth and then wrapped it around Raleigh's chest. Her skin itched as Thora pulled the linen tight. With it completely wrapped Thora fastened it with a clip. "You'll go out and lie on the stone slab, and the ritual will begin."

Raleigh took a shaky breath before following Thora back into the main room. The mood had shifted to one of silence and seriousness while she dressed. The Docents passed around the same chalice they used during the Convocation. Raleigh caught Tau's eye, and he nodded, so small that she wondered if he'd done it at all.

She had no time to consider the inducer. The Docents bowed their heads as she made her way to the stone table in the center of the room. She passed them, her feet heavy and her skin sweaty despite the cold.

The long slab could have fit someone a foot taller than her but wasn't very wide. Since it stood at about waist height she had to give a small hop to get onto it, not unlike an exam room bed. The gesture reminded her of how many times she'd faced medical uncertainty. In the past she'd been poked and prodded so much her skin had grown hard. This might be her first Docent initiation, but it wasn't her first time facing the unknown, her body reminding her of its mortality.

On the far side of the slab a pile of coals burned, emitting ripples of heat towards her. A welcome relief to the cold stone. She lay back, her hair falling around her face, but she didn't fold her hands over her stomach, instead she pressed them against the stone. Another wavering breath left her lips. Now was the time to be as brave as everyone claimed she was.

The Docents put down the cup of inducer and surrounded her. Tau, taller than many of them, didn't retreat back, staying firmly in sight. She stared into his blue eyes and gulped down her worry. Two older women came forward with low bowls full of some liquid thicker than water. They set them at the foot and head of the slab and then pulled sponges from their pockets.

A few of the Docents chanted, and the others picked up the words in turn. The women, one at Raleigh's head and the other at her feet, dipped the hard sea sponge into the liquid and then rubbed it over her arms, legs, and neck. The porous sponge abraded her skin, the oily substance easing the temporary pain. They used long stokes on her legs and tiny swirling ones on her hands. When they finished her front she flipped over onto her stomach and the process continued. When it was over she again lay on her back, her skin now pink and glossy.

With the bowls removed, and the women back in the group, the chanting stopped. A pristine silence filled the room. Then Thora moved to the head of the slab. "The body is a vessel for the Universal Soul. Now that you've been cleaned we shall separate the two, as a reminder that the body is temporary, the spirit permanent. In dividing the two we purify the soul and return it back. After that you shall be a Docent."

Raleigh slid her fingers anxiously together, the oil making them glide. Her back straightened on the slab, and her eyes flicked to Tau. His face remained stoic, his demeanor resolved. Raleigh faced the dome with eyes open.

The humming started with the men. Their deep baritone voices echoed in the space causing the muscles along her spine to tighten. As they hummed they craned their necks to face the obstructed sky and opened their arms so that their palms faced up to the heavens. Next came the women, their lighter voices joining the chorus.

The voices hit odd tones that bit against a harmony. The unruly dissonance made the hairs on Raleigh's arms stand stiff. The humming undulated, loud and soft, the concave ceiling catching and reflecting the sound so that it became a continual river of noise.

The vibrations bombarded her from all angles, and her head throbbed, anticipating the rhythmic ebbs to the song. A lightness crept into her chest as her body grew heavier against the stone. She experienced the sensation of being tethered to herself. There were points along her body where her soul seemed to lift up, the tension barely noticeable but there. Like the fine arc of a bubble over water, held delicately taut. Her body remained solid, trying to hold her back, and on a breath she felt herself go. The being inside ascended, insubstantial but real, over her body.

Now the two pieces of her, the corporeal and the immaterial, were on different planes. The unpleasant rawness of her skin remained behind. She became radiance, no longer encumbered by anything, allowed to simply exist. She was as insubstantial and as brilliant as a ray of light. Her essence held up by the waves of humming.

Below, she knew they touched her skin. They took a stylus from the hot coals beside the slab of stone and pressed it onto the skin directly under her collar bone. The pain seeped into her, like a drop of ink into a well of water, expanding its fingers across her and causing her body to gasp.

But she didn't feel it, not really. This event happened to the body below her, and her mind told her that it wasn't really her. An old man drew the stylus across her skin, creating a pattern, and continuing the distant agony that she somehow remained separated from.

When he finished his task he stepped back, and the sound of the humming grew louder, either because she'd become more aware of it or because it had increased in volume, she couldn't be sure. The sound cradled her and kept her afloat.

Then the joy worked its way into her. It slipped in like a warm breeze through a door, and she tumbled back into her body, acutely aware of how her heart beat, her skin ached, and her eyes blinked. The pain now shocked her, but the joy fought it off. An unseen battle where the happiness turned the burnt sensation into nothing more than an uncomfortable pressure near her shoulder.

She'd experienced a fraction of this completeness once before while hiking in Colorado. At the time when she was young and her problems so minor she couldn't recall them now. When she'd stood at a mountain peak, the clouds over a distant mountain range. Against the majestic backdrop she'd felt small and insignificant and at the same time linked to the world around her. That held true now. She was a drop of water in a vast sea.

The humming ended, but the elation didn't. Maybe the soul did exist, because she'd certainly understood the division between herself and her body during the ritual. Lucidin might be a tool to understand it. She sat up, and the Docents passed by her, holding up their hands to their foreheads, indicating that they shared the connection with her. A connection that had existed for Raleigh for some time.

Without a word, Raleigh's Docent initiation ended. Nothing in the room had changed, but the world couldn't be more different.

Thora came over and rubbed a salve on her burn. "This will help it heal. We'll change the bandages once a day." She taped on a patch of gauze. "Tonight you'll stay with the other Docents."

Raleigh slid off the slab and took a moment to steady herself on her feet. The few remaining Docents whispered their congratulations, and she moved over to Tau. She had so much she wanted to say to him. Had he sensed the magnitude of her experience? She opened her mouth and noticed his lips turn down into a frown.

How could he be so upset when at that moment she had such joy? If only she could erase his sadness and make him understand. Her finger rose up, as if not under her volition, and touched the corner of his mouth. His frown deepened. Maybe she was his sadness. "Raleigh, we need to get you dressed and then some fresh air."

"My soul, for a moment that's all I was."

"Good for you, but we still need to get you dressed. You'll be cold."

"My body, it's not important." She longed to experience the weightless hope she'd just had.

Tau shook his head. "It is, you're just not thinking straight. Come on."

"Would you like me to help?" Thora asked as the Docents cleared out.

"I've got it." Tau told her helping Raleigh to the small room with her clothes. "Get in and get changed. I'll be waiting here for you."

Raleigh started to take off the top before he'd even shut the door. She stood naked, her arms outstretched. Over the past months, her body had endured training with the Receps and abuse by the synthetic. Each of those memories lay in the fibers of her muscles. She flexed her arm, marveling at the musculature. Then she got dressed, her shoulder stinging when her shirt pressed down on the burn.

On the other side of the door she found Tau. They walked into the hallway where the lingering Docents spoke to each other and gave Raleigh small waves. She smiled, loafing near the doorway to the Docent's room, when Tau grasped her upper arm and led her down a small hallway to a door. He pushed it open and the January air nipped her cheeks. The door shut with a thud, and they were alone in the small courtyard.

She spun around grabbing his arm. "Did you feel what happened to me?"

"Shh," Tau said. "They'll hear."

Raleigh bounced onto the balls of her feet so she could put her hands onto his shoulders. "They're all inside. No one wants to be out here, it's dismal. But I don't care. I feel great."

"When you finished your out of body experience they flooded your system with endorphins and serotonin."

"We should tell Rho."

"No, you should sober up for a second."

"I'm not drunk."

"You're not normal."

She recognized the nuances of an endorphin high, the sensation that flooded her after a run and this wasn't it. "It's like that time you fiddled with my endorphins."

"No, it's not. I didn't hurt you and then mask the pain. I helped out a bit with your bruising in Italy. Nothing more."

Raleigh sat on one of the stone benches that lined the square. Tau sat down next to her. He leaned back and ran his hand through his hair. He bit his bottom lip, worried.

"You're handsome. Did you know that?"

"Stop, you'll say something embarrassing."

"Are you worried that you'll be embarrassed or me? Besides, you've always loved honesty."

He took a deep breath, considering something but then closed his lips. "Let's not talk about me."

"Do you want to talk about how my soul rose out of my body?"

"It didn't. They influenced your neuronal pathways to fire at specifically the right times. That caused you to think you rose out of your body. Then they burnt you and flooded your system with serotonin. Ecstasy works in a very similar way."

She kicked her feet against the stone wall next to the bench. "I should have guessed you'd have a scientific reason for it."

Tau's eyebrow moved up curiously. "You're upset? Would you have preferred the answer to be that your soul left your body? Do you even believe in the soul?"

Raleigh didn't, but she did want to believe that the happiness was authentic. Then she could own it, Tau's words made it seem less hers. "I guess not, what do you believe?"

"I don't believe in a soul. Maybe a sense of self, of consciousness, but not a soul. That doesn't mean that I'm right. But, I think you should consider what happened in that room as them manipulating your brain and not a religious experience."

"I suppose. But for a second there, I belonged, and everything was right." Maybe no one ever really belonged, maybe the best anyone could do was to fool themselves.

"Emotions are consequences of our minds."

"I guess that I wanted Lucid to have a purpose, for there to be a reason that I can do what I do. Why does it exist?"

Tau rubbed his hands on his jeans. "I would say to connect people, because that is what happens. But I don't think it's to connect our souls. It's another way to understand and perceive the world. Like our eyes or our sense of smell."

"Another sense then." Her shoulders sank. He'd managed to take romance out of it.

"Yeah, I guess. You're feeling better?"

"No. I'm feeling worse."

"You've returned to yourself. Happiness is better when it's real, not when someone has manipulated you to feel it. And you should be happy."

"Happy? All of us have our days numbered."

"We've been through worse. You've given us all hope. The synthetic is gone, and we're on much better terms with Grant and Able."

"And much worse with Sigma."

"They drank from a cup before they influenced you."

Raleigh perked up. "That's what they did before the Convocation."

"That has to be what Grant and Able spoke of. That has to be the inducer. Now all we have to do is get it."

C H A P T E R
18

RALEIGH'S ENDORPHINS FROM the Docent initiation had dissipated. Dread of telling Rho what happened, and about the scar, had sobered her up. She trudged behind Tau on the way back up to the rooms. She sensed Rho and Kappa behind the door to her room, waiting. Knots of worry tightened in Rho's back. She pulled her coat up higher, trying to cover the visible part of her bandage, hoping she could ward off the pain of it enough that Rho wouldn't suspect. Before she had a chance to rap on her door, Rho'd opened it.

"How did it go?" Rho ushered her and Tau into the room.

"It went well. They used the inducer again this time before the ceremony." Raleigh kept her voice causal. "And tonight they want me to room with the Docents, so I'll get more of a chance to see how they live."

Kappa pinched the top of his nose and let out an exasperated sigh. "Do you still think that you can leave whenever you want?"

"I believe it because I can."

Rho asked, "What about the ceremony? What did it involve?"

Tau spoke up. "They cleansed her body and then influenced her mind to produce an out-of-body experience." The last bit hung in the air. That wasn't all they had done. The pain of the burn throbbed against her tender skin.

"And you hurt your shoulder?" Rho asked Raleigh.

Raleigh gave Tau an uneasy glance and steeled herself to answer. "They etched a design into my shoulder."

Rho's eyebrows bowed together. "Like a tattoo?"

"They did it with a hot stylus." Tau made it seem simple and benign. "She didn't feel a thing, they influenced away the pain and made her think she was floating."

"It isn't that big of a deal." Raleigh shrugged.

Kappa coughed. "They branded you?"

"The burn wasn't as deep as a brand. They delicately applied it," Tau explained, and like Raleigh, kept his attention on Rho's face.

Rho's eyes darkened. "Can I see it?"

"It's bandaged. But sure." She pulled off her jacket and moved her shirt to the side. Then she peeled back the white bandages revealing the angry skin underneath. "It looks bad, but Anders's is now a shimmering white scar."

Rho took in an unsteady breath and then another. "And you knew they were going to do this? They told you in advance?"

"Yes."

"And you still *did it!*" His voice boomed through the small room.

Tau interjected, "Calm down, it was her choice."

"Don't tell me to calm down. I sent you to make sure that they didn't hurt her and she comes back to us branded."

Raleigh stepped between the two of them. "Don't get mad at Tau. We all carry scars, these you can see, but I've been hurt far worse—we all have."

"Yeah, but usually one of us doesn't stand by and mindlessly let it happen."

Tau shot back, "It wasn't mindless. We weighed the pros and cons before going in."

"Tau, you were sent to protect her, and you failed. Have both of you lost your minds? We need to leave tonight." Kappa's anger simmered in his chest. With Rho shouting he didn't need to yell, the tension hung in the air so thick that their words sat painful before her.

Raleigh tugged her jacket back on. "I didn't get this scar so the two of you could lose your courage. We'll stay until we get the inducer."

Rho tossed out his hand. "And if that takes years?"

Raleigh relaxed. She needed to diffuse this situation or they weren't going to get anywhere. "You said you understood. This morning you said you would have taken the boat over with me. Now you're demanding we leave?"

Rho ran a worried hand through his hair. His mood shifted, and she could tell he was thinking hard. "You're right. I did say that. This is more intense than I guessed. We can stay, at least for a few days more."

Kappa let out the anger he'd held in. "What? No! Rho are you crazy? They burnt her. It's a lot creepier than we thought, and my expectations were low to start."

"Just a few days, Kappa," Rho told him.

Kappa shot an angry glance at Tau and Raleigh, then stormed out of the room. For the first time she understood what he was saying. Rho chose whatever she wanted to hear. A poor habit and an abysmal trait in a leader. Still, this time it got her what she wanted. They would stay a bit longer.

She worked to keep a grimace from filling her face. The Rho

she'd gotten a crush on in Paris all those months ago would never have let someone else speak for him. This new Rho was worse than the one who tried to hold her back. The excitement of kissing him earlier turned sour. They couldn't have a relationship if only one of them participated.

Their incompatibility wasn't a conversation she could have with him right now. Even if Tau wasn't standing over her shoulder, this wasn't the time. If she ended things Rho might insist they leave tonight.

"I'm supposed to collect my things and go back down to the Docent building so Anders can take me over to the dorms." She went over to her bag. Tau and Rho both watched as she zipped up her pack.

"Do you want me to walk you back down?" Tau asked.

She wanted to tell him that she was her old self now, not blinded by the dopamine. "No, I'm fine."

"Be careful," Tau told her as she walked into the hall.

She took a few more steps in the direction of the stairs before Rho ran up and, reaching out, caught her hand. When she turned to assure him that she would be careful he kissed her. His warm lips startled her. They'd discussed being a couple but not in front of Tau. There hadn't been the time to explain to him. And now, her heart wasn't in it, so it felt like a needless injury to inflict. If Tau even cared.

Pulling back from Rho she left a hand on his arm as her eyes passed over his shoulder back to Tau. Surprise lingered on his face, the line of his mouth repressing the emotion that had been there a moment before.

"I'll report back tomorrow," Raleigh promised Rho and then headed down the stairs. There was no time to fuss over the two failed relationships, she had to focus on learning the secrets of the Docents.

ANDERS MET HER in the Docent building and this time took her beyond the dining hall to a stairwell that led to the dormitories. There he guided her up the curving stone steps, his feet light. They passed narrow windows where the courtyard came into view, and on the other side, across the way, was the apartment she'd stayed in the night before. Meaning that Tau, Rho, and Kappa weren't that far but not near enough that she could sense them or reach them quickly. Sharing the remaining corner of the courtyard was the Docent's entrance into the Convocation arena. Situated in the center of the town the Docents could spend their lives in near seclusion from the rest of the people. Images of medieval monks came to mind.

A child's laugh broke the air, and Raleigh stopped on one of the steps, staring at the landing. "Was that a kid?"

"The bottom floors of the dormitories house Docent families. There are fifty-three of us, and over half are married. It's easier to house them here than to have the Docents scattered across the town."

"Will I be staying with a family?"

"You'll be staying two more floors up in a room with the single Docent Women. I'll be one floor above you, housed with the single Docent men." Anders continued up the steps and motioned for her to do the same.

"So the singles are grouped together? You only achieve an apartment once you've been married?"

"It's not like that. We encourage Docents to have children and families to pass along our lineages. But being single doesn't make you a martyr. If you want an apartment all to yourself, you can have it. People here prefer to live together, we're not forced."

His response prompted a ping of guilt. Perhaps she'd been too harsh when asking about their living arrangements. Most of her high school friends had been excited upon learning about their dorm assignments. This wasn't terribly different.

"This is it." Anders stopped on a landing and motioned to the double doors. He knocked once but didn't wait for an answer before opening it. No locks. A relief after being trapped in the bunker, but it also meant that she'd be more vulnerable.

They stepped into the massive room. At the far end a fire crackled in a hearth, sending tendrils of warmth towards her. Reaching up, she pressed her cheek, relishing the warmth. The path to the fire divided the room into half, and each half was further divided into fourths by walls, not unlike the stalls of a corral. But instead of horses these cubical shaped rooms had a bed. Heavy curtains hung over the entrances, affording some privacy.

Anders strode in and pointed to the chairs around the fire. "That's the gathering area. Otherwise each of these nooks belongs to a different Docent. There's one open near the back. Meaning you'll be closest to the fire, but unfortunately that's where most of the chatter happens."

"That's fine." She craned her neck up to see the ceiling. It wasn't terribly high, making the room squished, but then the bunker had a high ceiling, and it had been stifling too. At least it would stay warm, and she found herself eager to shed her jacket.

She walked quickly back to her section of the room, pausing at the stall before it. The curtain was drawn half open, giving a glimpse into the space. Unlike the others that she'd passed this one was more than a bed and a handful of personal trinkets. Books lined the walls, their precarious stacks slanting against one another leaving little space to get around to the bed. Their spines had names in English. A surprise that made her stop.

"Your bed is the next one down." Anders waited, his head tilted in the direction of what presumably was to be her space.

"Whose bed is this?"

Anders face fell for a fraction of a second before he regained his composure. "Iola. She was one of the younger women at your Docent initiation today."

"The girl who looked upset?"

Anders nodded. "You'll no doubt meet her later tonight."

"You seem unhappy about that."

"Iola agrees with Ivar that you shouldn't be here. Don't take it personally, you'll win her over with time I'm sure."

"From her reading material I wouldn't think she would dislike outsiders." Surely someone so engrossed in this way of life wouldn't have so many foreign titles. Proving her logic were a stack of American classics near the opening to the room.

"She's from the UK. So no, not the same aversion to outsiders."

"She's like me then. New to this?"

"Yes and no. Her father grew up here and then married one of the people we healed. Since it had been generations since anyone in his family had heard the Universal Soul he decided to leave when she returned to England. They had a daughter and raised her with our beliefs. At fourteen she heard the Soul without help. That's when she came here."

Raleigh stared at the books, her heart picking up a fraction. "Heard without help?"

"Yes. Here children meet with the Sapient, and they see if they can hear the Soul. They're aided with ritual. That's how I learned to be a Docent. Iola heard it without help. A man at a market had a heart attack, and she felt it."

The pieces began to fall in place.

The Sapient probably gave the inducer to all the local children. Anyone who could sense was made a Docent.

The question was, how many could influence?

"Can everyone speak to the Soul?" Raleigh asked. "The way yours spoke to mine?"

"Fewer than can hear. Both are gifts. This is your space. There are some clothes in the dresser."

"Are mine not good enough?" The clothes she'd worn during the Docent initiation had been scratchy and stiff. Nothing like her cotton shirt and well-worn jeans.

"Yours are. We didn't know what you'd need. There's a purple scarf inside. To let the townspeople know that you are a Docent."

The townsfolk had observed her curiously at the Convocation that morning. How would they feel about her taking on one of their sacred roles? She stepped into her space. The comforter took up most of her bed, and a narrow window let a stripe of street light into the room.

"Get settled. Tomorrow you'll join us as a Docent at the Convocation. Have a good night." Anders offered her a kind smile before heading out of the dormitory. Raleigh stood staring at the bed. They lived a simple life, whose rhythm beat slower than the quick paced tempo she'd grown used to.

She sat down on the bed and winced at the lumpiness of the straw mattress. Of all the places she'd expected to end up in life this wasn't one of them. The last year had gone nothing like she'd planned. Memories of the dozens of rooms she'd stayed in from Sabine's house to the bunker ticked through her mind. She stood. The silence let too many unwanted thoughts trickle in. A distraction would be better. She walked over and stared at Iola's books. Surely the girl wouldn't mind if she borrowed one for an hour or so.

Without a door to open it only took one step for Raleigh to cross into the girl's space. It wasn't quite trespassing, and she ignored guilt over breaking Iola's privacy. Most of the titles she could see from the entrance anyway. Raleigh lowered herself so she could read the names. There were so many. Surely the bookstore on the mainland didn't sell her all these.

Tacked to the wall behind one of the towering piles was a picture. Tape covered the top bit and creases showed that it had probably traveled in a pocket at one point. Still, the image was clear enough. Iola, who stood with her long wavy dark hair and wide brown eyes next to a fairer man, likely her father, and a darker woman who had to be her mother. Many of the people on the island appeared Nordic. Ironically Iola appeared more Mediterranean, although who knows where her linage lay.

Raleigh sensed someone enter the larger room while she crouched down and read a title about poetry. She stood, moving towards the main section just in time to meet Iola at the threshold of the carved-out space.

"What are you doing near my things?" Iola accused.

Over the past few months Raleigh had been starved of female friendship. Agatha had been more of a mentor. The conversations last week with her sisters had been some of the few female talks that she'd had over the last year. Hopefully Anders was right, and she'd win the girl over, but this wasn't a good introduction. "You've got an impressive book collection."

"There is a public library in town. These are mine."

Raleigh twisted her fingers together, but she kept her face kind. "I didn't mean to offend you." She stepped around Iola closer to the communal area.

"You're not supposed to be here. You shouldn't have taken the Docent initiation, and you shouldn't be staying here now." Iola's brown eyes bored into Raleigh. The scowl on her face speaking more to frustration than hatred.

"I hear the Universal Soul."

"You don't understand. This place isn't meant for *you*. Or your friends. This isn't America, and you're not going to fare well here."

Ouch. The girl was blunt. "I'm meant to be here. Thora said so."

"You're making a mistake. The Universal Soul shouldn't have reached you. Next time you want a book, go to the library. I'm sure Anders will be keen to show you where it is." Iola retreated into her room yanking the curtain shut behind her. Raleigh was certain that if there had been a door she would have slammed it.

Walking over to her own bed Raleigh lay down. Iola and Ivar both wanted her gone. Who knew how pervasive the sentiment was? Maybe there was something extra to the reason Iola disliked her. With only fifty Docents there weren't that many in their age range, perhaps Iola liked Anders and considered Raleigh a threat. A simple jealousy, Raleigh would have to show that she wasn't romantically interested in Anders, maybe that would ease her mind. But not now, not after that chilly introduction.

Raleigh lay in bed, the lumps of the mattress pressing up awkwardly on her back. She didn't let her mind drift to Iola too long. It would have been nice to have a friend, but she wouldn't be here long enough for any of these relationships to matter. Or at least that was her hope as she drifted off to sleep.

CHAPTER
19

THE PURPLE SCARF chafed Raleigh's neck when she sat down to breakfast the next morning. Oatmeal again, like the day before. At least it wasn't something that came out of a box, and after her near starvation in the bunker, her stomach wouldn't dare complain about any food ever again. Digging into her breakfast she tried not to notice the wide berth most of the people gave her. This time she didn't have Anders to keep her company. Many of the Docents offered small smiles if she caught their eye, but their families and others looked upon her with fear and apprehension. When they spoke it wasn't in English, and her ears picked up on the syllables of their words, eager to eavesdrop and understand.

A momentary hush fell over the room. So brief that if she'd been chewing she might have missed it, but the temporary silence didn't escape her, and she straightened herself up, her eyes searching. Kappa had entered the room. The Designed never blended in well, but here, where they were also outsiders, the contrast was even more stark.

He sat down at the table across from her, his eyes glaring at the people who stared. Quickly they turned away, picking back up their conversation. "They stare at me like I'm an alien."

"They aren't used to outsiders. And you're handsome." It was the best adjective she could think up that wouldn't shine a spotlight on what he really was. "Did you want breakfast?"

"Someone brought us trays this morning." He glanced around again, his eyes lingering on the door.

"Are you allowed to be here?"

Kappa squinted at her. "I don't care where I am and am not allowed. But nobody has given us any rule about where we are to be if that's what you're asking."

Raleigh ate another bite. Something was up. Yes, Kappa had been annoyed with her yesterday, but the night should have cooled his temper. "What's wrong?"

"I had to find you, we found this on our door this morning." He slid a small piece of paper towards her.

Parchment was a better term for it. The consistency of it was grainy, as if pressed into shape by hand rather than a machine. Unfolding the thick paper she found one sentence inside.

Get her out now, she doesn't belong, leave before it's too late.

It was short, succinct, and damning. "I told you that some of the people weren't keen on outsiders, which they clearly think I am." Raleigh folded it and returned it to Kappa.

"This note makes it sounds like they're worried about you. They didn't tell us to leave, they told us to rescue you from this place."

"It's one line."

"These people don't want us here. What if they find out who we are?" The last part he barely spoke. He'd been letting his temper raise the volume of his words, but the muted, quiet bit had been the most worrying.

"They haven't, and they won't. And not everyone wants to see us leave, just a few." Although she wondered how large the group was, maybe Iola and Ivar were the tip of the iceberg.

"One person wanting us gone is too many. I need you to reconsider. Rho isn't listening to me. Tau's on the fence."

"I didn't go through yesterday so we could leave today. Like I said just a little longer—please."

Kappa leaned back and rubbed his hands along the legs of his jeans, thinking. "Fine. But don't be stupid, realize that something is up." Kappa grabbed up the note, shoved it in his pocket, and turned to leave.

"You're coming to the Convocation?" Raleigh asked.

Kappa nodded. "We all are." With that he strode towards the exit. Raleigh looked at her food but didn't eat. She couldn't shake the warning on the note. It hadn't told her anything she didn't know, but somehow the tone of it heralded danger more than the red paint on the door yesterday. Kappa was right, someone thought that by staying her safety would be at stake.

As Kappa left, Anders entered. The two made eye contact, but neither stopped to talk. Raleigh put down her spoon when Anders took the seat that Kappa had just vacated. "Your friend, he's upset. Is it because of the paint on the door?"

"And we got a letter this morning, saying I should leave."

"Sorry. Now that you're a Docent I thought things would calm down."

"I thought getting burned would do the trick too, but apparently not." She tapped her spoon on the tabletop. "Does it go beyond their distrust of outsiders?" When she asked the question she didn't know what answer she hoped to get. Would Anders bring up Grant and Able? Worse, would he say that it had something to do with the guys? The messages had started once they arrived, not that there had been much time before that.

Anders gulped and twisted his hands together. "Ivar is old."

"So he's being mean?"

"No, another Sapient will need to be named. Discussions have been underway for months. Iola and I, both the right age to take on the role, have shown the most promise. The plans have been laid for the Sapient Trial, where the Universal Soul will grant one of us the ability to lead."

"And people are upset about me because?"

"The soul has touched you deeper than any of us. Even Ivar, who the Soul has always favored, has never shown such ability. With the timing of your arrival, when we need a leader, it's fate."

Heat rose up Raleigh's neck. The conversation she'd had with Anders yesterday about her soul being drawn here had unnerved her. Having her become a Docent had been radical enough. Now he implied she would be a Sapient. "No wonder they're upset. I'm in no place to lead." Iola wasn't chilly towards her because she had a crush on Anders, she was angry that she was to take her position as Sapient. "And let me guess. Thora is in support of me, but Ivar wants it to be Iola."

"Ivar thinks the Universal Soul will choose Iola. But ultimately it's not up to us. Our people decide who will enter the Trial, but the Soul choses."

"You can tell Ivar, Thora, and Iola that I don't want it."

Anders face fell, and he reached out his hands, having them hover near hers. "Please, don't be so rash. I shouldn't have told you. Thora would have explained this so much better than I did. I only did because I wanted you to understand the notes and tension. Please. Don't make up your mind yet."

"Don't you want to be Sapient?"

He lifted his chin. "More than anything. But it isn't for me to decide. If Iola and I both fail the Trial, we'll be left without a leader, and that can't happen."

The Docents around them were getting up and heading toward the door. Even without a clock she guessed that it would be time for the Convocation. Raleigh could sense the flood of townsfolk flocking towards the arena one building away.

"What is it?" Anders said noticing her change in mood.

"The townsfolk, they're arriving at the arena."

"You can hear them from here?"

"There are a lot of them. Can you not?"

"I only hear people after the Convocation."

"For how long after?"

"Usually the middle of the night, then the Universal Soul retreats until the next Convocation."

The unspoken translation was he only heard people once he'd been induced to do so. Likely the only people who passed the Trial were those with a high enough receptor volume.

For the first time her stomach lurched at the thought of staying any longer. The decision to make her a Docent had been hasty, but they explained that she more or less qualified the moment she heard the Soul. To get anywhere near the inducer it seemed like the only option. But to become a *Sapient?* The very idea made her shudder. These people shouldn't want a stranger leading them. For them to consider something so outlandish only proved them to be more fanatical than she'd thought.

Anders stood. "We should get going."

Raleigh rose and put away her dishes before following Anders out of the cafeteria towards the arena. The conversation about the Sapient Trial would have to wait.

Right now she had to fulfill her job as Docent.

"During the Convocation you'll help the Universal Soul speak to the people. Convey its message of kindness and joy," Anders told her. "Seek these emotions out in the people, to relieve their suffering."

There was no secret then about what happened. The Docents knew they influenced the people even if they didn't call it that.

Raleigh stepped into the Convocation arena. On the opposing side of the vast space, beyond the doors where the townspeople entered, stood the villagers. Anders began the path down to the center of the room where the other Docents waited. Raleigh found a seat beside Anders, and Iola sat a few seats down from them, her body tense at their arrival. Thora and Ivar were in the center, and once the last Docents trickled in, they signaled for the doors to open.

People flooded in. Raleigh's eyes scanned the unfamiliar faces for those of the Designed, wondering if they'd changed their mind and chosen not to come. The variance in attendees made it difficult to see all the faces. Young children darted around the legs of their parents and caught her attention. The streams of people parted for the older, aged population, but the group crowded together otherwise. Like yesterday, greetings were exchanged and seats were taken.

"Here, take a long sip of this." Anders handed her the wide cup. "It's part of the ritual."

Raleigh's reflection bounced back to her as she stared down into the chalice. Her hands cradled the metal, knowing the value of what lay inside. What would happen if she took it? Would the inducer have an effect on her—would it prompt a blackout?

"It doesn't taste bad," Anders said.

She considered how to describe her concerns in a way Anders would understand. "Sometimes I hear so strongly that I have problems, like the other day on the boat."

"I think you'll be fine."

Taking it might very well overload her, but then again, it wasn't as if she were taking Lucid, like she'd done in the bunker in the attempt to create a blackout. The inducer shouldn't have much work to do in her, because she already made so much.

If she drank it she might remember enough about the flavor to recreate it. Oliver Able never mentioned getting to taste the drink. Bringing up the metal cup she took a long-drawn sip. The room temperature liquid might have once been hot, almost like tea, and the flavor had a nip of licorice or something like it. Mostly it tasted herbal, with a lingering bitter aftertaste. She passed it on and waited.

Nothing happened, she didn't sense the people any more than she usually did. The Docents continued to pass the drink, and she watched them. Then she focused her attention to the crowd. In the back, with space on either side of them, sat the Designed. Rho put up his hand and gave a half wave. She gave a short head nod in response.

Thora stood and spoke. Anders leaned towards Raleigh so he could translate. "She's welcoming everyone to the Convocation."

Yesterday Raleigh had fared fine without Anders to understand what was said, but she didn't refuse his help now. After the same short pleasantries as yesterday Thora said something that made the crowd go into an uproar. Anders paled beside her.

"What did she say? Why are the people so happy?" She sincerely hoped it wasn't her.

"It's the Sapient Trial, it's in two days." Anders began to sweat where the purple scarf wrapped around his neck.

Raleigh bit back her own worry. "You didn't make it sound that soon."

"I didn't think it would be this early. The day before the

nominations will be made." Anders stared at Thora. "All my life has led up to this. I'm not ready."

The audience applauded, and then Thora sat down. Anders tilted his head back like many of the other Docents. The time to consider the Sapient Trial had passed. Now the Convocation demanded her attention.

It progressed the same way as before. First the hearts found their matching rhythm. The townsfolk let out a collective sigh as their brains were flooded with dopamine and serotonin. Almost everyone had their eyes shut or turned to the ceiling, as if they could see the Universal Soul they believed so strongly in.

Raleigh found the Designed with both her eyes and then her mind. None of them broke cover by barricading. All three allowed the Docents to influence the feelings of joy and reward in their brains. Despite those emotions, Kappa's mouth bowed down in a frown. Raleigh turned away, hoping that his persistent skepticism wouldn't draw suspicion.

Ivar sat on the other side of the Docent seating. With each breath his lungs pressed against his ribcage, crushed by the osteoporosis of his spine. His oversized heart struggled to keep up with the unified pulse throbbing through the crowd. Then his eyes opened, and he stared at Raleigh. She turned away, masking her emotions.

The Convocation ended, and the voices began to chatter. People flocked to exits. The Designed fought to walk down to the front but were ushered out the back doors with the rest of the townsfolk.

Many of the Docents stood to go. Raleigh sensed Anders, his stomach turning and his mouth dry, as he hurried towards the door. The Sapient Trials scared him. She wondered why, after all, he seemed like he'd already heard the call to lead his people.

Thora walked over to Raleigh. "How did you feel your first Convocation as a Docent went?"

"Good. I do have a question, though. That drink at the beginning of the ceremony, what's its purpose?"

Thora's brow crinkled. "It's to help center you so you can better hear the Soul."

"And what's in it?"

Thora paused, and Raleigh wondered if she'd list off the ingredients right there. "A few different things. We can talk about it another time. I made the announcement in Greek, so I didn't know if you understood, our Sapient Trials will be in a few days."

"Anders told me, and he also said that he hadn't expected it to be so soon."

"Yes, it is time." Thora's eyes darted to Ivar before returning to Raleigh. "We've waited too long as it is. I should talk to you about the Trials, you would make a good candidate for Sapient."

Raleigh didn't want it. "No, I couldn't possibly. My friends and I should leave, we would hate to interrupt any part of this important ritual."

Thora shook her head. "You aren't an interruption. Besides, the boats won't travel for a week. We need to prepare the city for the Trial. This is a time of great celebration, and we're happy to have you and your friends as guests."

"No boats for a week?" Had they shut them down with the express purpose of keeping her here? "What about the pilgrim boats?"

"We'll halt those during this time. I wouldn't think you'd want to go back, you're just beginning to connect with us. The Trials, they are an important time. Come celebrate with us. Excuse me, I must go now, there is much we need to do." Thora put her palm to Raleigh's forehead in a blessing and then departed.

No boats for a week. This couldn't be good. If Anders and Thora wanted her to take the Sapient Trial it would be hard to get out of. Would they hold off the boats until she did? She'd bitten off a lot becoming a Docent, and that was already too much to ask. But if they made her a Sapient they would never let her leave.

Kappa had been right, things had gotten out of her control. She carried the burden of blame. Tau had been on the fence, and she'd manipulated Rho to stay. Now she would have to admit that she was wrong. A confession that she had to make quickly. She left the Convocation arena in search of the guys.

C H A P T E R
20

RALEIGH HEADED OUT through the Docent's hallway. Dread sat heavy on her shoulders. How would the Designed take the news that no boats would leave for a week? She could already anticipate Kappa's anger. Not that there was much she could do about it now. She sank a bit deeper into her coat as she reached the door that lead from the Convocation hallway to the courtyard.

"Stop there, we need to talk." Ivar's shaky voice wheezed out with each word.

Her hand tightened on the door handle, but she didn't open it. "I know you're upset that I've come here."

"Yes. Come talk. There is more." His feet scratched over the stony ground, his body heavy on his cane as he hobbled to an alcove near the door.

Raleigh didn't follow immediately, instead she paused, thinking, as Ivar waited. She'd be here all week, and eventually she'd have to talk to Ivar. Leaving the door, she joined him in the alcove.

"You aren't welcome here," Ivar said.

"I don't know what happened in the past to make you dislike outsiders so much…."

"You will not be Sapient. It isn't fate or destiny that you've come when my body is nearing its end. It's bad luck. The Universal Soul has always favored me more than the others. I know its wishes, and it tells me that you are not meant to lead us."

"I don't intend to lead your people."

"Then why are you here? I warn you now, there have been people in our past. People who claimed to come here to understand the Soul, who tried to control it in unnatural ways. Back then I let my curiosity get the better of me. Now I know that my intuition is better than anything else. My heart is telling me that you aren't to be trusted. Your friends and you are to leave on the first boat after the Trials. I don't care that you're a Docent, that honor should never have been bestowed."

Her chest loosened. If Ivar wanted her gone, surely he'd help her get off the island. "Because I'm a Docent will there be opposition to me leaving?"

"No. A fair number of us wish to have you go. I insist you leave after the Trials."

"I could go now, if you helped me get a boat."

"There are none, you will have to wait. And keep yourself out of our Trials. Don't underestimate me, my body is weak, but I am strong. The Universal Soul lends me its strength to defend it."

His eyes were unflinching, and his hostility rang out in his words.

"I will stay out of the way." She attempted to keep her attitude demure, to not incite his ire further. She stood and walked to the door, hoping the best way to diffuse the tension would be to exit.

Ivar froze her legs mid-step. A trick that she'd used more than once, and she knew influencing well enough to know that was done to her now. Twisting where she stood, her eyes met Ivar's. So they didn't just use influencing to entice the townsfolk to stay. Her mouth opened, there were no words.

"Go, tell your friends to pack their bags."

Raleigh's legs were once again under her control. Fury rose up her neck, warm and hot. People had hurt her before, but no one had been so brazen as to influence her like this. Not when she herself could inflict far worse. The thought of the people she'd harmed slammed into her. No, Ivar wouldn't be one of them.

"We'll leave as soon as the boats are allowed to travel." Raleigh yanked open the door and stepped out into the cold January morning—she needed to find the Designed.

The misty air spattered her skin alerting her already heightened senses. The adrenaline made her steps long, her legs still reeling from the insult of being influenced. Nearby the trees and bushes that lined the courtyard reached their thin dark hands to the clouds. The image of the Docents, with their slack mouths facing the sky sat uneasily in the back of her mind. She shook off thought of them, their rituals, and the fear of being on the island for a week.

Kappa, Tau, and Rho stood outside the courtyard. The wall here was shorter than it was lower down in town where it blocked the view. Here it came up to their shoulders, giving a glimpse of the horizon in the distance. She walked over to them, the drop off into the water reminded her of the journey Rho had taken to get to her all those months ago in Belgium. For a long time now, living had been more about survival than anything else.

"There are no boats for a week," Rho said evenly.

At least she didn't have to say it out loud, because even though she couldn't have predicted it, their situation was her fault. And Rho's. If he'd had more of spine he would have pushed her to go. Blame didn't help. "Who told you?"

"Thora announced it," Tau told her. "That was part of her little speech at the Convocation. We speak enough Greek now that we could figure it out."

"You've already picked up that much?" Raleigh often forgot how intelligent they were.

Tau said, "We don't know enough of the language to understand why they've stopped the boats."

"They're having Sapient Trials, when they decide on a new leader. That's why," Raleigh said.

Kappa swore lightly, the wind dragging the words menacingly across the air. "This is bad timing. I'd rather not be here for their cult rituals."

"It's not a coincidence, is it?" Tau asked ,and both Rho and Kappa stiffened.

"No. It's not a coincidence." Raleigh took a deep breath of the cold air, coughing a bit as she did. "Anders wants me to become a Sapient, so does Thora. Before you guys get upset, it's my choice to take the Trial, and I've already declined."

Kappa snorted. "Unless they somehow force you. No boats, that means we can't leave. We should find a way off right now...."

Raleigh said, "No. We sit tight. Ivar is adamant we leave. Once the boats run again he's made me promise we'll be on the first one. So we just have to sit tight and not make any waves."

"I agree with you," Rho said before Kappa could speak again.

But did he? Raleigh couldn't help but question his motives. His compliance rubbed her the wrong way. Kappa was right, he seemed too eager to side with her.

Tau too winced at Rho's words. "Either way, with no boat we have a week. Let's find out all we can about the inducer before we leave. There's a greenhouse. Any herbs they put into it must be grown there. You've tasted it now, so that should help."

"Did you get a burst of Lucid after drinking?" Rho asked.

Raleigh shook her head. "But I already make so much. Would the inducer work if I'm already making it?"

Tau shook his head. "I don't know. It's hard to say. Let's go check out the greenhouse."

Kappa said, "Rho and I will explore the library. The town has one. It might not be a huge help, who knows how many of the books will have any information. But it's better than explaining all four of us hanging around the greenhouse if were caught."

"Fine," Tau said. "We'll meet up later tonight and discuss what we've found."

No one disagreed with the plan, so Kappa and Rho broke off from Tau and Raleigh. She watched them head back down the path towards the outskirts of town. Raleigh stayed close to Tau. "This is a good idea, the greenhouse. I just wish I knew more about plants."

Tau withdrew a small book from his pocket. "It's a basic book of herbs used in ancient medicine. Complete with pictures, so we'll know what we're looking at."

She accepted the small book and ran her hands along the spine. The binding was stiff, the pages flat and new. "And it's in English. Did you find this in their library?

"No. I picked it up in Denver. When we decided to head this way I thought it might be a good idea. After all, it makes sense that they'll use some kind of plant. It seemed like a good thing to have. You can hold onto it. I've been studying it the last few days."

"You're brilliant. I didn't think of any of this. Grant and Able aren't looking into plants. I wonder why."

"They've probably given up. It's been near thirty years since they've been here. If I had to start from scratch I would probably look at a gland that produces Lucidin and work backward from there trying to stimulate it."

"Right. But it can't be that easy either, or they would have figured it out."

Tau turned up a side street. "Yes, which is why I'm eager to see the greenhouse." The large glass building came into view, but Tau stopped her before they got too close.

Raleigh opened her mouth to ask what was wrong when his fingers grazed the mid of her neck. Her heart leaped into her throat, as if trying to find his fingers.

"Your scarf," he said sliding the purple out from under her sweater. "Let's make it as obvious as possible. Surely a Docent will be welcome to walk through the greenhouse, right?"

Raleigh gulped down the butterflies, embarrassed that Tau might have sensed them. "Yeah, good idea."

With the scarf fully out, Tau studied her one more time before going over to the door. The structure didn't follow the stone motif of the others. Instead it had old glass, warped by time. The overcast day reflected white against the cloudy exterior. Green plants pressed against the windows, hinting at the jungle inside. Tau pulled open the door, and the smell of dirt and flowers rushed out.

She entered first, and they both paused letting the door shut behind them. A few birds chirped and then darted across the high ceiling. The town was made up of thousands of grays, and here it was all greens. Brightly colored, broad leaves dipped down near the door, practically hiding it. Smaller ferns peeked out from the taller trees. Rows of metal tables sat with planters.

The smell of lavender brought Raleigh's mother to mind. She'd spent enough time in her mother's flower shop to know most of the flowers. Many afternoons she'd found herself helping out after school. Now she neared one of the plants, looking into the dirt it was rooted in. A year ago her fingernails almost always had soil trapped up underneath them, no matter how many times she'd scrubbed them.

Tau asked, "Are you all right? You seem upset, I know it's a big task, but we're just hoping to collect whatever information we can."

"My mother is a florist. This reminds me of her shop."

Tau's face softened. "That's right, it should give us an advantage."

"Yeah, although it would be easier if it were spring. So many of the plants stand out because of their flowers, or at least the ones I'd recognize do." If only Raleigh's mother had grown more herbs. Florists were more concerned about the aroma and appearance of flowers, not their ancient medical uses. "I could taste some of them."

"A lot of plants are poisonous. I think that we'll have to look them up in that book before you try anything. You're right, though, about the season. I wonder if the ingredients for the inducer are things they could grow year round, or if they were seasonal and they had to store up what they made."

"But they probably couldn't heat things so well seventy years ago. Those solar panels are pretty new technology, relatively speaking."

"And they hail originally from the North. It means we probably aren't looking for anything too tropical. Let's start cataloging." Tau handed her a small notebook with a spiral along the top and a small pencil. "If you can't find the name jot down the characteristics and sketch a bit so we can figure it out later. I'll take this half, you take that one. Reference the book." He removed his coat and slung it over one of his arms. Then he walked over to a plant and began scribbling down information.

Raleigh started on the far side. They had the whole greenhouse to themselves. The crowd had been excited about Thora's announcement, most of them were probably getting ready for the Sapient Trials. Raleigh's first entry was a small fern with waxy leaves. She sketched a rough drawing of leaf shape. There was no point in trying to discern the various bushes right now, if they were caught in here, they might be asked to leave. She considered barricading but decided that it would be more suspicious if they were found. She went to the next specimen.

Hundreds of plants decorated the space. Twenty minutes in and she'd only collected maybe thirty names, and some of them likely were incorrect. A sobering thought discouraged her, what if the preparation, and not just components, was important? The small book had information on how to make medicine from the herbs, and the detailed descriptions hinted that this process would be more detailed than she first assumed.

"Raleigh, come over here," Tau said from a few benches down. His voice broke her concentration.

She walked over to find him plucking something from a plant. Its starlike shape nestled neatly in his palm. He opened it up, removing the seeds from their case. He cradled the seeds delicately. "Taste these." He took her hand, his fingers warm against her chilled ones and dropped them in her palm.

Shouldn't he be against them eating the plants? His eyes watched hers and drifted down to her mouth. She opened her lips and tipped the seeds in. "It's licorice."

"It's anise. This one I'm familiar with. Do you think that was in the drink?"

"Yeah, maybe." The first sign of hope, quickly dashed by the thought that there could be a lot more ingredients. This one might only be used to mask the flavor of the others. "It tasted bitter, too."

"A lot of poisons are bitter, that's going to be harder." Tau told her. He focused his attention on a nearby bloom but didn't move away. They stood close enough that his comforting smell outdid the flowers.

Being this close to him physically hurt. She bit her lip to trap her confessions of liking him. Yesterday she'd kissed Rho, how could her heart still pine for Tau? Where was the fairness in that? Tau remained still, not saying anything or hinting in any way that he felt the same.

The skin on her arm closest to him tingled from proximity, begging to be touched. The anise on her tongue bit back the bitterness of not being able to have him. The birds infringed on their silence chattering overhead. The humid air weighted down her breaths, which came out unsure and dissatisfied.

Tau stepped away. "We should get back to work."

Raleigh returned to her section of the greenhouse. She forced her attention back to the task of cataloging. There was work to be done, she didn't have the time to daydream about what she wished would have happened with Tau.

CHAPTER
21

A DAY LATER, Raleigh waited outside in the courtyard before the Convocation. The dirt from the potted plants yesterday dusted her coat sleeve. The smell of flowers no longer lingered in her hair, it had been replaced by the burnt odor of a distant fire. The night before she'd slept in fits, her muscles achy from the hard mattress and the burn on her shoulder that had yet to heal.

Now she stood, gazing at the sky. For once it was blue, but the sun somehow made things colder, as though the clouds the day before had acted as a blanket. The light drew attention to the stone walls and caused the trees to cast shadows. The chill iced her nose and cheeks, but instead of shrugging deeper into her jacket, she lifted her chin up, letting the air wake her. She sensed Thora exit into the courtyard but kept her eyes ahead.

"It's a beautiful day." Thora took a step near her.

"Yes, but it feels colder."

"Then you must keep your feet moving." Thora motioned with

her arm for Raleigh to walk. Together they progressed with measured steps around the square. Silence drifted in around the women, only broken by the occasional distant shout or nearby coo of a bird. When Thora finally spoke her words took up more space.

"We are without someone to take over Ivar's position."

This was the conversation that she'd promised Raleigh they would have the day before. "I thought you had Anders. And if not Anders, Iola."

Thora gave a sigh. "If our leaders were elected to the position, either one would be a fine choice. However, it is not the people, but the Universal Soul that decides. It's particular about who it allows to be Sapient."

"And the Trial... it's how you test who the Universal Soul will accept?"

"Yes, the Universal Soul will either favor a person or not. I begged it for a better candidate than those two. In my heart I don't think either will pass."

"But both of them can hear and speak for the Soul."

"Yes, but the connection isn't as strong as the one I had with it, and my bond was never as sturdy as Ivar's. Up until a day ago I thought that Ivar had the most significant relationship, but then the Universal Soul touched you and let us all hear. Its tie to you far exceeds even the one it has with Ivar."

"I suppose."

"The Soul brought you here. We needed a leader, and it sought you out. It's your destiny to become a Sapient."

"No it isn't." Raleigh needed to bury the absurd idea. She'd been hoping that Anders was wrong, that Thora would realize that her presence wasn't enough to nominate her. But apparently all of them were eager to find meaning in the coincidental. "I'm not one of your people, not really. I don't believe in destiny."

"Why else would you be here? Fate aligned your path with ours."

"The position of Sapient is meant to go to Anders or Iola. Wouldn't you prefer one of your people?" Raleigh doubted that these people would want a stranger to oversee them, they likely wanted her to lead less than she wanted to do it.

"Like I said, my decision isn't the one that matters." Thora's eyes grew glossy, and her voice grew softer. "Anders will likely fail. He's my nephew and means a great deal to me."

"It's not the end of the world if he fails, right? Iola will try to take it. Surely one of them will pass."

Thora's steps quickened, breaking the leisurely pace she'd kept before. "During the Trial, the candidate's soul joins with that of the Universal. Then they achieve the knowledge and return to their body. Those who don't pass fail to return to their bodies."

Raleigh no longer needed the chill to wake her. Every hair on her body stood on edge. Thora couldn't mean what Raleigh thought she did. "You mean they die?"

"Not right away. The body takes a few days to follow the Soul. But yes, that is the end result."

"Why risk that? I can't imagine that the Universal Soul wants you to sacrifice your people. You should just name a leader, and they can guide the people as you have."

"That isn't how it works. The Universal Soul fortifies me, as it does Ivar. Without the Sapients, the unification with the soul isn't as strong. Without it, our people will not succeed."

This is why Thora was eager to nominate her. She'd rather sacrifice Raleigh than one of their own. "And you're asking me to do this, for me to risk death?"

"It is a risk I myself have taken. I know the fear and uncertainty that comes with undergoing the Trial. The Soul favors you, and it brought you to us. You must take it."

"So I don't get a say?"

"Of course you get to decide. I'm confident that you will make the right choice."

Raleigh shook her head. "I'm not going to participate in the Trial. I know we are alike in many ways, but I'm not meant to be your leader."

"Our way of life is shocking to you. I wish that you'd arrived sooner and had more time to adjust. As it is we've pushed back the Trials too long and can't wait longer. You'll be a good leader. If the Soul has confidence in you, so do I."

"I have a life in America. A family. I can't stay here forever." How did Raleigh argue against such flawed logic? Thora's conviction was absolute. Even if Raleigh explained Lucidin and the rational explanation behind sensing and influencing she didn't know if the woman would dispel her belief in the Universal Soul. Was that the real reason Grant and Able were banished? She didn't dare bring it up now.

Thora watched Raleigh's face. "You're in love with one of the men you brought?"

Raleigh jumped a little at the question. Was she asking about Tau? Or Rho? "Why do you ask?"

"If you're Sapient, you could have him stay. I was young and in love once, we wouldn't want you to be unhappy. We don't accept outsiders often, but in this instance we can make an exception."

"Thora, I...."

"Don't decide now. The Trial is tomorrow, consider taking it. There is no point in running from fate, it always catches up with us in the end." Thora put a hand up to Raleigh's forehead. She smiled and turned to leave the courtyard, entering into the arena for the Convocation. Raleigh stayed a moment longer. There was no way they were going to get her to participate in the Trial, she would hold firm and be on the first boat out.

THE GUYS HADN'T been at the Convocation. Raleigh had searched the crowd with both her vision and sensing and came up empty handed. Only Docents were expected to attend, but she'd still expected them to be there. Now she headed up the stairwell to their apartments. Hopefully they'd missed it because they'd made some progress on the inducer. When she hit their floor she sensed them, their shoulders tight and their feet heavy. Their bodies were unsettled, hinting at a bad omen rather than good news. She rapped on Rho's door eager to know what troubled them.

Rho opened it and pulled Raleigh into a tight embrace. His hands clutched her, like he expected her to slip away at any moment. Panic cemented in her stomach. Something bad had happened. She could feel it. Then he released her, kissed her head, and shut the door.

"What's wrong?" Raleigh asked Tau and Kappa who were sitting on the bed.

"Last night someone influenced me," Kappa told her.

Raleigh walked further in. "Like during the Convocation?" Kappa had been moody since arriving, maybe one of the Docents had tried to make him happier about staying.

"No, they tried to stop his lungs." Tau's eyes were dark. "He woke up gasping. I felt it from next door."

"I barricaded, stopping them," Kappa said.

Raleigh sucked in a breath. They'd agreed that the Designed wouldn't display any of their Lucid abilities for a reason. If the Docents hated Grant and Able enough to close their doors what would they do to their creations?

"It was either that or let them kill me," Kappa said. "Hopefully whomever it was will just think they lost their hold."

"Did you sense who it was?" Ivar was the first suspect that came to mind.

"It woke me up from a deep sleep, I wasn't paying very close attention. It wasn't the old Sapient if that's what you're thinking." Kappa would easily have recognized Ivar's grizzled body.

Raleigh's heartbeat pounded in her ears. Someone tried to kill Kappa in his sleep. If he hadn't been Designed he wouldn't be here right now. And whomever it was couldn't possibly know he was Designed. "They must not know who you are, if they did they would have attacked you a different way."

"Yes, but they might know after the barricading." Rho let out a long sigh and then ran a hand through his hair.

"Why would they want to kill Kappa?"

"It's no secret that a lot of the people don't want you here, don't want us here," Rho whispered.

Raleigh gulped. This was no good. "Do we dare try and stay the week?"

"No. Not if someone wants us dead," said Tau. "We checked out the boats, the docks are empty."

"We could swim." Kappa wasn't smiling as he spoke. He was actually being serious.

Raleigh shook her head. "I couldn't. I can't even cross a pool. You can though, if you need to. I can stay here alone. It's my fault that we're in this mess."

"I'm not leaving you here with these freaks," Kappa said with conviction. "We'll just have to figure out a way off this island."

Rho said, "If we're not going to swim, and there are no boats, I don't see how. Our phones aren't getting a signal, and even if they were, I'm not sure how'd we convince a boat to come for us."

"Then we'll take turns staying up tonight," Tau said.

"If someone figured out that Kappa barricaded, they could figure out that you're not what you seem." Raleigh couldn't derive a convincing reason to explain why Kappa could barricade if the Docents asked.

Rho shook his head. "What are they going to say? I tried to kill him and it didn't work? No, it's likely that whomever it was isn't going to speak up even if they think something is off. Not when Thora is so firmly on your side. If it wasn't Ivar, who else wants you gone?"

"Iola. A girl from my dormitory. She's in line for the Sapient position, she's been standoffish. If I had to guess, it would be her."

"Thora should let her be Sapient then. I can't understand why they are so eager for you to take it," Rho told Raleigh. "Even if you are phenomenal at sensing. You would think there would be more politics around it."

Raleigh tugged her shirt sleeves taunts with her hands. Better to tell them the whole truth now. "Thora thinks that both Iola and Anders will fail, and if you fail the Trial, you die."

"So you get to take the fall!" Rho asked.

Raleigh flinched at his anger. "She thinks I'll pass, because the Soul favors me."

"We need to figure out how to get off this island." Kappa stood up. "Rho and I will work on calling the mainland or figuring out how to get a boat. You guys go back to the greenhouse. We came here for that damn inducer. See if you can't figure it out."

Raleigh looked to Tau. She'd never have put Kappa's life on the line for the inducer. Her own maybe, but not his. "Our priority is to get off the island."

"Yeah, but two people working on it should be enough," Rho said. "Everyone watch your backs, influence if you have to. We'll meet back here later."

C H A P T E R
22

THE SECOND TIME Raleigh and Tau went to the greenhouse, they only had an hour to jot down plant observations before they were forced to leave. Townsfolk came in to collect flowers for the Sapient Trials and without a good reason to be there they didn't dare stay. With their data collecting interrupted, they headed back to the apartment to see if Rho or Kappa had made any progress with the boat.

Tau let out a long yawn as they climbed the stairs.

"Did you guys get any sleep last night?" Raleigh asked.

"After what happened to Kappa, not really."

"Maybe you should take a nap. We could head back down to the greenhouse later?"

Tau rubbed a hand across his chin, considering. "Fine. But wake me up if anything interesting happens." He then gave her a small head bob goodbye and headed to his room.

Raleigh went over and knocked on Rho's door. He opened it so she could enter. She asked, "Did you guys figure out a boat?"

"No leads yet. There are no public phones. These people like their isolation. Kappa's still working on it."

Raleigh chided herself for getting them into this mess. How could she have been so stupid? She should have insisted on staying alone, a possible option even now, but none of them would cross without her. If only Rho would have spoken his mind he could have talked her out of her bad decision. They could be flying home from Athens right now.

"How did the greenhouse work out?"

"Not good, we had to leave."

"Going after the inducer has always been unrealistic." Rho pressed his lips together as if fighting not to say more.

Raleigh's shoulders sank. "Yeah, and the greenhouse stuff isn't really getting us anywhere, either. Coming here was a mistake. Staying was a mistake. And it's all my fault. And now Kappa almost died."

"Kappa didn't almost die. It wasn't hard for him to barricade."

"Someone still tried to murder him."

"You made the decision to come on your own, but we also chose to stay."

"But your vote doesn't count."

Rho lifted an eyebrow. "What?"

"You didn't really want to stay, you only said we could because you're going along with whatever I want."

Rho's face dropped. "I know Kappa says that…."

"He says it because it's true. And I knew what you wanted, and I selfishly chose not to care. Since Tau remained neutral it would have meant leaving, so I didn't encourage you to be honest."

"So you're saying it's my fault we're here?" Rho squinted at her.

"No, it's entirely my fault. I knew that you'd go along with what I wanted."

"No offense, but I'm tired of Kappa—and now you—thinking that I can't make decisions for myself."

"You can't. You're not thinking straight. This relationship we have, it isn't working. Not if you can't be true to yourself."

Rho waved one arm angrily in the air. "But when I voice my opinion it's me holding you back. It can't go both ways. You can't not want to be with me because of my choices and then not want to be with me when I side with you."

"Don't you see? We aren't meant to be. You're you, and I like you, Rho. You're a good friend and a great leader. But as a boyfriend? You're either too much of a pushover, or you want me to be someone I'm not."

"But I'm in love with you, Raleigh."

She pinched the bridge of her nose. This wasn't love. Infatuation, yes. Exciting, yes. But her attraction to him paled in comparison to the way Tau made her feel. Even though Tau wouldn't have her, she could never go back to pretending that love was anything less.

"You don't love me," she told him simply. "You feel indebted to me for saving your life. And we work well together, when we're both leaders. Yes, we butt heads, but that's a great thing. We balance each other. That works for leading your brothers and getting things done, it doesn't work romantically."

Rho took a long breath. "We're meant to be."

"Why is everyone so into fate? I'm not going to let the Docent's notion of destiny make me take that test, and I'm not going to have you or me be who we aren't so we can fulfill some notion that we're meant to be."

Raleigh could both see and sense his despair. His brow dropped, and a sharp ache twisted through his chest. To keep his pain private, he barricaded. They weren't supposed to, a careless decision if anyone walked by and knew there were two people in the room. Still, she could tell by the way his shoulders hunched that she'd hurt him. Maybe she deserved to experience that pain that she'd inflicted, but she was grateful that he'd spared her.

The room pressed in on her, the space no longer large enough to fit both of them and their heartbreak. Regardless, it had to be done. Now they'd be free from having to make something work that never would. He'd see it too, once he got over the rejection it would be a relief.

Kappa knocked on the door once before pushing it open. "Rho? Sorry, I didn't mean to interrupt anything. I thought only Raleigh was in the room. Why are you barricading?"

Rho straightened his shoulders and let the barricade fall. His whole body was taut as a piece of hide stretched over a drum. One hit and the whole of him would reverberate with anger.

Kappa flinched. "Did you guys have a fight? Should I go?"

Rho relaxed a bit. "No, we didn't fight. I need to apologize to you. I haven't been very honest. It isn't going to be a problem anymore. Raleigh and I are no longer a couple."

"I didn't mean to break you up."

"It wasn't you." Raleigh said. "So what's up? Did you find anything out about the boatman on the shore?"

Kappa shook his head. "No. But while I was working on getting his number and finding a phone Iola came up to me. She's the one that painted the door and sent the note."

"And tried to kill you?" Rho asked.

Kappa shook his head. "I didn't bring it up, and she didn't confess. But I know it wasn't her."

"We don't know that," Rho said. "We have to assume it could be anyone. She's the most likely if it isn't Ivar. Maybe she could tell you barricaded, and she confessed to that other stuff so your guard is down."

Kappa twisted his fingers. It wasn't often that he acted meek, but Raleigh couldn't think of a better term for his disposition now. "She offered us a boat. She did all that because she thought that Raleigh would be nominated for Sapient, and she wants to save her from it."

"Or take the title herself," muttered Raleigh. "But either way. If she has a boat, we can leave. This is great news."

"Where is it? I haven't seen any," said Rho.

Kappa said, "It's hidden. She built it when she first arrived here. Initially she had a hard time acclimating to their culture. She built a boat, so she could leave if she ever wanted to. I told her to leave with us, to not take the Sapient Trial."

"Of course she'll take the test," Raleigh said. Or maybe not? If Iola had really been so cold to Raleigh because she wanted to save Raleigh, that put everything Iola did in a different light. The girl wasn't power-hungry but kind. An idea that Raleigh couldn't immediately wrap her mind around.

Kappa fidgeted with his hands. "She'll go through the Trial, but it's out of duty. She confided in me that she wishes that the Universal Soul had never called to her, but it had, and she couldn't drown out its voice now." His nerves reminded Raleigh of the Receps, she wondered what was up with Kappa. Anger seemed to be his emotion of choice, not anxiety.

Raleigh said, "She's been brainwashed." A bitter taste sat on her tongue. They'd been hoping to do the same with her.

Rho shook his head. "Brainwashing isn't the right word. She doesn't have a good explanation, and she's reluctantly taking the only one she can get. At least she's not so far gone that she won't save Raleigh from the same fate."

"Should we tell her?" Raleigh asked. "About Lucidin?"

"No, for all we know, she might clam up. If Grant and Able had no success, we won't. No point in risking it." Rho's face looked apologetic. "They'll want Anders to take the test first, won't they? Maybe he'll pass, and she won't have to do it."

The color drained out of Kappa's face and Raleigh asked, "What's wrong with you?"

Kappa blurted out. "I messed up our cover!"

"What?" Raleigh and Rho asked in unison.

"I told her that she should come with us. She told me that line about the Universal Soul. I told her that she couldn't die for it. Then she kissed me."

"She *what?*" Rho's mouth opened. "Like a kiss on the cheek?"

"Like a full-blown kiss. The kind of kiss a person gives when they think they might be dead at the end of the week."

Raleigh knew those kind of kisses. The world is ending, but at least I have this one good thing left. She also knew that they didn't fare as well once the world wasn't ending, at least her and Tau's hadn't.

"And you stopped it, right?" Rho said. "Before she tasted the Lucid. You stopped it."

"No. She asked if I could hear the Soul. She said that she could tell it touched me in some way. It freaked her out. She ran."

Rho threw up his arms. "What? To Ivar?"

"No idea. But yeah, maybe." Kappa grabbed his head. "And I don't know where her boat is. I never got the information from her."

"How could you?" Rho's voice echoed in their small space.

"It was a balancing act. Being nice enough for her to give us the boat. I must have crossed a line. It's not like she isn't a pretty girl. It was light flirting. I didn't know she would kiss me." Kappa grew red in the face.

Rho threw up his arms. "I can't believe you fucked up everything over a *girl.*"

"Look who's talking, Rho. We're only here because you let your hormones get the better of you."

Rho's face scrunched up, and he took a step back from Kappa. "We're going to have to swim for it. If she tells Ivar and the others and they come after us, we're screwed."

"We're all better at influencing than them." Raleigh would rather attempt to control the whole village than face the open water.

"Yeah, but there are fifty of them. I don't like those odds. Not to mention, I can't stomach having their blood on our hands. Grant and Able were one thing, these people are creepy, but we can't take out their whole culture. Raleigh, with the help of the three of us, you should be able to cross."

"Have you seen the water today?" Kappa said. "It's choppy because of the wind."

"It's never going to be perfect." Rho went over to the window. Raleigh figured that if he squinted he might see a narrow strip of blue past the rest of the town, but they weren't near enough to gauge the danger.

Raleigh wouldn't swim. She'd have the guys go across without her. They'd be much more likely to make it if they didn't have her to drag them down. "Iola might not tell. If she really did all that stuff to try and save me, she might not be willing to hand us over right away. I would consider my options if I were her, and I bet that's what she's doing. Let's find her and tell her the truth."

"That'll only get us in deeper. It will link us to Grant and Able." Rho rubbed the back of his neck, frustrated. "Dammit."

"There's no fixing what happened." Raleigh interjected before Kappa circled the conversation back to his regret. "Let's lay all the cards on the table. She didn't grow up here and might jump on a scientific explanation. It saves her from having to follow the Universal Soul. It gives her a reason to not take the Trial. Let's hope that's enough."

Rho set his chin and went to open the door. "If it doesn't work we swim. Today. I'll go wake up Tau, let's all search for her. I hope she can see reason."

Raleigh's eyes darted to Tau's door before she headed down the steps. Hopefully Iola hadn't already sealed their fate.

CHAPTER
23

THE TOWN PREPARED for the Sapient Trials. Cloth streamers flapped in the wind while winter flowers peeked out from windowsills and sat in baskets lining the streets. The people hurried past Raleigh, jubilation bubbling in their chests. Their excitement was visible in their toothy smiles and exaggerated gestures. Nerves tempered the outright enthusiasm. This sacred event only happened once, maybe twice, in their lifetimes. When she passed they offered her greetings, some already bowing to her the way they did Thora. Apparently, they too assumed that she'd arrived with the intent of leading them.

She'd checked the dorms and Docent rooms first. The guys couldn't enter either, and they seemed like the best bets. Both had been dead ends. Now she ran down the streets, with no clear plan. Each moment that passed gave Iola more time to make up her mind and side against them by telling Ivar.

Frantically she searched pausing on a flash of dark hair poking out from a woolen cap, a purple scarf sitting not too far below the tresses. Iola stood near the wall, her eyes staring out over the sea in the direction of the mainland. Raleigh neared her slowly, not wanting her to startle.

Iola's brow was knit in thought. Then she turned, her stoic scowl quickly trying to erase any traces of emotions on her face. She opened her mouth but didn't say anything.

Raleigh cleared her throat beating back her worry. "We need to talk."

"We do. You're going to explain yourself now, and that's going to happen in private." Iola headed down the road.

The relief of finding Iola vanished when Raleigh considered that she would be the one to divulge their secrets. All of the story, from Grant and Able to the Designed, to the Receps, and her needing the inducer, was damning. It wasn't possible to put it into a better light, because the story was too dark to weave into anything else. The only thing she had going for her was that it was the truth, and she'd wouldn't underestimate the value of honesty.

Iola took her to a courtyard with a fountain, turned off for the winter. The buildings around them had windows with lace, through which homes could be glimpsed. All of them were shut tight against the cold. Their voices would travel up, and there was a risk they'd be heard, but it was better than any of the places she'd seen thus far.

"The kids play in the fountain during the summer, but people don't come here in the winter." Iola put her hands on her hips. "Tell me what's going on."

"You should take a seat. It isn't a short story."

Iola perched on the ledge of the fountain, folding her hands in her lap before she turned her set of angry eyes on Raleigh. "There's something up with your friend. The one who has the initial Kappa."

"That's his name, not just his initial. And I guess the first part of the story. Do you know why your doors were closed thirty years ago?"

"Outsiders tried to damage the Universal Soul. I'm not sure how, but it must have been bad, because anyone old enough to remember is still upset. Aren't you supposed to be explaining things, not me?"

"The people were scientists named Grant and Able. They came to figure out the reason your people could hear the Soul and see if there was a genetic cause. You know about genetics, right?"

"I didn't live in a box in England."

"Right. Well, they figured out a biological explanation and a number of genes that increases the likelihood."

Iola's face remained distrustful. "And what exactly were these scientific answers?"

"There is a hormone called Lucidin. Most people don't make much of it, only in times of stress. But a lot more people have receptors to use it, about half of the population. And all someone needs is receptors to feel Lucidin's effects."

"And those effects are hearing the Soul."

"Grant and Able call it *sensing*. Fewer still can influence or send messages controlling what another person's body does. You call it speaking to another person with the Soul. It's the same concept, just different terminology."

"I've never heard of any of this. Why wouldn't our people be happy about an explanation? Why close our doors?"

"The scientists made a version of Lucidin, a synthetic, that isn't very good. So they took the genetics, and they made twelve people who created a lot of Lucidin and had receptors to use it. They also made some people who just made Lucidin, but that's not really important right now."

"Made people who could hear the Universal Soul? You expect me to believe that?"

"They named them after Greek letters. Because they were an experiment."

Iola's eyes grew wide, and she stiffened. "Kappa. Rho."

"Tau. You probably tasted the Lucidin in Kappa's saliva earlier. That's how you knew he was like you, like me."

"I felt the Universal Soul move in me."

"His Lucidin tickled your receptors. Not very much, there's more in our blood, that's why Grant and Able put ports in our arms." Raleigh flipped her arm over and lifted her sleeve to show the puffy scars.

Fear flashed briefly in Iola's eyes. "You're created to make it, too?"

"No. I'm an anomaly. I make a ton, but have no relatives that do. It's like cancer, it can be inherited or you can just get it. The created people are called the Designed. They all are kinda eerily-perfect looking, and they are smart."

"Yeah, I noticed." Iola stared down. "Does Ivar know about them? Did your scientists tell our people?"

"No, only about the synthetic. We assumed Ivar doesn't know what they did with the genetics. Please don't tell him."

"I'm not. But our people should know about Lucidin. It makes a lot more sense than the Universal Soul. I can't believe Ivar has kept this hidden."

"So you believe me about Lucidin?"

"Of course I do! Honestly, I never believed any of this Soul rubbish, anyway. My parents went on and on about it. Then I heard that man with the heart attack. It kinda became impossible not to believe, but it's always been weird. Why do you think I built that boat?"

"Does your offer still stand, can you get us all out of here?"

"Yeah. It's not that big, but it should work. Why did you guys come here in the first place?"

"A lot of bad stuff has happened." Raleigh didn't sugar-coat telling Iola about the Receps and their addiction, the synthetic trade, or that some of the Designed were evil. Iola would learn all this the moment they got a hold of Gabe, and she should know what she was getting into.

When the story was over Iola said, "Ivar was right about one thing. Grant and Able should never have tampered with it." Most of the hope that had been in Iola's eyes darkened. Raleigh imagined she looked very similar when Rho had laid it all out for her months ago. "That still doesn't explain why you're here."

"None of your people are addicted like the Receps. You all have Lucidin in your systems, and none of you have their problems. The drink you take at the Convocation, it's why we've come."

"Really? You risked everything for that?"

"It could help stop the addiction, that's no small thing. The Receps are being ripped apart."

"Sounds like they deserve it."

"Some of them are my friends." Raleigh paused. She'd already asked Iola for a boat and didn't want to push her generosity too far. "Can you get the recipe for the drink?"

Iola lifted an eyebrow. "Yeah. I should be able to. I know who mixes it up. It's not like it's a secret."

Incredible. All Raleigh had to do to get the inducer was to ask the right person. A lot had changed in thirty years. The people had been so cut off they'd dropped their guard about the drink. It wasn't perfect, after all, they might not be able to find the ingredients once out. What if they didn't use the same name for common plants? Raleigh couldn't think of that now. Iola's silence about the guys and the boat had been her main objective. She hadn't gone into the conversation with intent of bringing up the inducer, let alone Iola agreeing to get it.

"Tell your friends to meet us by this fountain tonight. They need to be quiet. We'll slip out of the dorms after everyone is asleep." Iola shifted and her eyes raised to the buildings around them. "A lot of people are watching them. It won't be easy."

"We can barricade," Raleigh told Iola.

"What's that?"

Raleigh drew up her barricade, and Iola's eyes grew wide.

"You're sitting right there, but my soul can't hear yours." Iola reached out to touch Raleigh, then pulled her hand back.

"Yeah, it means you can't speak to my soul, either." Raleigh dropped the barricade. "Can your people not do it?"

"Not that I know of. It goes against our beliefs. It's the Soul that connects us all, no one is able to separate from that." Iola's mouth scrunched. "More evidence against what we've been taught. To think they wanted both of us to endure a test that may kill us, when they knew that there was another explanation all along."

"Ivar knows, but do you think Thora does?"

Iola shrugged. "She thinks Anders will fail the test. Do you think it is because he has fewer of these Receptors?"

"No clue. Do you think we should tell Anders?"

Iola let out a long breath. "I've always felt shaky on the Universal Soul, but not him. What if we tell him, and he responds the same way as Ivar? Ivar clearly understood and banished those scientists as a result. What if Anders ignores the evidence?"

"But he'll understand what he is risking his life for." Since learning of Lucidin, Raleigh's life had been in constant danger. It would be easy to regret ever meeting Sabine. But in her heart she was happy to know. Before she learned the truth she'd been sick and weak. Now she'd used Lucid to become strong and formidable.

This path may very well lead to a shorter life, but it would be one lived on her own terms.

Iola said, "You're a threat to our way of life. The people believe us Docents are in contact with their life force. If that's not the truth, then why should they stay?"

"Because your people induce them to feel happy with serotonin and dopamine."

Iola's face faltered. "That's what happens during the Convocation. I really didn't mean to do it. I thought we were lessening their burden."

"I know, none of the Docents seem to be intentionally doing it to hurt the townsfolk."

"We can't tell Anders. I want to, but I think he will go against us, and that would mean turning Kappa and the others over to Ivar." Iola stood up. "Go tell them to meet us here at twelve thirty and to barricade so they aren't sensed. I'll get the drink. I'll see you back at the dorms. Don't speak to me, I don't want people to question why our relationship has changed."

When Raleigh left she headed in the direction of the apartment. Iola went deeper into the town. She had to tell the guys the plan. Hopefully they would reconvene in the room sooner rather than later.

CHAPTER
24

RALEIGH DIDN'T HAVE to worry about anyone noticing her change in demeanor. They were too invested in setting up for the Sapient Trial. People rushed by, an anxious joy in their muscles. Anders and Iola's names popped out in the Greek speech. Everything hummed, and all Raleigh had to do was keep her head down.

The guys had opted not to come to dinner at the Docent dining hall. Since Kappa had been influenced they figured that no one really wanted them there. So Raleigh sat with Thora and Anders, holding down a pleasant conversation about the traditions of the tribe.

Both of them were kind to her. Thora acted like Lana, Raleigh's older sister, giving her knowing smiles. Fortunately, she didn't ask Raleigh for her answer again, but the question of Raleigh becoming Sapient seeped into their conversation, a topic both of them danced around. Ander's restless smile begged her to save him. Iola was correct, they couldn't tell him about Lucidin, but Raleigh still wished he knew.

The sun eventually sunk down over the horizon, painting the world in beautiful hues. Raleigh couldn't wait for the dark, when her actions would be concealed. When she retired to her bed she intentionally avoided eye contact with Iola. In a handful of hours they'd be making their escape. From her time in Italy, Raleigh understood that even the best laid plans could unravel. She no longer entertained all the scenarios that could go wrong. When things went bad it was impossible to predict how they'd play out.

Raleigh's lumpy mattress tried to entice her body to fall asleep. Her warm blanket settled down on her, masking the rise and fall of her chest. The pillowy comforter looked the same with or without a person underneath. But the Docent women who shared her floor had sensing, and Raleigh had no idea how long the Convocation's dose of inducer would last.

One by one the women drifted off. Only Iola, on the other side of the wall, remained awake. At twelve-fifteen Raleigh tore off her covers, sensing Iola at the entrance to her space before her eyes could focus in the meager light to see her. Iola held her fingers up to her lips, but Raleigh didn't need the reminder, they needed to be quiet.

Raleigh positioned her pillow so the head of the comforter would be higher, hopefully mimicking her head. Then she pulled on her barricade. Between that and the dark, she became nearly invisible. By the time she reached the entrance to her space, Iola already stood by the exit.

The door creaked when they opened it, and Raleigh stretched out her mind. Everyone remained asleep. They sneaked out, pulling the door shut quietly behind them before heading down the stairs. Iola's leather shoes hit the steps noiselessly. Raleigh tried her best to plant her feet quietly, but the occasional clomp echoed down the spiral stairwell.

Adrenaline flooded Raleigh's system. She gripped the rail near the steps. It had been three days since her last episode, she was due, and her nerves only increased her chances. If she blacked out, her mind would funnel all the sensations. It wouldn't matter if the inducer had worn off or not, that kind of shout was sure to be heard.

All the more reason to get out faster. She gave up caring about her noisy footfalls and made up the distance between her and Iola. They got to the door, opened it, and slid through to the outside.

The moon hung bright overhead. Craters and imperfections ran the length of its pearly face. As a child she'd always cut out yellow moons and taped on bats. Now she saw that she'd been incorrect, this white moon was eerier, as if drained of blood and hope.

All the lights in the Designed's apartment building were out. Only the streetlights buzzed with electricity. The two set off in the direction of the dried-out fountain. The straps of Raleigh's bag containing her street clothes bit into her shoulders. Her locator chip promised that even if she were trapped Gabe and the others could try to come for her. Thoughts of the bunker faded in the icy air. A breeze reminded her that she was above ground.

They arrived at the fountain, and the three tall silhouettes of the Designed came into view. Her feet froze in place between strides. They stood tall, their broad shoulders and sharp lines demonstrating a strength that she needed. They turned and came towards her and Iola. No one took any time to extend a proper greeting, the guys fell in line behind Iola alongside Raleigh.

Tau neared her, his coat smelling like the mint leaves he'd rubbed through his fingers that morning in the greenhouse. She wanted to turn to him, to see if he also felt a sense of foreboding. Was her conscious mind aware of something logic couldn't grasp? Or was it that so many of her other best laid plans had fallen through?

They headed to the corner of the stone wall, a place where

brown ivy gnarled over the stones. Iola's hands stretched into the brambles, and then surprisingly, slipped through the wall. Raleigh stepped closer, finding a narrow passage. Kappa went directly after Iola and then Rho. Tau touched Raleigh's elbow, indicating that she should stop. She paused but kept her eyes ahead watching the others descend.

The path down was built of uneven stone steps only two feet wide. On one side stood the wall. There was no railing or hand grips, nothing to help her if she began to pitch forward. On the other side a drop-off promised a painful death falling on the white sand beaches below.

"You're overdue," Tau whispered. "Stop barricading. I'm going to calm your heart, but I can tell that you're on track to black out."

She let her barricade fall, and he placed his hands on her shoulder—half shielding her from the drop. If she fell, she'd take him too. In her chest her heart tried to race, but he was true to his word, slowing her down. They continued to descend the precarious steps until at last they were on the beach.

Iola ran over to the side of the stone wall and pulled a tarp off a pile of wood. She reached down and started to tug on the ropes that held the logs in place. Exasperated, she flipped her hair over her shoulder. "Kappa, help me bring it to the water."

Calling the craft a boat was generous. It was no more than a full-scale replica of the popsicle stick rafts Raleigh used to race down the gutters during the summer with her brother. Kappa went over and heaved it towards the water. If they all crammed they might fit on the small plank.

Raleigh ducked her head close enough to Tau that only he could hear. "How is that going to make it across?"

"The water isn't that rough right now. It's better than swimming."

Right. Only marginally.

Rho walked down to the edge of the water where the waves licked the front part of the raft. "Come on, we don't have much time." He held it steady while Iola and Kappa got on.

"You won't drown," Tau assured her. "And if you black out, I will be right beside you and won't let you go."

"This boat will be slow." Raleigh put her right foot on board. Even with Iola and Kappa weighing it down it swayed beneath her.

Rho said, "We're in luck. With no boats here, they won't be able to come after us. They'll have to call the shore first."

Raleigh scooted onto the boat, the water slopped up between the cracks. But it remained afloat. Rho and Tau climbed on. Iola handed Kappa and Rho oars. Once everyone was sitting, Rho pushed off from the shore with his paddle. They were at sea.

Tau wrapped his arms around Raleigh. There was nothing romantic about it. His arms sheltered her from the spray of the water as they moved forward. The journey would take a while.

Midway across and Raleigh's teeth chattered. She'd stopped caring what Rho might think and huddled so far into Tau that she had to strain to see past him. In the distance the island stood cold and dark. Iola sat pressed between Kappa and Rho. Her adrenaline kept her warm, and her thick fur coat didn't hurt.

As they moved, the lights on the opposing shore went from being small dots to larger bulbs. Rho and Kappa didn't tire as they kept a fast pace rowing. All of them were doused with water, but none of them had fallen off, and the large surface of the boat meant that it was unlikely to capsize.

Soon the water became shallow, and the two could plant their oars into the sandy bottom and glide the boat the rest of the way to shore. One by one they got off. Tau released the influencing effect he'd had on Raleigh's heart. The adrenaline she'd been resisting rushed her system.

Her mind tore down the Designed's barricades. She could sense the cold on all of their cheeks. The nervousness that Iola hid so well in her face tightened her shoulders and squeezed her stomach. Rho and Kappa's arms ached, and their hands were sore from holding the rough wood of the paddles, the physical effects of their trip shown through in little aches and pains. The sensation of all of them swam through her. In the nearby city she could sense people sleeping in beds. Warm and unaware of their ordeal.

The sensations whipped around her like the wind and the salty air. They cascaded down into her mind overwhelming it. Tau's arms gripped tightly around her, the last thing she was conscious of as the whole world turned black.

———————

"SHE'LL BE FINE. Like Rho said, even if they sensed her on the island, they have to call the mainland to get a boat. We'll be long gone by the time they manage to figure out that we've come across," Kappa said.

Raleigh sat up. Kappa put a hand on her back to stabilize her.

"Are you all right?"

She dug her fingers into the coarse sand. The boat rested on the shore a few feet away. Iola stared at her, worried, on the other side of Kappa. Tau and Rho were gone.

"Where's Tau? And Rho," Raleigh asked.

"Getting their car. We made it across. I haven't seen any boats leave this side of the shore since your spell," Iola said. "We think that we have a decent chance of getting away."

Raleigh pushed herself up and with Kappa's help stood wobbly on her feet. "We made it?" So many plans had gone so terribly wrong, and this one had worked out. This one that had involved an amateur built boat and less than a day of planning. Raleigh let out a laugh. She'd never felt so light. They'd actually escaped.

"Thanks for waiting until we were on land to faint," Kappa said with a grin. "We're going to make it to Athens. Gabe and Adam should still be there. We'll get tickets and go home."

Iola stared down at her feet, not saying much.

"You're coming with us, right?" Raleigh asked. She hadn't given too much consideration to Iola's future beyond their escape.

"If that's okay. I really don't have anywhere to go. My whole family will be disgraced once it's learned that I've defected. I haven't any money, and the only job I've ever had is as a Docent."

Kappa jumped in. "Of course you're coming along. We owe you for getting us off that island. I'm sure it wasn't easy. Your boat was great! It got us all the way across." He smiled at her. It was the kind of smile that Tau had given Raleigh on more than one occasion. The kind that made her knees go weak, and from where Raleigh stood, she could feel butterflies in Iola's stomach.

Kappa and Iola couldn't date. Iola had a lot of receptors. Enough to sense and influence. The Designed and her couldn't date people with high Receptor volume, because the risk of addiction was too real. Maybe the inducer would help, but she'd hate to see Iola shift to being jittery like all the other Receps. Raleigh opened her mouth, considering the best way to frame her concerns. Better to end things before they really had a chance to start.

Then she stopped. Tau or Rho could remind Kappa of the rules. Right now they could all be happy, at least until tomorrow, when they'd have to face all the problems that they'd temporarily left behind. Like Quinn and the growing threat that was Sigma.

"You have the inducer right?" Raleigh asked.

Iola pulled a flask from her pocket and held it out. "Here, complete with the list of ingredients just as you asked."

Raleigh took the glass bottle. It must have been made on the island, because its surface was warped. It reflected the streetlights from the road up the hill. The pint-sized vial was full, it and the list should be enough to recreate it.

A car approached and then stopped right at the side of the road. Rho sat in the driver's seat, and Tau walked around the front of the car, the headlights outlining him. The look on his face mirrored how she felt. They'd actually made it, and for once it seemed as though everything would be okay.

Raleigh beat back the cynicism that told her that she should never get her hopes up. She didn't care, a smile broke across her face as she headed towards the car.

CHAPTER
25

THEY REACHED THE Athens hotel at three in the morning. Rho had called Gabe and told them that they were on their way. Even at that early of an hour, they encountered the occasional person darting across the street or leaving their home for the day. The five of them piled out of the car and walked into the lobby of the hotel. A lone receptionist sat bored at the desk, paying little attention to them as they went up to Adam and Gabe's room.

Rho only had to knock once, and the door opened. Gabe stood on the other side, wide awake despite the hour. Adam waited for them a little further in, stifling a yawn.

"You're back," Gabe paused when Iola reached the door. "And *you're* from the tribe."

Raleigh met his eye. "She's a Recep, falling somewhere above the ninety-fourth percentile because she can influence."

"She's also the only reason we made if off that island in one piece." Kappa pulled the door open a little wider, making his stance clear.

Iola was one of them now.

Gabe stuck out his hand. "We're thankful you got them out. We had no idea that things there had taken a turn." He welcomed them all into the room before asking, "What exactly happened?"

Rho gave him the rundown. Raleigh added her two cents when she knew more, but for the most part the description was succinct. The Docents didn't appear to suffer from addiction, but their rituals and daily life were worrisome.

"So they influence the townsfolk to be happy?" Adam asked. "That's messed up, isn't it?"

"There are worse things, and to be fair, they see it as helping the people feel better. It's not done maliciously." Iola stood up straight, not showing any guilt.

Gabe chose to focus on a different part of the story. "They believed that fate brought Raleigh to the island and not anything she learned from Grant and Able?"

"Yeah, our arrival timed perfectly with their Sapient Trials." Rho crossed his arms.

Gabe grimaced. "But you got the inducer out?"

"Yes." Raleigh pulled the bottle Iola had given her from her pocket. "The Docents take a few sips of this, and moments later they can influence and sense."

Gabe grasped the vial, holding it up so the light could bend through its liquid. He turned to Iola. "And you've done this?"

"Yes. Every day."

"And she's not edgy like any of you or the other Receps." Tau watched Gabe's eyes. Deep down in his heart did Gabe realized the extent of his addiction, or did he prefer holding on to his denial?

"May I have some?" Gabe asked Raleigh, as he tugged out the cork stopper.

"Yes."

Gabe took a hearty sip and waited. The bedroom clock's bright green numbers counted four minutes. "Nothing. I feel no different."

Raleigh's stomach sank. "Try some more." She too had noticed no change upon drinking the concoction, but surely that was because she made Lucid already.

After another long sip they waited longer. "Adam, you try." Gabe handed him the bottle. "I've got nothing."

Adam took two long drinks and then closed his eyes. Much like Gabe his face slid to disappointment after a few minutes. "I don't feel anything, either."

"Maybe it's something unique to the tribe." Kappa took the bottle and handed it to Iola. "You take it."

Iola did, and they waited in silence. "It didn't work this time. I don't feel any different."

"How is that possible? Why is it not working? Iola's taken it before, it should at least work on her." Raleigh grabbed the bottle and smelt the mixture, now a quarter gone. Not that it mattered if it didn't work.

"Where is the list of ingredients? There has to be something special in this that effects the Lucidin production," Rho said. Iola handed Rho the list that she'd brought along with the bottle. Rho scanned it. "There's nothing that interesting in this. If I didn't know better, I'd say it's just tea."

Gabe rubbed the back of his head. "Oliver Able said that they passed around a drink and that enabled them to use Lucidin. This is the same drink, right?"

Raleigh gripped the bottle tightly. This *had* to be it. "Yeah. Before their daily Convocation the Docents drank this, and then they're able to influence and sense. I swear. You could *feel* the change in them. People like Iola can only use Lucidin during the Convocation and after. She's not like me, she can't sense all the time."

Iola nodded. "That's right, I've only sensed without the drink once before. You're certain it is what you're looking for, the Lucidin inducer?"

Gabe's mouth turned down. "Obviously not. Do you think they would have given you the wrong drink? Maybe they realized that it was going to be stolen and brought off the island so they supplied you with a false one."

"No, not a chance. This came from the same vat that we used that morning," Iola said. "Why would they lie to me anyway? It's not like they ever kept the drink a secret."

Raleigh sank down hard onto one of the beds and fell back, the soft blankets reminding her of the night's sleep she'd foregone. They were missing something, but her frayed nerves and tired brain didn't have the wherewithal to figure it out at that moment. She got off the bed and took a swig. "This is definitely what I drank at the Convocation. It has the bit of licorice and the bitter taste underneath."

"And it affected you at this Convocation?" Gabe asked.

"No. It didn't. But I figured it was because I made so much to begin with. I'm already creating so much Lucidin, I can't imagine this would cause that big of a change."

Gabe sighed. "You're probably right. We'll get the lab workers this information. Maybe it's something about temperature or something like that."

It wouldn't be. Gabe was grasping at straws now. For whatever reason the inducer no longer worked once it left the island, but there was nothing special about the island that would have changed its properties. Not anything that she could think of.

"Why don't you all get some sleep? You look like you've been to the bottom of the sea and back." Gabe pointed at the beds. "We've booked a second room when Rho said you'd be coming. Sleep and shower, and maybe we can figure out what went wrong."

Because something always went wrong. Raleigh kicked the side of the dresser. Nothing came to them easily.

"At least we got away," Tau said to her.

Yes, and she had to admit that was something. But otherwise they'd gone there for no reason. Other than to save Iola from the Sapient Trial. But life as a Recep wasn't one anyone would envy. Would Iola joining them lead to a better life than the one she'd had? Raleigh couldn't say for sure that it would. Maybe Anders was lucky that he didn't know the truth. Plopping back down on the bed, Raleigh couldn't think about it anymore. If she got any more frustrated, she'd probably kick a hole in the wall. Turning on her side she pulled up one of the blankets. The guys were sorting out the sleeping arrangements as she slid into slumber.

THE BACK OF Raleigh's eyelids turned orange as the sunlight slid through the window. The sun sat relatively high in the sky, it was already afternoon. Blinking against the rays she covered her eyes. The saline smell of her jacket and the sand rubbing against her legs from the folds of her jeans reminded her of the night she'd had. Sitting up she let out a long yawn. Iola slept on the other side of the queen-sized bed. Her mess of curly brown hair covered her face, but even without seeing her eyes Raleigh could tell she was sleeping.

Gabe was right, the rest had dissolved some of her frustration, but it had little effect on her curiosity. What part of the puzzle was she missing? Her mind stretched back to remember the conversations that she'd had with Thora and the other Docents. The most recent, and probably most upsetting, had been about the Sapient Trial.

The bit about how lethal the Sapient Trial could be had captured her attention. That and Thora trying to convince Raleigh to participate replayed over and over in her head. The fervor of the day erased much of the what had been said, but one thing rose up from their conversation—the Sapient helped the Docents unite with the Universal Soul. Could they do something to help them create Lucidin? The answer came thundering towards her. Yes. They could. If a drink could cause a brain to produce Lucidin, why couldn't influencing? These people practiced the Sapient Trials despite the risks. There had to be a reason. Thora implied that the people couldn't continue without it.

The pieces fell into place. Thora and the other Sapients were always present at the Convocations. Likely they played a part in the rituals that Oliver Able had seen too. Yes, the drink was part of it, but it was just another ritual like them facing their blank eyes to the sky. It didn't actually matter in the long run.

Raleigh tossed off her covers and searched the ground for her shoes. What was she going to do with this information now that'd she'd discovered it? She stopped with her hand shoved under the bed wrapped halfway around her sneaker. The answer was nothing. Stealing a liquid inducer was one thing. Her mind could barely wrap around what it meant for a person to have that kind of power.

No wonder people died for it. Raleigh slid back on her heels and crouched on the ground in thought.

Iola yawned. "How long have we been asleep?"

"Could Thora and Ivar *be* the inducer?" Raleigh asked.

"What are you on about?"

"Could they induce you... speak to your soul... so it actually makes Lucidin?"

Iola rubbed her eyes. "Yesterday you thought it was that drink."

"But it wasn't. Then I started to consider everything they've said. About helping foster the Universal Soul in people."

Iola rubbed the back of her neck, her eyes squinted against the steady light. "Maybe. Sapients are always connected to the Soul, they always can hear and speak, even without the Convocation. That's the purpose of the Trial, to achieve the bond."

"So they upped their own production."

"I'm not really sure what you mean. But yeah, the Soul is in constant contact with you once you become a Sapient, and you help all those around you hear and speak to it."

"And a Sapient is present at every Convocation?"

"Yes, and they will help a Docent during the day if they lose communication."

"What happens during the Sapient Trial that makes them able to do this?"

"I have no idea. The Sapients are very secretive about it. Why?"

"It would be good if we could recreate it."

"Have you already forgotten that half the people who take the test die?"

Raleigh froze. "But there must be a reason some people pass. Thora mentioned the Soul favoring some people. Is it receptors?"

"From what I can tell, that isn't the only factor. It doesn't matter now. We're free of them. I just got my life back, I don't want to think about it." Iola curled back into the blankets and pulled the pillow over her head.

Raleigh left the room. She had to tell Rho and the others. Even if they weren't going back this news meant something. Thirty years of experiments had failed because they hadn't been looking at the right thing. The answer lay in the mind—*not* in a vial.

CHAPTER
26

RALEIGH POUNDED ON Rho's door. Tau opened it, his hair matted down on one side from sleeping. It was his face that caught her attention, worry streaked across it, the relief of leaving the island nowhere to be found. Inside the room Gabe, Adam, Rho, and Kappa all wore the same foreboding expression. "What happened?" Raleigh felt her lips moving, but her voice sounded foreign when she spoke.

Tau shut the door, and two seconds of silence ticked by as Gabe collected himself. "I got the call from my men this morning. Sigma made a move."

Her mouth went dry. She thought of her sisters, her parents, the Designed, and the Modified. There were so many people that she cared about, so many ways for that man to hurt her. "Who?"

"Sigma took Dale."

Dale. She reached out grasping the dresser. Her lungs pressed in, making it hard to breathe. She'd promised him that she'd keep him safe and left him with Gamma and Upsilon. They'd been hiding and doing a good job of it. At least she thought they had been. "How? They were hidden."

Gabe cleared his throat. "It was Collin. He's sided with Sigma, and he told them where Dale was."

"Collin?" A breath of air came into her, but instead of releasing the pressure, it ignited with the sudden hatred that filled her. She'd never trusted him, never like him. "Collin betrayed us. He's always been awful."

Rho lowered his head. "Yes, he's been struggling since we cut him off. Sigma offered him Lucid, and he chose that over us. Over Dale. Over…." Rho's voice trailed off.

"Over what?" Raleigh couldn't imagine anything worse that Dale being kidnapped.

"He killed Gamma." Gabe's eyes lowered, in condolence. Raleigh wasn't sure she believed it, though. Grant and Able had been trying to capture or kill the Designed for years. Surely Gabe's sadness was over Dale.

"Gamma's *dead?*" It wasn't possible. She could picture the way his cheeks framed his brown eyes when he smiled. And he smiled often, she remembered how they'd played cards with Upsilon and Dale.

"He was a good man," Gabe said. "And despite our difficult relationship with the Designed, Agatha wants you to know that he will be mourned."

She couldn't listen to this. Her ears rang with rage, and her chest twisted in sorrow. Kappa, Rho, and Tau watched her. "If we hadn't been in Greece," she whispered.

"Don't do that," Kappa said softly. "You're not responsible for this. Collin would have given away your location, too."

"Or he might not have risked it at all." Anger squeezed her throat. She'd never felt such hatred for anyone.

"You can't watch everyone," Rho said. "Gamma wanted to watch Dale, they were friends. Both he and Upsilon insisted."

"We're headed back tomorrow," Gabe told her. "We can take your friend Iola with us."

Raleigh turned her attention to Adam. He stood near the window, out of the way. He'd never known Gamma, but there were months where he, Raleigh, and Dale had gone running. He stood back now, holding onto his pain.

Lucidin had ruined all these people. The Designed lived precarious lives. Adam and Gabe would never stop wanting Lucid. She'd been lucky by comparison. She'd learned to live with the blackouts. What would happen to Iola? She'd lived a lie with the Docents, but here, the truth was malicious and unkind.

"We're going to undergo extractions." Rho studied her reaction. "I know it's not what you wanted, but it's necessary."

"Collin wasn't the only one to side with Sigma, Dustin did as well," Gabe announced. "The Receps need Lucid."

Dustin going to help Sigma didn't surprise her for a second. They were the two people she disliked most in this world, and their alliance fit. Dustin would do anything for Lucid and esteem, two things Sigma doled out to control his underlings.

For the first time Raleigh thought they would lose. Since teaming up with Grant and Able their prospects had improved. With the synthetic gone they'd defeated a difficult rival. While they'd been working on all these things Sigma had been plotting. Now he was many moves ahead in a game that she didn't know the rules of.

Raleigh didn't have a way to solve this, didn't have a solution to the pain that raked her. No one spoke further on the topic, because there were no answers to be had.

"We should get some food. The flight back tomorrow will be long," Gabe said. "Is Iola up yet?"

"No. Let her sleep." Raleigh could keep her from this for a few more minutes.

Kappa said, "I'll stay here so one of us will be here when she wakes up. Will you pick us both up something?"

"Sure," Rho said, and they filed out of the room.

Tau and Raleigh were the last two leave, and Tau gently took her hand before she could go. "It will be all right."

"It won't. Sigma is going to defeat us. Gamma won't be the only one to die."

"We're going to supply Grant and Able's remaining Receps with Lucid. Once Sigma is gone we'll figure out how to wean them off. We can fiddle around with the recipe for the inducer. I can't help but feel like there is something we missed."

That was it. The inducer. If she could become an inducer, the Receps on Grant and Able's team would be far more stable than any that Sigma had. How much Lucidin could they realistically stockpile? Sigma had his Designed, Dale, Quinn, and probably some of the synthetic if she had to guess. Far more than Grant and Able had these days, they'd be hard pressed to compete. But with the inducer they'd surpass him. Not to mention the Receps they retained would be content, like the Docents.

"What are you thinking?" Tau stepped closer to her.

She couldn't admit it to him, not when she could barely grasp what she planned to do herself. The only option to win this was to become an inducer. If she took the Sapient Trial she could fight Sigma. Then she'd have to return to the Docents to lead, but maybe she could usher them into a more honest way of life by blending what they believed with the truth. There was no reason belief couldn't supplement science. They'd work to heal disease not just alleviate it.

The Docents were right, everyone was connected. They felt each other's joys and pains. Lucidin made the understanding more urgent and acute. And that was another thing. For her and the Designed to thrive, Lucidin had to be an agent for good. And the Docents were the closest to getting that right.

"I'm just thinking of Dale," Raleigh lied.

"Kappa's right, it's not your fault. I know you'll want to beat yourself up over it, but you can't. Promise me you won't."

"I promise."

Tau was correct, chastising herself didn't accomplish anything. Action moved her forward. That's what Sigma had over them. He'd been moving while she and the Designed had become stagnant. This plan of his was part of a large scheme that started long before Raleigh met him, maybe when he first met his brothers. He'd found Grant and Able's weakness, and he'd discovered ways to exploit it.

If she succeeded in becoming the inducer, she'd throw a wrench in his plans.

Raleigh followed Tau out of the room. She'd have to head back to the Docent's soon before Anders took the Trial. When Iola woke up she might tell them about Raleigh's realization. There would be no leaving them then. And she had to go alone. Allowing them to come last time had been a mistake. This was her duty, not theirs.

She stopped Tau as he headed down the hall. "I'm staying here, I need to take a shower."

"Are you sure? Aren't you hungry?"

"Not so much, the Dale stuff is making me queasy."

"Do you want me to stay too?"

"Don't be silly, get some food. I have Kappa and Iola here. Plus, you won't be gone long." She stared up into his blue eyes, wishing she could say goodbye but couldn't risk it.

"All right." Tau rested his hand on her shoulder and squeezed over the chip implanted there. Their sign. "Stay strong. It's a shock, but we'll get Dale and Quinn back."

"I know."

Tau turned and headed down the hall. Raleigh dashed back into the room and grabbed her bag, fishing out the emergency money Rho insisted she carry. This should be enough to get her there. Her hand hovered over the car keys, did she dare drive? With her blackouts she'd never been confident to try for her license and driving abroad had its own challenges. No, she'd have to take a cab. She glanced at Iola still sleeping and then sneaked out of the room.

———————

FOR THE SECOND time that week she found herself en route to the shoreline village across from the island. She shifted in the backseat as the driver took the roads quickly. The cabby didn't speak with her. Either he spoke no English or he didn't want to have a conversation. The silence suited Raleigh just fine. It gave her time to think.

She'd have to find her way back onto the island. Iola's raft was probably still sitting on the same stretch of beach that they'd left it. In the haste of last night it had been discarded. It would be difficult to make it back across with just her rowing. The maiden voyage had been dicey, and that was with two hearty rowers. There would be less weight with only her, but it would still take a long time. How long did she have?

Iola must be up by now. She'd tell them what Raleigh said, and it wouldn't be hard to piece together where she'd gone. Tau and Rho would come after her. They'd be dead set against this, which is why she'd left without telling. She had to assume that she didn't have much time. The boatman would have to take her.

She paid the driver to let her off in front of his house across from the docks. The boatman's cottage had its shutters closed tight.

Her courage was as thwarted as her spirits. The captain would know about the week-long ban on boats. How would she convince him that she had to cross? Anders's paper permission slip lay scrunched in the bottom of her pocket. Pulling it out she flattened it in her hand. The watery passage had drenched not only her, but it. The ink of the words bled together, sloppy and illegible.

With a heavy hand, she knocked against the door. No answer, so she rapped a second time. He must be out running errands because it was midday. She sat down on the step and wrapped her arms around her legs. Resting her head on her knees she considered the raft again. Her chances of blacking out two days in a row were slim. Still, a lot could go wrong. Where was the fate now? How come things only fell into place when they shouldn't? She let out a long sigh.

She looked up to find a young man standing in front of her, his silhouette backlit by the sun. He said something, and she brought her hand up to shield her eyes. Under his weathered coat his arms were strong and his hands rough. The smell of fish lingered on him, it was not hard to place him as a fisherman.

"I don't speak Greek."

"You're American." He smiled as though that explained a lot. "The man who lives in that house is on vacation. There aren't any boats allowed across."

"But I need to go. Please. It's an emergency."

"They have some kind of religious holiday. No pilgrims are being taken across. You'll just have to wait to the end of the week."

"Do you have a boat?"

He nodded. "Which is why I know the island is closed."

"I could pay you."

"They work with the devil, girl, and I won't be cursed taking you there."

Raleigh stood up and squared her shoulders. "But they will

be thankful you took me. I am one of them." She pulled back the corner of her shirt and peeled back the bandages. The scars pronounced red and angry that she belonged to the Docents.

His face contorted in momentary horror. "That doesn't mean anything. You'll have to wait a week." He turned to go.

Raleigh influenced him to stop, Ivar's trick of showing just enough of your hand to get what you wanted. A sweat broke out across the young man's back. She spoke clearly. "The Universal Soul speaks to me, and it tells me that I need to go across to the island. You will take me." She held out the rest of her money, likely more than he would have asked. But she needed that trip.

He stared at the island and then back to her, no doubt sizing up which was worse. Then he snatched he money from her hand and led her down to the docks. "I'll take you, but you explain to the islanders why I took you. I don't want any curses put on my family."

Raleigh held her tongue on how stupid it was to believe in curses. Right now she needed him to fear her enough to take her across. Idle chitchat about the futility of superstition didn't seem the best conversation.

The fishing boat was smaller than the ferry but much larger than the raft. Nets hung over the sides and seaweed clumped in the corner of the deck. He motioned for her to take a seat, not offering her a life jacket, and untethered his boat from the dock. Then they were off.

Of all the trips across the channel this had been the least frightening. Maybe because she'd had a bad track record thus far, or perhaps she was finally starting to become used to it. Most of the time she faced forward towards the island. Every now and then she turned back to the shore. Would Rho and the others find their way across? Hopefully not, their presence would only hinder what she needed to do.

C H A P T E R
27

ONCE AGAIN SHE neared the island, its gray exterior and high walls all the more intimidating knowing what was housed inside. "I'm going to take you to the main entrance, no one will be at the pilgrim's side one. It's likely they will be upset. Remember to tell them that you made me do this," the fisherman said.

They pulled up to a much larger dock than the one she'd been to before. She imagined that before Grant and Able this was the way that everyone arrived. From this vantage point she could see more of the city, spiraling up to the sky, the tall Docent dorms and Convocation dome impressive against the clouds.

The fisherman was correct, someone waited at the dock ready to turn away anyone who came. He stood up upon seeing their boat and left his small hut on the side of the pier. Worry and confusion knit his brow, and he waved his arms, his meaning clear—they needed to leave.

They didn't heed his wishes, the fisherman driving his boat

closer, the waves choppier near the island. Soon they were close enough to hear the townsperson's shouts, urgent and in Greek.

Their boat thudded against the dock, and Raleigh braced against the jolt. The fisherman moved from the helm to the front and shouted back. He turned to Raleigh, motioning for her to show her scar. Raleigh peeled back her coat, the Docents markings commanding on her shoulder.

The townsperson fell mute at the sight. His eyes raked over her, and then he lowered into a humble bow. Nodding his head he moved back so that she could move around him to the dock.

The fisherman didn't bother to tie his boat, and Raleigh had to balance the gap between the side and the wooden planks of the dock. With a large step she made it onto the island. The boatman drove away the moment she stepped ashore.

She was left with the townsperson who now knelt before her. She held up her hand ready to give the Docent blessing. With her palm near his forehead she stood watching him, his eyes closed. For good measure she influenced a small burst of dopamine. The lines of his face smoothed, and then he rose.

"Thank you for letting me ashore. I need to find Thora." The townsman didn't seem to register her words. She nodded kindly and then decided it best to go directly to the Docent buildings.

Each time she passed through the village she saw it through a new lens. The first time it was that of awe, the next time fear, and now ownership. If she took the Trial, and she hoped that there would still be time, then she would be their leader. The people she passed now would turn to her for guidance. A heavy responsibility, and one that she would meet.

Garlands strewn with flowers lined the streets. Colored scarves hung over doorways, and petals littered the ground. The colors reminded her of spring, but the cold air lacked the dewy freshness of renewal. Instead the icy air spoke of winter and death. An unsettling omen on a day she'd be either reborn or die.

The nearer she came to the Convocation arena the more people she encountered. They, like the town, adorned themselves in metal jewelry and flowers. A few of the children that ran by clanged bells as they passed.

A woman grabbed another woman's arm upon seeing Raleigh, and like the man at the dock, she wilted to a kneeling position. Seeing the gesture the second woman quickly followed suit, and before long all the people in the street knelt with their faces turned up towards Raleigh.

The commotion that had echoed down the stone street ceased, and Raleigh's steps remained the only clear noise beside the bells. With too many people to individually approach, she had no way to convey a blessing. So she swept through them face forward and feet assured. Hopefully they greeted her this way because Anders had yet to take the position of Sapient.

Raleigh bypassed the townsfolk entrance to the Convocation arena. Instead she wound further up the spiral street until she reached the back entrance, the square that was overlooked by Rho's old apartment and the Docent dormitories. Firmly, she tugged the heavy wooden doors open and slid inside the Docent building.

Inside, her eyes took a moment to adjust. The blanket of flower petals on the ground muffled her steps. A few had already dried in the cold air, crunching under her shoe like autumn leaves. The aroma of spices and flowers combined to produce a sweet smell, almost tart. Her nose scrunched as she fought back a sneeze.

"Raleigh?" Thora stepped out from a shadow. She had her long hair pinned back by flowers, and a belt of twisted gold and silver encompassed her small waist. "You weren't at the morning Convocation. The whole town has been searching for you and Iola."

"We left." There wasn't any sense in trying to deny it. "Late last night, Iola had a raft, and we left."

Thora's face contorted in confusion. "But why? To avoid the Trial? I told you that the decision was yours to make."

"Someone tried to hurt my friends using the Universal Soul the night before."

Surprise crossed Thora's face before changing to concern. "Are you certain?"

"One of them woke up, the breath being forced from his chest. He recovered, but we were concerned. We suspected Iola, since she's been against me becoming a Docent."

"It's because she fears her calling and wanted to save you the burden of being a steward of the Soul."

"I know that now. She wasn't the one who tried to harm them."

"I can't imagine that anyone would. What would be the purpose?"

"I don't know. But I had to see them to safety. Then I came back."

"And Iola?"

Raleigh shook her head.

Thora's shoulders sank, and her eyes scanned to the door. "She was supposed to take the Trial today. Her leaving is a great loss to our people."

"I've come to take it, if you'll still allow me."

"Of course!" The worry melted from Thora's expression. "You've finally accepted the intentions of the Soul?"

Raleigh nodded. "Yes. I'm meant to lead people. I'm meant to heal others and assist others in doing the same." Her voice came out with conviction. It wasn't a lie, these were Raleigh's deepest desires—to become a doctor and heal. She hadn't anticipated this route to achieve her aims, but it could get her there nevertheless. These people were misled in their explanations, but they wanted the same thing as she did. "I'm not too late, am I?"

"No, Anders is preparing for the Trial. The villagers are thanking him for his calling. Now you too shall be recognized."

Thora led Raleigh into the Convocation arena. From the top of the steps the empty rows of seats appeared like ripples from the center stone platform. Normally it would have been crowded with the fifty or so Docents, but now only Anders sat there. A procession of townsfolk entered in the far door forming a line down to see him before turning and heading back out.

Thora and Raleigh proceeded down the Docent entrance. With each step the tension inside Raleigh built. In a few hours she'd either be a leader of these people or she'd be dead. There had been a time, back in the bunker, that she'd faced death head on. Back then she hadn't been prepared, she'd needed to give her family her farewells.

Now, she'd reached a better place with her sisters and parents. It was true, her relationship with her mother remained strained, but at least Raleigh had said her piece. If she died, she wouldn't have the same guilt over abandoning them with no answers, and she wouldn't regret how she'd left things.

Dale. The promise she'd made about keeping him safe had been broken. If she failed the Trial, she'd never be true to her word, but this gave her the best chance at leading the remaining Receps in fighting Sigma. It was for him that she did this, so he couldn't blame her.

When she stepped onto the platform her thoughts went to Tau. Last time she'd braved her fleeting mortality he'd held her hand. The bittersweet love that had existed between them had made her feel things so acutely that she'd pulled through the numbness of those dark days. Now he was gone. This time she'd face the process alone. She didn't believe in fate, but somehow it seemed fitting.

Anders turned to her, his eyes lighting up. His pale skin shone with a clammy glow. It wasn't because of heat. With a full audience the arena warmed due to so many people, but the line of visitors didn't suffice. No, his appearance was a product of fear. The pungent smell of flowers made his stomach roil, and desperation sat pinched tight in his chest. Blue rimmed his sunken eyes.

Raleigh gave him a smile and then went over to the spot beside him on the pedestal. Thora retreated back up the steps, and Anders returned his attention to the people as though death had already wrapped one icy hand around him. Raleigh smiled and tried to fight her own butterflies. No point in losing her gumption now.

A townsperson ascended the steps to the platform and went to Anders. She whispered something before clasping his hands. The timber of her voice held both gratitude and sadness. These people loved Anders, and they understood that this might be a farewell.

Raleigh adjusted herself on the chair before sitting with a straight back. She didn't know what to do with her hands, or what words she should say in response to them. The woman who'd thanked Anders moved towards Raleigh. With a smile, the woman bowed and reached out her hand, as unsure as Raleigh about what was to be done, evidence that Anders would be better at Sapient. Reaching out, Raleigh took the woman's thin fingers in hers and squeezed them. Her way of promising without words that she would carry the mantle of Sapient to her best ability.

The woman bowed and then left, and the next townsperson in line replaced her. Person after person followed. A few of them placed flowers around her, others brought her bangles. She slid the cold metal onto her wrists. This copper had been pounded into shape, the small hammer marks each a loving imprint of the work that had gone into making the gift.

The townsfolks' imploring stares and lingering touches beseeched her. Without words they asked her to lead, to guide them through the next fifty years. They requested her to give them strength when they were weak. Raleigh had spent the early years of her life chasing hope, finding it, and then during the last year losing it again. This was the first time that she embodied the sentiment. Yes, Grant and Able had plans for her, but to these people she was more than a girl sitting on a pedestal, she was a life raft that would navigate the storms ahead.

And it remained her intent to lead them if she succeeded. But she'd have to leave first. Because she'd made a promise to Dale, and Grant and Able were right, she was the only one who could beat Sigma. He and Rho were even, and in real life, good intentions didn't hold a candle against the urge to win despite all else. A dirty fight lay ahead, and Rho would be too pristine to fight it. But she could. She'd trudged through the sinister underbelly of Lucidin, and she'd traded in lies more often than the truth. There was no point in denying who she'd become.

When it was over she'd come back. She'd fulfill her promise to Dale, and then she'd repay these people for giving her the gift of Sapient by teaching them the true nature of the Universal Soul. All of these faces that passed would become family.

Eventually the procession tapered off. Anders and Raleigh were left sitting in the large amphitheater, their thoughts echoing off the high walls. Breaking the silence, Raleigh stretched her legs and rose.

Anders turned to her. She could feel the cotton of his mouth as he gulped. "Wait."

She moved closer to him but didn't sit. "Are we not allowed to leave?"

"No. I have to speak to you. You left, but you came back?"

"I did. I can take the test first if you'd like. I'm not scared. It's all been leading to this, and I'm a fool for thinking it would ever go another way."

"You should go first. You'd be a better leader."

Raleigh scrunched her nose. "Don't sell yourself short. You'd make an excellent leader."

"No. It isn't true. Before we face the Trial, I must confess something to you."

A stone formed in Raleigh's stomach. Would else could there possibly be? The test already had the potential to be fatal. What haunted Anders now? Did she even want to know? "I'm taking the test either way."

"Yes, and if you succeed you'll be my leader, and I have to have you know the truth, now, when we're still equals." He twisted his fingers, his neck muscles tight.

"All right."

"The other night I went to the dormitories that housed your friends. I knew that they were pressuring you to go. I've always known that I wasn't meant to take the Trial. Iola's always been a good second choice, but you were the first person that could ever replace me as first in the Trials."

He stopped talking, taking a deep breath. Sweat broke out on his brow, and he looked as though he was going to be sick. She asked, "Are you all right?"

"No. I communicated with the Universal Soul. I used it to try and hurt your friends. Without their disapproval I hoped you would take the Trial. But then the Soul withdrew from him, suddenly. Proving to me that I shouldn't have done it. To force the Soul to satisfy our wishes, rather than its own, it's a grave sin."

"You were the one who tried to kill Kappa?" Anger flared in her. If Kappa hadn't been Designed he'd be dead right now. Anders didn't know that he could barricade, it had been a lucky chance that he hadn't passed in his sleep.

"I feared my own death."

The raw honesty of his words made her flinch. Right now he sat a few feet from her, every part of him laid out for her to see and judge. Repressing the rage of what he'd done, it wasn't hard to understand his motive. "And you're telling me because you want leniency?"

"No. I'm telling you because if you are my leader, you will choose the proper punishment. And if you die… then I am likely to take the test, and I don't want to leave this world with that hanging over my head."

Raleigh had an impulse to let him take the test first. Let him embrace the fate that she was to save him from. But she couldn't do that. She'd let the ends justify the means herself.

"I'm not asking for your forgiveness, just your understanding."

"That's good, because I don't know if I could forgive you. But, I can definitely understand."

Anders bowed his head. "Now there is nothing left to do but take the Trial."

CHAPTER
28

THE SAPIENT TRIAL took place in the same room as the Docent initiation. This time only Thora waited at the head of the stone bed. Before, with fifty people, the space had been small and suffocating. Now, with only Raleigh and Thora, the area was comically large.

What Raleigh wouldn't have given for a window, for a sliver of sky to bolster her strength. Thankfully, the room wasn't underground, but her mind was inclined to pick up on similarities to the bunker rather than the differences.

The main thing that differentiated the two was that the door she passed through now had no locks. Only her sense of duty kept her walking over to Thora. Raleigh's bravery had acted as motivation many times, driving her into good and bad situations. Would this fall into the former? Raleigh didn't believe in an afterlife, and if she failed, she wondered if she'd even know.

Her death would be felt, even if not by her. Her mother would be proved right, Raleigh's choices would be her demise. She considered Thalia, lying in that hospital bed with her legs paralyzed. The pain at seeing her sister in that state had cut deep. Now she'd be gifting her sisters and brother that torture of losing a sibling. Her passing would hurt Rho and Tau. Ironic—she did this to save others, and if she failed, her last act in life would leave a sour taste that overshadowed everything else.

"Are you ready?" Thora asked.

Could a person ever be ready for this? Raleigh'd become used to violence. She'd killed that man back in October when he'd tried to kidnap Gamma. A lifetime ago. The synthetic trade had made her hard, made her ready to die in battle, even though her war wasn't traditional. This though, this wasn't in the trenches. Silence gave her mind too much space to think.

"I'm ready."

"Lie down, and I will guide your soul to join with the Universal one. From there it's your choice to remain or to come back."

Raleigh deduced that Thora would make it so that Raleigh could influence the portion of people's mind that made Lucidin. How exactly that worked she didn't know. If she had to guess, something about the process short-circuited the brain. You either woke up from it or you didn't. The process involved no real choice for Raleigh, beyond getting onto the stone slab.

A lot of questions about consciousness remained. For all Raleigh knew about the body, she'd not given enough consideration to the mind and what made her her. Because that was really what she was in danger of losing, because her body would make it through regardless.

Raleigh lay on the block. "Have you done this before?"

"No. But once you've walked through that door you know how to unlock it for someone else."

Another benefit if Raleigh made it through this, she could

make other people inducers. Unlike the tribe she wouldn't have to wait every thirty years.

Raleigh stared up at the woman's slack face, whose eyes had fluttered close. "Thora?"

"What?"

"Can you tell them that I'm sorry? Tell them that I had to do it?"

"Who?"

"My friends."

Thora's thin smile filled the left corner of her face. "You will make it through. And you will always be connected to them, even if you aren't in your body anymore. But yes, I will convey your farewell if it is needed."

Raleigh didn't close her eyes. She wanted to face death head on. Not cowering, not hiding but wide-eyed and ready.

The ritual around becoming a Docent had been elaborate and sensory. Her skin had burned, her mind had wandered, aromas had tickled her nose, and the humming had resonated in her ears. This experience was the lack of everything.

Her nose no longer picked up on the subtle herbal smells of the room. The silence remained pristine with the exception of her breaths. Staring up to the ceiling, her eyes unfocused. Warm, but not hot, her body relaxed into the hard stone in acceptance. She had to hold onto the details or they blended into the room. There was nothing to distract her.

She retreated into herself. Thora was there. Raleigh felt something in her mind. Buried deep inside, near the back of her skull. Or at least she thought it was there. The brain wasn't like skin, it didn't have dozens of receptors to analyze the world around it. Instead it relied on the input from other organs. It wasn't accustomed to speaking for itself, and when it did, like now, it spoke in a language she wasn't familiar with.

The world became light and white and freedom all fused together. Then it folded in. The darkness grew from a speck and spread out, drenching her mind. There was no sound, no smell, and her skin no longer ached against the rock. She became this one spot and nothing more about her existed.

Reasoning went next, and for a brief moment she was. Then her heart slammed in her chest, and her lungs fought for breath, as though reminding her that she depended on a series of systems for life. Lucidin swirled through her wanting to make it so it wasn't just her heart and her lungs but everyone's that she touched. The world became wide as it always did before a blackout.

No, not now. The darkness rushed towards her as she gripped onto the small light near the back of her skull. A futile gesture, like trying to keep a candle lit in the midst of a tornado.

It went out, and so did she.

CHAPTER
29

A DROP FELL against her cheek. It glided down the side of her face, clung for a moment on her skin, and then slid off. In its wake it left a salty trail. For a moment she thought the tear was hers, that she'd been crying, but when another fell she realized they weren't hers.

She opened her eyes, and they stared into Tau's blue ones. Their glossy surface reflected her own back. Where was she? She tried to talk, but her arid mouth fumbled to shape the syllables of her words. Instead she coughed, the rotting smell of damp flowers made her nose crinkle as she inhaled.

"You're back," he whispered.

The dizzy sensation of starvation muddled her thoughts. Her hands rose to brush the quilt of flowers off her. The Sapient Trial. The small location in her brain that sparked like a match now begged her attention. She pressed a finger to her forehead. Then she turned to Tau. Folded deep inside his brain she could sense the same spot in him. It wouldn't take much to ignite it, no more effort than flicking a light switch.

"You need water. We've been giving you sips, but you're dehydrated." His right hand helped raise her to sitting as the other brought a glass of water to her lips and brought relief to her parched mouth. The muscles of her throat constricted, and she coughed a bit but then tried again getting a good drink. "Not too much, you can't introduce liquid too fast or you'll upset your electrolyte balance."

"What happened?"

"You took the Sapient Trial. Don't you remember?"

"Yes, *that* I remember." She turned from Tau and peered through the meager light. Low archways scattered across the room. Candles, not sunlight, made it so she could see. The room smelt of rotting flowers, and she brushed more from her abdomen. Her hand grasped the stone edge of the bed she lay in. A deep bed, more akin to a tub, that kept the flowers piled in around her. Her hands gripped the side in an attempt to hoist herself out, but the weight of her body and the extraction machine tubes stopped her. "This is a coffin."

"Everyone thinks you died. As far as they know, you failed the Trial three days ago when you took it."

"Three days? I've been out for three days?"

"Yes. After talking to Iola we pieced together what you'd discovered, about the Sapient being the inducer. Once we figured that out we knew you'd come here. We came as quick as we could, but by the time we got here you'd already failed it."

"And Anders took it?"

Tau's eyes drifted over her shoulder to her right. Her eyes followed his, finding Anders in a similar coffin to her own. Flowers were strewn across his ashen body. "I can't sense him."

"No, he died."

Raleigh forced her eyes away from Anders. "He knew he wouldn't pass. He was the one who influenced Kappa that night."

"What?"

"He confessed to me before I took the Trial. He was desperate for me to go before him, and he felt that Kappa wouldn't let me do it, so he tried to harm him."

"At least he confessed." Tau didn't bother to say what an unforgivable action it was. It didn't need saying, and Anders was dead now.

"Where are Rho and Kappa?"

"In the Convocation arena attending your funeral. Rho's been inconsolable about your death, and Kappa is furious and torn up at the same time."

"But I'm not dead."

"No, but I couldn't very well tell them that. I could tell that you weren't brain-dead like Anders. I believed that there was a chance that you were simply overloaded with Lucidin. So much that your body didn't clear it, creating an extended blackout. That's why I snuck down here with an extraction machine and reapplied your port. I didn't know if it would work."

"But you didn't tell Rho or Kappa that you were going to try?"

"I couldn't tell them without drawing suspicion, we've been watched closely since we've arrived. It took some work to get a boat and be accepted over here, but after both you and Anders failed Thora needed Iola to come back."

"Iola took the test?"

"And passed. She is Sapient now. That's the reason you're down here and not still in the Docent's room withering away. When Anders died, I went to her and told her that I thought I might be able to save you with an extraction. Since I couldn't very well perform it up there with everyone watching she announced that you died so that you'd be brought down here."

"Couldn't they sense that I was still alive?"

"Thora and the Docents believed Iola. The people who brought you down weren't Docents, and they didn't question the word of a Sapient. Meanwhile, I told Rho and Kappa that I couldn't bear going to your funeral. Iola had a boat come and pick me up to bring me back to the mainland. There I got an extraction machine from Gabe and a fishing boat. I drove it back myself and parked it on the far part of the island, where Iola originally stashed her raft. Then I came here and gave you the extraction."

Much had happened over the course of three days. "Iola is a Sapient. Can she induce?"

"Yes, And control how much Lucidin she herself produces."

"I believe that I'll be able to induce, too, I can sense the part of the brain that creates Lucid."

"Then I guess it was worth it." Tau bowed his head.

Raleigh lifted an eyebrow. "Are you angry at me?"

"I was upset. But unlike Rho, I know why you didn't tell us. None of us would have been willing to sacrifice you to this cause. I would have held you back, but it wasn't my place to decide, it's your choice. I'm not mad that you made it. But it was painful to see you lying there beside Anders."

Tau turned his head and wiped away a stray tear that graced his cheek. His chest shook. He barricaded, but she could imagine the sob wracking through his lungs.

She said, "I had to take the Trial. If we're going to survive we have to make sure we're on the right side of things, and we can't do that as long as Lucid is a blight."

"I know. But I would have been selfish. I would have wanted you to stay." Tau brushed some of her hair behind her ear. "Like I said, I understand why you did. I only wish that I would have had the strength to instead."

"You took on the synthetic for me."

"I took it on for Rho. You were just the only upside to doing it."

"Was I the upside? I figured you regretted it."

"Falling in love with you? No. I could never regret that."

Raleigh's fingers touched his face, his cheek warm beneath her fingers. "I don't regret any of it. Well, maybe actually being trapped in the bunker but not...."

She couldn't finish. Tau pressed his lips to hers. She clasped her hands around his neck to lock in him place, so that he couldn't pull away or take any of it back. When they finally separated, he traced a line of kisses along her jawline, lining the path he'd taken before, when they didn't have to worry about Rho.

"Wait." Her hand on his shoulder was enough to stop him. "You're not just kissing me because I nearly died. I don't want you only to be with me when I have one foot in the grave."

"No. That's not it. Rho's foolish, he loves the idea of you. But not you. The bravery, the wildness—all the part of you that he should love, he doesn't."

"And you like all that?"

"Part of what makes you who you are. Without it you'd be some-one else. I'm not happy you nearly died, but I admire your bravery."

The sound of a footfall echoed through the cavernous room. Tau pressed her shoulders back down into the coffin. "Don't speak."

Raleigh sensed a woman, who was warm in her heavy robes. "Did it work?" Iola's voice filled the darkness.

"Yes. It did, she's fine." Tau reached a hand towards Raleigh bringing her to sitting again.

Iola approached the side of the coffin resting a hand on the stone side. "Everyone thinks you're dead. I can't believe you made it."

Raleigh straightened herself in the casket. "Thanks for hiding me down here."

"No problem. Did Tau tell you? I'm a Sapient. I can induce the people, as you suspected."

"I am able to, as well." Raleigh pointed her finger to the side of Iola's head.

"Yes. Suddenly the tradition of the Sapients raising their hands makes more sense." Iola smiled, but it was wan, as though the joy didn't fully reach her eyes.

"So you're staying to lead your people as Sapient?" The last time she'd seen Iola the girl had been joyous about her escape.

Iola's shoulders sagged underneath the weight of her responsibility. "Yes, I must. After both you and Anders failed I had no choice. These people, they're misled, but they are good people. As Sapient I will be a leader. Hopefully I can introduce the idea of Lucidin to the people in time."

"Will that go over well?" Raleigh considered how upset Ivar had been.

"I will not mislead them, I'll explain that it can do harm. There is no reason for them to have to abandon their tenets. Lucidin is simply the means by which we connect. Even if there is no Universal Soul, it still allows us to communicate in important ways. Really, things don't have to change that much."

"I suppose. So the Sapient Trials will continue?"

"Yes, and you know the importance of them now. I have a favor to ask. Go to the scientists, see if you can't figure out what makes some people end up like Anders while other succeed."

"Yes. I promise, let's hope Anders will be the last to die." Sapients would have a role to play in the story of Lucidin, but after seeing the duality of how it was used Raleigh didn't yet know what that role was.

"You have to go. If they find out that you've ascended to Sapient they may make you stay. Go save your kidnapped friend."

Raleigh gripped Iola's hand. "I will come back. I won't leave you here."

"Kappa has already promised to return as soon as possible."

Kappa? Raleigh fought down the surprise on her face. Of all the brothers he'd been the most desperate to leave. Now he'd pledged to come back? Iola's brown eyes and the wisp of smile held the answer. Raleigh squeezed Iola's hand a bit harder. The girl had made the brave decision to stay so Raleigh could leave.

"All right, Tau, let's go."

CHAPTER
30

THIS TIME RALEIGH made the crossing piled under burlap sacks and fishing nets in the back of the boat Tau drove. A few leftover fish remained, dead in the shallow film of water that covered the floor. The smell of the fish competed with that of the dead flowers that still lingered on her skin. Unlike the last time she'd escaped no one would be looking for her. She'd watched Iola seal up both her and Anders's caskets. As far as anyone on the island knew she was just another poor soul lost in the search for the Universal one.

Tau didn't say anything during their passage over. Either because he was focused on the steering, or because he didn't want to give any hint that there might be a stowaway in his craft. It gave Raleigh time to reflect, and her thoughts drifted to Anders. On the one hand he'd been willing to kill Kappa, but on the other, it was because he knew he wouldn't pass. Why hadn't he? His ability to influence put him in the top six percent, if that wasn't good enough to make Sapient, what was? Was it the mindset? Raleigh should have questioned him more, but his mysticism made any answers obscure and hard to apply to the actual science.

Eventually, the boat shook as the hull scraped the sandy shoreline. A moment later the nets were lifted off her. She imagined that she probably didn't look much better than the dead fish lying around her, but Tau had seen her look much worse, and she didn't really care. It wasn't possible to face something as frightening as death one day and then fuss over a bad hair day the next.

"Are you all right?" Tau asked her.

"Hungry."

"Yes, Gabe and Adam are in the hotel Dr. Alexiou recommended. We didn't dare bring them to the island for your funeral, not when we didn't have a reasonable way to explain them."

Raleigh pushed herself up, peering over the side of the boat at the island in the distance. In her mind she tried to imagine what her own funeral would look like. She would hate to go to Rho's, and the pain of Gamma's death was still fresh. "When will Rho and Kappa come back?"

"Now that they think you're dead, they'll definitely be back tonight." Tau stabilized her forearm as she stepped over the side of the boat onto land. Her legs wobbled beneath her, but her resolve was strong enough to compensate. She waited for him to grab the extraction machine, and they walked up the beach.

As they headed up to the hotel, Tau shrugged off his jacket. He gave it to her to pull on. Underneath she still wore the Docent's tunic and loose pants, but the jacket made the outfit stand out less. With the hood up, she didn't appear remarkable.

After checking to make sure the coast was clear, Tau ushered Raleigh into the hotel and up the stairwell. It was doubtful that the hotel owners would care if she was there, or that she was supposedly buried on the island, but they didn't need to have any witnesses know the truth about her survival. Rumors could be dangerous things.

Tau didn't bother knocking on the hotel room door, opening it and rushing her in before anyone could happen upon them. Gabe and Adam both glanced up at their arrival. Silence hung ominously in the room, Adam's eyes red around the edges—he'd been crying. He stood up slowly, his eyes widening at the sight of her. "Raleigh?"

"Hey."

He stepped closer to her drawing her into an embrace, his arms so tight around her that she lost her breath. When he let her go he stared at her for a long moment, evaluating her face and sniffing against the smell of dead fish and flowers. Earlier that year he'd pledged his friendship to her, promising to leave Grant and Able if it came to that. Their bond stood strong, despite their frequent separation. Now she offered him no words, only a faint smile.

Surprisingly, Gabe hugged her shortly after Adam. "We thought you'd died."

"Nearly."

"It was just an overload, as I suspected." Tau put the extraction machine at the foot of the nearer bed.

Raleigh had spent a lot of time in both Gabe's and Adam's company when she'd trained with them at Grant and Able, but this was the first time she'd ever felt that small part of their brain where the Lucid was created. It stood out to her, as clear as the noses on their faces. How she'd not noticed it before, on anyone, seemed a mystery.

Adam was content enough to stare at her and have her stare back, but Tau guessed the meaning behind her gaze. "You can feel the spot can't you?"

"Yes." Somehow the Sapient test had opened her mind to that little bit of knowledge.

Tau turned to look at Adam. "Can you describe to me where it is on him?"

"I could, but that won't help. To show you I'd have to show you on your own mind," Raleigh said.

Tau let out a sigh. "And that is what would make me an inducer. *That's* the Trial."

"Right."

"And there is something about that process that kills."

Raleigh shuddered at how something could be both simplistic and lethal at the same time.

Adam lifted up an eyebrow. "So you're the inducer? That's how it works?"

"Yeah, there's a portion of your mind that I can tell makes Lucid." Raleigh lifted a finger to her own head.

Gabe stood up straighter. "Have you tested it out yet?"

"No," Tau said. "Adam, do you want to let her give it a try?"

Adam took a step back. "What if it goes wrong? People can die, right?"

Raleigh shook her head. "I'm not going to make you an inducer. But I can see if I can increase your Lucid production."

Adam shifted uneasily and said. "All right, but just that."

Raleigh focused on his mind, on the newly discovered area, and influenced it. Lucid itself didn't have a presence she could sense, but its effects were clear now. Adam relaxed. It wasn't the soothing wave a dose caused, this was more a gentle nudge towards normalcy. This wasn't addictive, because this was his body making what he needed, not supplementing.

Adam stared at her. "You're barricading, so I can't sense you, but I can sense Gabe. I could influence too if I needed."

Raleigh turned to Gabe. "You want to try?"

"Yes." He stood up straight, bracing himself.

"It won't hurt," Adam said.

Raleigh applied the same pressure in Gabe's mind, watching as his shoulders relaxed when she did.

Gabe said, "It works."

"This is amazing!" Adam grinned. "With this we can arm as many men as we need. And the healers! Just *imagine* what we can do."

Raleigh's uncle's concerns dogged her now. In a world with unlimited Lucid there would be the haves and the have nots. And even though she could increase Lucid, she didn't have any control over receptors. This complicated things further.

"Can you make me an inducer?" Gabe asked her.

She flinched at the question. "What?"

"An inducer."

"But you could die, we still don't know what makes people survive it."

"But most of them do, don't they?"

Tau shook his head. "We're not going to risk that."

"Why not? I've risked my life for my men before. I'd be a more adept teacher if I could induce them. Imagine how much better their training would be. We need to get Dale and Quinn back. Some of us are going to have to take risks. Raleigh, back me up, you know how important this is, you've put your life on the line for it."

Yes she had, but Gabe was the face of Grant and Able. He embodied their mentality of charging ahead with Lucid and considering the consequences as an afterthought. If she gave it to him, he'd pass it along. Receps would die, and Lucid would become abundant. Her uncle's warnings about the future wouldn't be a far-away siren but a close deafening blare.

"No. I'm sorry. I won't do that. I don't believe that people are experiments."

Gabe's eyebrows knit. "I don't, either."

"But Grant and Able do, and you're a part of their cause. There will be more inducers one day, but first we have to understand how to make it nonlethal. Then we have to figure out who will not abuse it."

Gabe opened his arms. "Raleigh…."

"I'm not going to risk it, Gabe. I just woke up an hour ago a foot away from a corpse. It's a slow, horrible death. I'll induce you, I'll help you and the Receps break free of addiction, but I won't make you an inducer. Not today." What she didn't say was that it might be never. Gabe was too ambitious, too power-hungry, to entrust with something so revolutionary.

Gabe's face fell. Raleigh understood in that moment how similar they were. The decision to become an inducer wasn't one that she'd taken lightly, and neither did he. They were both willing to sacrifice to get there. But all she'd had to do was cross a channel and implore a cult to help her. Gabe would have to convince her, and that was going to be a lot harder.

"Fine." Gabe took a step back, his shoulders relaxing. He didn't get it, but he wasn't going to argue right now. Later they would have to discuss it. Once they'd been a team, but now they were simply on the same side. There was a difference, one that she grasped the full meaning of as she looked to Tau.

Tau spoke up. "She needs rest. I'm taking her next door and getting her some food."

"I'll get the food." Adam grabbed up his coat from the hook near the door. "You get her settled."

With that, Raleigh and Tau went next door. Once inside, Tau bolted the lock, and Raleigh, exhausted, sat heavily on the bed. He came over and sat down next to her, his fingers brushing the length of her jaw from her ear down to her chin.

How easy it was with him. She leaned forwards and kissed

him, and he didn't push her away, kissing her back. Wrapped up in his arms she appreciated that the sunlight streamed in from the window, that they weren't in a bunker or in any immediate danger. This wasn't him being with her because the world was ending.

"You made the right choice," he said after pulling back from her.

"I never really thought Rho was the right one."

Tau's brow furrowed. "I *meant* about not making Gabe an inducer, goober."

Embarrassed, Raleigh glanced down. "I'm sorry, I thought you meant Rho. I shouldn't have brought him up."

"Don't be. But my brothers are going to see it the way you did. They're going to see it as a choice between me and Rho. They'll make the wrong assumption like I did, that you're only not with him because of me."

"But that's not it."

"I know that now, but they won't."

Raleigh hated lying, and she'd been bitter towards Tau for burying what they'd had, but now she could see the logic. Kappa and the others adored Rho. They liked Tau, but Rho was the golden boy. She'd already hurt him when she broke up with him. This would be worse, and he'd be devastated. His brothers would rightly be upset about the harm she caused. Her actions prickled guilt in her stomach. How could she expect them to understand something overnight that it'd taken her months to sort through? "Then they can't know about us."

Tau exhaled. "I guess you're right. But we can't keep it a secret forever. Somebody's going to figure it out."

"We'll face Sigma, and then when Dale is back, and this is all over, then we'll tell them."

Emotion brimmed in Tau's eyes. "Then they're going to know sooner rather than later, because the next step is to go after Sigma."

Raleigh straightened her spine, ignoring the hollow feeling of her stomach and the weakness in her muscles. It was time, and she was ready to fight.

Lightning Source UK Ltd.
Milton Keynes UK
UKHW011833170621
385713UK00008B/687/J

9 781633 736405